REBELLION . BOOK TWO

WEAPONS OF WAR

M.R.FORBES

Published by Quirky Algorithms

Seattle, Washington

Cover illustration by Tom Edwards

http://tomedwardsdmuga.blogspot.com

1

THERE WAS NOTHING IN SLIPSPACE. No stars. No planets. No dust. No light. There was only pitch black, pure and perfect in its simple depiction of nothingness. A place positioned somewhere outside of reality, where time and space changed meaning, and sometimes it seemed as if anything were possible.

Gabriel had flinched as the Magellan had reached the surface of the Earth. He had felt his stomach clench, his body reacting to his sudden fear and tension. He had thought that he was going to die. That everyone on board the starship was going to die.

He thought his father had failed him. Had failed them all.

And General St. Martin would have had Gabriel not reached the bridge when he did. He didn't have to think it. He knew it, as sure as anything.

The ship had made it into the aether, riding the waves of phased distortion through the planet and out the other side. Maybe his first thought should have been to jostle his father, to remind him to command Maggie to get them out of this place and back into realspace, to keep them from riding the crest too far, too fast. Maybe he should have given the command himself, and hoped the starship's intelligence would obey, even though he already knew it wouldn't. Maggie only listened to one person, and that was the General.

Besides, it was so peaceful here. So quiet. So calm. After the chaos and fury that had seen him escaping from the planet with one of the Dread's weapons only to nearly crash back to the Earth, he was anxious for the break and eager for the suggestion of possibility.

He welcomed this place outside of time where he could believe his mother was still alive, and his father was still fit for duty.

He wished at least one of those statements were true.

He counted four heartbeats. Five. Six. He wrenched himself from his inner dialogue, his eyes casting out around the bridge, to the men and women manning their stations, the same look of fear and surprise on their faces that he was sure was written all over his.

It had been that close.

"General," he said at last, remembering what Reza had said.

The Earth's gravity would intensify the strength of the stream, and in turn, would send them further, faster. The Magellan had means to sustain them, but not forever. And besides, they had woken the sleeping giant, drawn one of the Dread's massive, city-sized starships to leave its moorings on the surface and give chase. Maybe they had escaped. Maybe they hadn't. Either way, they had gained an advantage against Earth's usurpers that they had never held before. They had captured a weapon that could defeat the enemy's shields. A weapon that could damage them. A weapon that could kill them.

Retaliation, no matter what form it took, was inevitable.

"General," Gabriel repeated, loudly this time.

His father jerked as if taken by surprise. He was as lost in his thoughts as Gabriel had almost been. His eyes darted to Gabriel, an embarrassed expression crossing his wrinkled face. It vanished in an instant as he gathered himself. The fact that Gabriel had seen the emotion at all told him he wasn't wrong in his assessment that his father was losing it. Was it his age? The pills? A momentary lapse? He had been concerned when he saw Theodore bent over and vomiting in his quarters. Their near death had proven that the General's judgment was impaired. Hadn't it?

Could he afford to risk that he was wrong?

Could the crew?

The Magellan shuddered suddenly, a warning tone sounding across the bridge. It was a sound Gabriel didn't recognize, but he could tell by feel what was happening.

The ship was coming out of slipspace of its own volition.

"Maggie?" Theodore said softly.

"Slipstream velocity lost," Maggie said. "Quantum phase generator powering down."

The stars expanded in front of them until everything looked normal once more.

Except nothing was normal. Nothing would be the same. They had scored their first victory against the aliens who had stolen their home world. He had seen a clone of his mother among the rebels on the ground. He had witnessed a Dread gun cutting through Dread armor like cloth. They were alive.

Thank God, they were alive.

The bridge was silent as the starship came to a full stop. Nobody moved. Nobody dared to breathe. Gabriel stood next to his father, waiting for orders. He would have to confront him, he knew. He would have to challenge him on his lapse, and on the potential for future lapses.

Not now. Not yet. He was a good soldier and a good son. Some things were better discussed in private.

"Damage report," General Theodore St. Martin shouted, breaking the silence as he finally leaned back in the command chair. Gabriel caught the grimace of pain as he did.

"Data is still filtering in," Abdullah said, watching his screen. "We had a hull breach on Deck 17. The emergency bulkheads have sealed it, but we lost a power conduit. We won't know how that will hurt us until we have a better picture of our overall status."

"Understood, Sergeant," Theodore said. "Casualties?"

"None reported, sir," Spaceman Miranda Locke said.

"Only 'cause the old girl is four-quarters empty," Theodore said softly to himself. Gabriel still heard it. "That was close. Too damn close." He looked at Gabriel. "You saved all our bacon, son."

"General-" Gabriel started to say. Theodore put up his hand.

"I'm tired, son. Suddenly so damned tired. Came at me like a snake in the bayou."

"General-" Gabriel tried to speak again.

"Colonel Choi, you have the bridge," Theodore said.

"General?" Choi replied. "What about-"

"Captain St. Martin, I'll expect you to provide the Colonel with a full debriefing," Theodore said, ignoring her protest. He leaned forward on his hands again, his arms shaking from the exertion. "The rest of you, thank you for a job well done. Especially you, Mr. Mokri. For a civvie, you sure have a big set of balls."

"Uh, thank you, sir," Reza said.

Gabriel could feel the tension on the bridge, and it only grew as the General swung himself into his wheelchair and rolled away without another word.

2

GABRIEL LOOKED AT CHOI. HER face was hard, her lips a taut, thin line.

"I should go talk to him," Gabriel said.

"No, Captain," she replied. "Give him some time. He's never been in this situation before either."

Gabriel looked back the way his father had gone. He knew Choi was right. Even so, it was hard for him to stand there.

"Colonel Choi, I've got an update from engineering, ma'am," Abdullah said.

"Go ahead, Sergeant," Choi said.

"According to Corporal Rogers, the blown conduit can be rerouted through one of the internal circuits, getting us back to full power. There's also some damage to secondary plumbing that is causing a loss to water reserves."

"What kind of loss?"

"Zero point three percent per hour at the current rate," Abdullah said.

"How long to patch it?"

"Three hours, ma'am."

"Not bad. Get on that first. Right now, water is more valuable than engine thrust."

"Yes, ma'am."

"Mr. Mokri," Choi said, calling out Reza. The scientist was sitting at his station, checking the star charts. "Do you have any idea what just happened, or where we are?"

"I think we hit a dead zone, Colonel," Reza said.

"Dead zone?"

"Yes, ma'am. There are areas in space the slipstreams don't cross. I'm still calibrating, but I think we're in one of them. It would have been easier to pinpoint if we had a target for the slip."

"Understood. Interrupt me whenever you have our position."

"Yes, ma'am."

Choi returned her attention to Gabriel. "So. Do you have it? The weapon?"

Gabriel nodded. "I left it with O'Dea. We'll have to bring Reza to take a look at it."

"It really works?"

"It does. I saw the ground forces take down armored Dread soldiers that my guns couldn't touch." Gabriel lowered his voice and leaned in closer to her. "There's something else. They had a girl there with them. I think she was one of the enemy's clones. They copied her, Vivian. They copied my mother."

Colonel Choi froze, her surprise obvious. "If they copied her-"

"It means they captured her. I know. As if things aren't going to be hard enough with Theodore. When he finds out about this-"

"You can't tell him, Gabriel."

"I have to. He's going to ask for news about her. You know he will. He almost cared more about Rodriguez updating him on her whereabouts than he did about recovering the weapon."

"It's going to break his heart."

"His heart is already broken. It's going to piss him off, make him irrational. He's already not thinking clearly."

"That's the medication."

"It doesn't matter what it is; he isn't thinking clearly. That's dangerous territory considering what we just did."

"I know," Choi said. "Like I said, you can confront him on that later."

"Colonel Choi," Reza said, standing at his station. "I have it."

"So where are we, Mr. Mokri?"

"There's some math involved here," Reza replied. "So the projection may be slightly off. I've had to recenter based on the position of Earth in relation to the rest of the known universe, and then estimate the wave speed based on the data collected by the QPG nacelles."

"The short version, Reza," Gabriel said.

"Uh. Right." He smiled. "About six hundred light years beyond Earth."

"Six hundred light years?" Sarah Larone said. "We were in the slipstream for what? Twelve seconds?"

"Thirteen seconds," Reza said. "We traveled approximately forty-three light years per second."

"Are you certain that's right? At that speed, we would be able to reach Calawan in less than two seconds."

"From Earth. Not from here."

Gabriel had been too busy to look out the viewport ahead of them. He did so now, staring out into the expanse of emptiness beyond. It was difficult to differentiate from any other part of space. There was a red dwarf star nearby, close enough to be a little more than another white dot against the black backdrop. Otherwise, there was nothing.

"It would still only take about twenty-two days," Choi said. "We have more than enough reserves for that."

"Yes, ma'am, that's true," Reza said. "There is one complication."

"What is that?"

"I'm scanning for streams, ma'am. As near as I can tell, there aren't any."

Gabriel forgot about the view. His head snapped toward Reza, as did every other head on the bridge.

"Excuse me?" Colonel Choi said, not quite sure she had heard correctly.

"I know," Reza said. "It seems impossible, but there's nothing."

"We came here on a stream," Gabriel said. "That means there has to be one in this area. Doesn't it?"

"That's not how slipspace works, Captain," Sarah said. "The paths aren't random, but they also aren't constant. Are you familiar with the tides on Earth?"

"Caused by the gravitational pull of the moon, sure," Gabriel said.

"Slipstreams are like the tide," Reza said. "During high tide, they'll extend further than during low tide."

"It's only been five minutes."

"For us, Captain," Sarah said. "Remember, slipspace sits outside of our conceptualization of time. We know a lot about how it works, enough that we can plot courses with some measure of accuracy, but only to a certain point."

"And we're beyond that point," Reza said. "It was nothing but insane luck that we were able to even find a slipstream to ride that was passing through the Earth. We should all be dead right now. That stream has crested, though. It will pass through here again, but without a point of reference, it may take weeks to figure out when that will be."

"What's the bottom line?" Choi asked.

"We took a calculated risk to escape the Dread the way we did," Reza said. "That part of it worked out for us, and we made it out alive."

"But?"

"But Captain, unless something changes, we're stranded out here."

3

"IT CAN'T BE MUCH FURTHER," Major Donovan Peters said, pushing past another bit of low-hanging brush. His eyes drifted above him, to the wisps of smoke illuminated by the starry night sky. They had been tracking the fallen starfighter for the better part of two hours, making their way back down the mountain toward the area where they had seen it touch down in a controlled crash.

"Wait," Ehri said, grabbing his shoulder to slow him down. "Look."

She pointed through the trees, to where a large shape stood sentinel. At first, Donovan thought it might be one of the bek'hai mechs, before realizing it was too small. An armored Dread soldier.

Where there was one, there had to be more.

"I've got a clear line of fire," Lieutenant Renata Diaz said, hefting one of the Dread Hunter's rifles to her shoulder. "One shot, one kill."

"At ease, Lieutenant," Donovan said. "We don't know how many more are out there."

Of course, the bek'hai had reached the site before them. They were on foot and tired, while their enemy had powered armor and genetically enhanced human clones to send out to survey the scene of the crash. Had they already found the pilot? Captured him? Killed him? They had moved as fast as they could to reach him ahead of the Dread.

They were too late.

Donovan motioned to Diaz. "See if you can find a good line of sight that way. Don't shoot until I do."

"Yes, sir," Diaz said.

"Ehri, you're with me. Matteo, stay low and out of sight. If you get in trouble, don't be afraid to use that thing."

Matteo glanced down at the Dread rifle. Donovan could see his friend's hands were shaking slightly, but the tech didn't complain.

"Okay," Matteo said. Then he took a few steps back to hide behind the brush they had just pushed past.

Diaz headed off to the left, vanishing into the woods a moment later. Donovan kept an eye on the Dread soldier, making sure it didn't notice the movement. It continued to sit motionless, watching whatever was taking place near the wreckage. Donovan was sure he could hear soft voices now, coming from that area.

He headed to the right of the Dread soldier, creeping slowly through the brush with Ehri right behind him. She was so close he could feel her breath on the back of his neck, calm and even. Did anything make the bek'hai scientist nervous? He doubted it.

It took a few minutes for him to get a better vantage point. He stopped when he caught a glimpse of the source of the wisps of smoke, the side of the starfighter where a scorched hole in the fuselage had burned through one of the thrusters and left it unable to climb out of the atmosphere.

"There," Ehri said, tapping his shoulder and whispering into his ear.

She pointed to the left of the fighter, to a small area in front of it. Two female clones were kneeling beside a man laying on his back. The pilot. They had pulled his flight suit down to his waist and were talking quietly to one another while they placed a bandage over his abdomen.

"What are they doing?" Donovan asked.

He continued scanning the area. A second armored Dread soldier was standing perpendicular to the first, at the edge of the small field. A handful of clone soldiers stood in formation beside him. None of them seemed concerned that they might be attacked, or that they were in any danger.

They had to know what had happened up on top of the mountain. They had to know their Hunters had been defeated, their weapons falling into the rebel's hands.

Didn't they?

"He must have been wounded," Ehri replied. "The salve is similar to the restorative bath the drumhr use to keep their skin healthy. It will heal most of the damage within hours."

"Why are they healing him? Why not kill him?"

"Why do you think, Major? The Domo'dahm will want information about the ships. Especially where they came from. The bek'hai have been monitoring the activity for years, but were never concerned enough by it to seek out the source."

"Until tonight."

"If they escaped with the weapon, then yes. Until tonight. To use a human expression, the tides have shifted, Major. Yesterday, the bek'hai were invincible to the human rebellion. Now, they are not."

"Thanks to you, in part," Donovan said. "Those soldiers don't seem that concerned to me."

"They have grown complacent over the years. Some will take the threat more seriously than others, at least until you start winning more battles."

"Which I have every intention of doing," Donovan said, his thoughts drifting to his mother. Had the Dread discovered her and the children? Was anyone from their base still alive? "We can't let them take him."

"No."

"What about the female clones?" Donovan asked, putting his eyes back on them. They were nearly identical to Ehri, created from the same base DNA. "Are they a threat?"

"They can't be permitted to escape."

"Is there anything else you can tell me that might be helpful?"

"The armored soldiers. Aim for the helmets. Severing the connection to their oxygen supply will kill them. Be careful not to hit the tanks. At this distance, you'll wind up killing the pilot."

Donovan remembered the explosion that had followed when they had killed the bek'hai Hunter, Orik. "Affirmative. I'll take the one on the right. Can you hit the one on the left?"

Ehri raised her rifle. She had confided that she had trained with Orik for a number of years. She knew how to fight, better than he probably ever would. "Of course."

"On my signal. I expect Diaz will open up as soon as she sees the plasma."

"Affirmative."

Donovan lifted the Dread plasma weapon, sighting along it to the armored soldier, getting a bead on the helmet. He focused on his breathing, making sure to keep himself centered and steady while he took aim. He couldn't afford to miss. Not this time.

He was about to take the shot when a flash to his left broke his concentration.

A scream pierced the night.

4

"MATTEO," DONOVAN SAID, LOWERING THE rifle and breaking back toward where they had left him.

His motion drew the attention of the Dread soldier, and a moment later a heavy plasma bolt hit a tree right in front of him, sending hot splinters into the alien cloth he was wearing. The second skin absorbed the attack, deflecting it without harm, and he continued to run.

A second bolt came a little closer, flashing past his chest, nearly cutting him down. He dropped to his stomach, sensing the light and heat of the third shot crossing over him.

The shooting stopped.

He got back up, running toward the trees. He could see the light of rifle fire to his right, back at the clearing. It had to be Diaz and Ehri covering him.

A face appeared to his left. A clone soldier, nearly on top of him. He didn't hesitate, swinging the Dread rifle like a club, smashing it across the soldier's jaw. The clone collapsed into a heap, replaced with a second a moment later. It tried to tackle him, but he fell to his knees, turning the rifle and shooting, catching the clone in the chest. He rolled away before the body fell on top of him.

"Matteo," he shouted. The enemy already knew he was here; it didn't matter if they heard him.

"Donovan," his friend replied.

"Where are you?"

"Help!"

Donovan followed the sound, rushing through the trees. He had managed to break away from the attack, to escape the Dread's attention.

He caught sight of Matteo a moment later. The tech's back was against a tree; the rifle cradled in his arms. His expression was fearful and tense. A dead clone was on the ground in front of him. Three more were approaching his position.

Where had this group come from?

Donovan dropped below a stump, resting his weapon on it and taking aim. He didn't have time to worry about accuracy. He started firing, sending bolts of plasma across the distance and into the enemy line.

One fell. Then another.

Something came at him from his left, cracking through tree branches and landing right beside him. A bek'hai warrior. It kicked the rifle away from him, giving him just enough time to stumble back and fall onto his ass.

"Shit," Donovan said, eyes frantically searching for a way out. The soldier said something to him in the alien language as it approached, rifle pointed at him. Why didn't it shoot?

"Surrender," the soldier said, switching to English.

Information. That was why it didn't just kill him. The rest of the Dread didn't know everything that had happened on top of the mountain, but they wanted to.

"Go to hell," Donovan said. It probably wasn't the smartest thing to do, but he wasn't going to tell them anything.

The soldier came at him, faster than Donovan could believe. It grabbed him by his throat, lifting him easily and shoving him against a tree. "Druk'shur. How did you defeat Orik?"

"He had help," Ehri said, appearing from the brush.

She fired, the bolt tearing through the Dread soldier's helmet and head and passing out the other side. Donovan felt the pressure on his throat release, and then he slid down the trunk as the soldier collapsed.

"Thanks," he said, looking back to where he had last seen Matteo. He wasn't behind the tree. "Where's Matteo?"

"I didn't see him," Ehri said.

"What about the pilot?"

"Diaz is with him."

"The enemy soldiers?"

"Dead."

"Your clones, too?"

"I told you, they couldn't be permitted to leave."

He watched her face for signs of remorse. There wasn't any. Death didn't have the same meaning to the bek'hai as it did to humans. Not when they reproduced like toys in a factory, instead of unique living, breathing, feeling creatures with hearts and souls. Ehri was starting to see the truth of that perspective, but she wasn't there yet.

He found his rifle on the ground, picking it up before heading over to the spot where Matteo had been standing. He was half-afraid to find his friend's corpse among the dead clones, half-relieved when he saw it wasn't. Where had he gone?

"Matteo," he said as loudly as he dared. "Matteo."

There was no reply.

"Did any of them escape?" he asked.

"I didn't see any fleeing, but their numbers are hard to judge in the cover and the darkness."

"Did they take him?"

"It is possible."

Donovan cursed, leaning against the tree. If the Dread had ordered Matteo to surrender, it was likely that he had. Matteo was smart, creative, resourceful. He wasn't a soldier.

"What am I going to tell Diaz?" he said. He felt responsible for losing him, and he knew she was going to blame him, too. Even if she didn't admit it. Even if she would never say it. He had been so close. He should have protected him.

15

"It isn't your fault," Ehri said. "He may still be out here."

A soft rumble in the sky caused Donovan to look up. A Dread fighter streaked overhead, momentarily blotting out the stars.

"We don't have time to look for him," Donovan said. "They're going to send more soldiers."

"Mechs," Ehri said. "I can hear them in the distance. We don't want to be near here when they arrive."

Donovan wasn't going to run away from his responsibility. He led Ehri back to the downed fighter, where Diaz was positioned over the pilot, keeping an eye out for more of the enemy.

"Diaz, we have to move," he said, approaching them. He glanced down at the pilot. He was small and thin, with a delicate frame and a kind face. "Can he be carried?" he asked, looking over at Ehri.

"Do we have a choice?" she replied.

"Where's Matteo?" Diaz said.

He kneeled down next to her. "I'm sorry," he said.

She kept her expression flat. "Dead?" There was no emotion in the question.

"I didn't find his body. They may have taken him. I was close. I should have-"

"Shut up, D. We're not going there. We're all doing our best." She blinked away a tear that found its way to the corner of her eye.

"I'm sorry," he said.

"I told you to shut up," she replied. "We need to get this guy out of here, or we lost him for nothing."

Donovan nodded and then lifted the pilot over his shoulder. The man was unconscious, but he groaned slightly as he was moved. The Dread fighter passed over a second time. It would be sensing their heat, communicating their position. They had done well so far, but they were nowhere close to being safe.

How the hell were they going to get out of this alive?

5

TEA'VA DUR ORIN'EK STOOD IN the antechamber to the court of the Domo'dahm. His mottled face was wearing what he intended as a scowl but was distorted by the overall structure of his flesh and bone into something closer to a smile. It was an unfortunate side effect of the cloning process that had made him, and of the in-between state of the bek'hai and human genetic splicing. He was ugly as both a pur'dahm and a human, trapped in a phase of change that had left him alienated from the other dahm, while at the same time revered by the scientists that had created him.

Beauty was in the eye of the beholder, and to them, he was the future.

The Domo'dahm's antechamber was a dark place, lit only by a thin line of luminescent moss that had been compounded and packed into narrow channels along the surface of the lek'shah; the material that was used in nearly all of the bek'hai construction. Super strong, impervious to nearly everything, it was the only reason they had survived for as long as they did. From what Tea'va had learned, when their homeworld had started to die, it was the lek'shah that had saved them.

That was all history. Ancient history. For hundreds of cycles they suffered under the weight of their failures, each rotation of time leading them closer to the final destiny.

And then they had found this Earth. A planet rich in resources, including an intelligent life form that had not only overcome its failures, but that held the key to saving them as well. It had taken the prior Domo'dahm little time to decided that the planet would be theirs and that these so-called humans would be both savior and slave.

So it had been for fifty of the planet's cycles. They had first conquered the humans and then begun to use them, harvesting the strong to assist in their splicing experiments, using the middling as labor while they replenished their strength, and breaking down the weak for sustenance. Of course, some of them had evaded their grasp. They were intelligent life forms after all, able to think and reason and learn. It didn't matter if some escaped. It didn't matter if they tried to resettle their planet, to learn to live alongside their masters. And the bek'hai were the masters. They both knew it.

Most of them, anyway.

A hatch slid open. A female lor'hai in the traditional white robes of the sur'Domo'dahm, the servants of the Domo'dahm, stepped through it to meet him. Unlike many of the clones within the capital, she wasn't a copy of the un'hai. She was one of the Mothers, a larger-framed model that was being produced for their higher levels of fertility and genetic compatibility. The idea of the clone type was lost on Tea'va. Some of the dahm, like Tuhrik, had been adamant that the key to their survival was to re-learn to reproduce in the fashion of the humans, a method they had abandoned long ago. He could still remember Tuhrik's impassioned plea for Tea'va to open his mind to the idea. He was one of the few pur'dahm who had fully functional genitals, and who had the potential to impregnate a Mother.

The idea of it disgusted him, and as a pur'dahm he couldn't be forced. Turhik had gone so far as to attempt to lure him to first experiment with his si'dahm, Ehri, a clone of the un'hai. Rorn'el had always been infatuated with the human who had sourced Ehri's genetics, and some of the other pur'dahm had found the si'dahm particularly intriguing. He wasn't one of them. The bek'hai had abandoned sexual reproduction for a reason.

"Domo'dahm Rorn'el is prepared for you," the Mother said, smiling widely at him. Her face was soft and gentle. He saw nothing appealing in it.

Tea'va followed behind her, into the court. It was a large, open room, though the lek'shah here was molded thickly to protect their leader, hanging from the ceiling in wide spines and covering the floor in intricately carved plates. There were a few other pur'dahm already present, those that had positioned themselves into the top ranks of their pecking order. One of them would be the next Domo'dahm within thirty cycles.

Tea'va knew he should have been standing there with them, instead of approaching them under these circumstances. He had played the game differently than the others, his more successful splicing leaving him with no choice but to prove that he was, in fact, superior to them. The scientists wanted to believe that he was because it would validate all that they had done since they had found this planet. Subjugating another intelligent race had never been a desire.

It had been a necessity.

The assembled pur'dahm stood beneath the warm glow of bright lamps that mimicked the sunlight outside and cast shadows across the space, shadows that hid the Domo'dahm from clear view. It was a tradition that had continued after the death of Kan'ek, the Domo'dahm who had brought them to Earth. The original bek'hai form was against their laws to be gazed upon. It had been decreed that the human design was their future and that looking upon their past would predispose them to reject it.

Tea'va understood why Kan'ek had made it so. He had never seen what a true bek'hai looked like, and he still rejected being more human. He knew he wasn't alone in that. Though Rorn'el had been taken with a human slave, he had little love for the rest of the lesser species. It was the reason he had decided he would no longer tolerate their presence on the planet. They had what they needed from them, and their consistent uprisings were a wasteful distraction. There was no logical reason to risk that they might ever find a way to overcome the lek'shah.

Tea'va lowered his head at the thought, staring at the floor plates as he approached the gathered pur'dahm. They had been etched with a written and pictorial history of the bek'hai, from the early days before they had invented an alphabet, to their first forays into space, to their arrival here on Earth. Parts of the design had been scorched over; the images that had once depicted the original bek'hai body.

"Domo'dahm," Tea'va said, reaching the front of the room. He fell to his knees, prostrating before his Master.

6

"PUR'DAHM TE'AVA," DOMO'DAHM RORN'EL SAID. His voice was light and scratchy. He spoke in English, though it was difficult for him to do so. "Rise."

Te'ava got back to his feet. He forced himself to make eye contact with each of the other pur'dahm. They glared at him with flat expressions. They knew what he had done. All of them knew what he had done. It wasn't all his fault. Tuhrik had a hand in this. A bigger hand than his? It was difficult to say. Difficult for him to judge. It was up to Rorn'el to determine that.

Of course, Tuhrik was dead, and his si'dahm was a traitor. Rorn'el should never have allowed Ehri to study the humans so closely. He had tried to do right by Kan'ek, to continue the work the prior Domo'dahm had started and bring them closer to full integration. The failure was as much his as it was Tea'va's.

Not that he would ever suggest as much. To do so would mean challenging Rorn'el's wisdom, which in turn would mean matching the Domo'dahm in a game of intellect. A game Tea'va knew he couldn't win. A loss that would mean his immediate death.

"Domo'dahm Rorn'el," Tea'va started. He would be aggressive, speak first and state his case before any of the assembled pur'dahm could take the opportunity to twist his words and use them against him. They all wanted to take Rorn'el's place, and discrediting one another was part of the game. "I believe the latest human activity has proven that my initial concerns were accurate. Allowing the external-"

"Silence," Rorn'el said softly.

Tea'va stopped speaking.

"Why do you suppose, after fifty years of absence, the human ship returned?" Rorn'el said.

"Domo'dahm?"

"Something made them bold, wouldn't you say, Gr'el?"

"Yes, Domo'dahm," the pur'dahm replied. "Perhaps it was related to one of our gi'shah pilots giving chase through the mesh?"

"A desperate attempt to destroy another of the human's small starcraft," a second pur'dahm, Orish'ek, said. "To what end, when we have already destroyed so many, and still they continue to come?"

"You didn't question my motives at the time," Tea'va said. "You believed it wise to try to destroy the one you call Heil'shur. The one who has always evaded us. You believed he could be dangerous."

"I told you the pilot's success was a minor concern," Rorn'el said. "If he could teach the others to defeat our defenses so regularly. A minor concern, Tea'va, because they still couldn't harm us."

"Tell us you weren't trying to prove your worth as a Hunter, Tea'va," Orish'ek said.

"Tell us that you weren't trying to prove that you are better than we are," Gr'el said. "Because you can breathe their air without assistance. Because you can mate with the Mothers."

"Why would I ever want to mate with the Mothers?" Tea'va spat. "You insult me."

"The scientists believe our future depends on it," Rorn'el said. "Whether you agree with the practice or not, the potential of your splicing cannot be ignored. You insult us with your pride."

"A Domo'dahm must be proud," Tea'va said. "To make the right decisions, a Domo'dahm must be strong in their beliefs. That is what the pur'dahm are taught. That is what all of us were taught."

"Being steadfast and being stubborn are two different things, Tea'va," Rorn'el said. "That is why you are here as a disgrace, instead of standing among us."

"I almost had him," Tea'va said. He regretted the outburst immediately. He couldn't win the game if he couldn't keep his emotions in check.

"Pride, again," Rorn'el said. "What has your pride gotten us? One ship escaped from Kan'ek. One ship capable of riding the slipstream. One ship capable of returning to this planet."

"It is only one ship," Tea'va said. "It cannot defeat the lek'shah."

"That is what even they believed before you fired so recklessly into the mesh," Gr'el said. "You showed them that the lek'shah is not invincible, that there is a way through it. That we are vulnerable."

"The smallest light of hope soon grows into a star," Rorn'el said. "Letting the humans remain was a risk I no longer wished to take. That is why we have expanded our patrols. That is why we seek to root them out."

"And that is why you allowed Ehri her experiment?" Tea'va said. He tensed as he realized he was doing more harm than good.

"We could have kept her under control. Even with the weapons she stole, without the help of the external forces she would never have held them. Even now, I expect that we will have her back here before long."

"Back here? Don't you intend to kill her?"

"No. I want her back."

"Why?"

"She is different. I am curious."

"Domo'dahm, that is a mistake."

"You should not be the one to judge mistakes. Ehri exhibits many of the same traits as the un'hai. I wish to understand how that has come to pass."

"None of this would be a concern if the ship hadn't returned," Gr'el said.

"Or if the pilot hadn't escaped," Orish'ek added. "Again."

Tea'va bowed his head. It was his fault the starcraft had made it back to the larger starship with the weapon. He had hit one of them, but it had been the wrong one. The human had escaped him a second time. Then, the forces he had sent to retrieve the downed pilot had been overcome by the freshly armed human rebels and the lor'el that Rorn'el was so infatuated with. Everything had been spiraling out of control for him since he had given chase through the mesh.

It was a mistake he didn't know if he could recover from. He had to try. First, he had to stop letting his defensiveness get the best of him.

"Domo'dahm," he said, bowing his head deeper in further submission. "I accept that my actions have threatened the security of the bek'hai, and given the humans that light of hope of which you spoke. I take responsibility for the deaths of the other pur'dahm, and for my failure to destroy the Heil'shur on two occasions." He looked up, barely able to make out the Domo'dahm's form in the darkness. "I implore you, Domo'dahm. Allow me to take command of the Ishur, and I will find the humans. I will destroy them before they can learn how to defeat the lek'shah. I will hunt them to the ends of the Universe, and I will not fail you again."

"Take command of the Ishur?" Orish'ek said. "You wish to be rewarded for your failure?"

"I wish to redeem myself," Tea'va said. "Domo'dahm, you have held the belief that the success of my creation is a herald of our next age. Please, allow me to prove that your trust is not misplaced. I have erred in the past. I will not do so again."

A silence fell over the court. The other pur'dahm's eyes suggested they were furious that Tea'va had asked. Tea'va didn't care. His advanced genetic makeup was the only thing he had to bargain with; he wasn't going to waste it. And, if he could find the human rebellion and destroy it, he would be able to return to Earth as second in line to the Domo'dahm.

"You intrigue me almost as much as she does," Rorn'el said at last. "I will acquiesce to your request on two conditions."

"Domo'dahm," Orish'ek said. "You can't-"

"Do not presume to tell me what I can and cannot do, Orish'ek," Rorn'el snapped. "It took you ten years to reach this cell. I can expel you from it in seconds."

Orish'ek cast his eyes to the floor and lowered his head.

"What are your conditions, Domo'dahm?" Tea'va asked. He would do anything for the chance to recover from the failures Rorn'el believed he had made.

"First, Gr'el will accompany you as your si'dahm. He will report your experiences back to me. If I see a need to remove you from command, I will do so without hesitation."

Tea'va glanced at Gr'el. He hated the idea of having someone watching over him. He also knew he had no choice. The former Hunter was an easier choice to live with than Orish'ek, who was more likely to let personal grudges guide his thinking.

"And the other?" Tea'va asked.

"When you return, you will mate with the Mothers. As many and as often as needed to further our learning."

Tea'va felt the distaste rising in his throat. He fought against it, though it was almost enough to break his resolve. Was he willing to submit himself to something that disgusted him for the opportunity?

"Very well," he said, unsure if the bitterness was held from his voice. "I agree to your terms, Domo'dahm."

"Good," Rorn'el said. "The Ishur is yours. She is waiting in orbit while we calculate the stream patterns. The human's strategy was unorthodox and effective, but it will not prevent us from catching up to them."

"Yes, Domo'dahm."

"Do not fail us again, Tea'va. It would be a shame for all of us to have wasted these years on the wrong genetic considerations."

"Yes, Domo'dahm."

Tea'va glanced at each of the pur'dahm and then turned and walked away without another word. When the Mother met him at the end of the chamber to escort him out, it was all he could do to keep himself from throwing her against the wall. He would take the Ishur, find the humans, and destroy them. Then he would return not as a triumphant pur'dahm, but as a challenger to the bek'hai leader.

Nothing was going to get in his way again.

7

DONOVAN GRUNTED, SHIFTING THE UNCONSCIOUS pilot on his shoulder so that he could take aim at the Dread clones behind them. He fired a few times, appreciating the lack of kick on the enemy plasma rifle. If he were carrying a standard issue Resistance weapon, his entire arm would be bruised and sore.

Even so, he was exhausted, and the pilot he was carrying seemed to gain weight with every heartbeat. He was so heavy by now that Donovan was surprised he was still able to stand, still able to fight.

When the other option was to die, it made things a little easier.

"Where are we?" he asked. They had been running for so long, fighting for so long, he had lost all sense of bearings. They were somewhere in the jungle near what had once been Mexico City. That was the best he could do.

They had chosen the direction based on geography. There was a river somewhere to the south of their position that would offer their one, slim opportunity to make a good break from the Dread forces that were pursuing them. Forces that by all rights should have killed them a hundred times already, but had always eased up at the moment he believed they were about the be obliterated.

Ehri had told him that she believed the Domo'dahm wanted her alive, and he had no reason to doubt her. Their continued survival wasn't accidental, and it wasn't because of anything special they had done. The fighters that continued to pass overhead didn't risk strafing them and hitting her, and the mechs had remained further back while the clone soldiers harassed them with their more precise fire. It was fire that had damn near killed both him and Diaz a couple of times already; plasma bolts that had split hairs to find their way between the foliage and Ehri.

"The river should only be another few hundred meters ahead," Ehri said.

"You have global positioning built-in?" Diaz asked. Despite her efforts to push reality aside, losing Matteo had made her understandably upset, and she was taking her anger and frustration out on everything around her. Donovan had been forced to order her to turn over her Dread weapon out of fear she would expend the power source that made it work.

"I have studied this area extensively," Ehri replied. "If we make it to the river, we can become much more difficult to track from above."

"And then what?" Diaz said.

"We lose or kill the clones, and then we find somewhere to hole up for the night," Donovan said. "Hopefully, this guy will wake up at some point and be able to walk on his own. At that point, we go back to base and see if that Hunter was lying about killing everyone."

"What if he wasn't?"

"We keep fighting, Diaz. That's all we can do."

They continued through the trees. Every step Donovan took hurt, his legs and shoulders burning. A part of him had been tempted to abandon the fallen pilot more than once, knowing he was slowing them down. He would never have done it, but he couldn't avoid the thought. He gritted his teeth and kept going, one step at a time, refusing to quit. They were almost at the river, and then they would have a chance.

Bolts continued to light the area around them, pulses of plasma striking the foliage on either side, each explosion of sparks and smoldering wood a reminder of what would happen if any of the shots landed. Donovan and Ehri continued to fire back from time to time, their attacks measured, their goal to disrupt the clone soldiers more than to hit and kill them. They pushed on until Donovan could hear the soft churning of water over rocks, the signal that they were in the final stretch.

One last step, and then Donovan found himself on a steep slope, the river spreading out below the bank. He almost collapsed right then and there from his exhaustion, and would have fallen over if Diaz hadn't grabbed his shoulder to keep him upright.

"We made it," she said with a smile, even as the Dread fighters passed overhead once more. "We'll be invisible to their sensors by the time they circle back."

"But not to line of sight," Donovan said, pointing to the trees where the clone soldiers were still approaching. He took a few shots at them before stumbling down the incline a few steps.

"We can lose them in the current," Diaz said. "Come on."

She continued down the slope ahead of him, putting her arms out to balance. He followed behind, each step threatening to knock him to the ground.

He was almost to the water when he realized Ehri wasn't with them.

He looked back. He hadn't seen her get hit. He hadn't heard her cry out. Where was she? Had she decided to rejoin the bek'hai after all? Or had she sacrificed herself to help them escape?

"Where's Ehri?" Diaz asked, her sudden concern surprising him.

"I don't know," he replied, still scanning the tree line.

The grade and distance had given them a short respite from the Dread soldier's harassment fire. He could hear the fighter's engines growing louder as they approached for another pass. He heard something else now, a crashing sound from the other side of the bank a hundred meters distant. It was the sound of tree branches breaking against something substantial.

Something like a mech.

"Hurry," Donovan shouted, giving up on trying to keep his balance. He scrambled down the slope, slipping onto his back, barely managing to maintain his hold on the pilot. Diaz moved ahead of him, reaching the water's edge and wading into it.

Was the water even deep enough for them to hide?

The trees on the other side began to part, the Dread mech making its way through the foliage. Donovan looked back over his shoulder. Ehri was still nowhere to be found. Where could she have gone?

She had abandoned them at the worst possible time. Without her, the mech would have free reign to open fire.

He got back to his feet, skipping the last few meters to the water's edge. Diaz was in up to her waist and had turned back to face him, holding out her arms to help him in. The mech was clearing the trees, its arms swiveling to target them.

"Get down," Donovan said, throwing himself into the current.

Then he was submerged, his ears hearing nothing but the rushing of the water as it began to carry him away. He lifted his head to take a breath, shifted his body to ensure the pilot's head was clear. The echo of the mech's weaponry discharging drowned out his hearing again, rounds splashing into the water behind them as the machine's driver worked to get completely clear. Donovan looked around frantically, searching for Diaz, finding her a dozen meters ahead of him, letting the current carry her away.

The Dread clone soldiers reached the edge of the bank, and suddenly Donovan found himself under fire from both sides. Plasma bolts joined with projectiles, striking the area around him and vanishing in gouts of steam and bursts of water. He knew he was hard to see and hard to pick up on sensors submerged the way he was. It didn't matter. The volume was more than enough that he would be struck sooner or later.

He tried to swim a little, to push himself further and faster, to escape the range of the attack. He felt a biting in his leg, a bolt sinking into the water and hitting him, striking the Dread cloth at a reduced strength, burning him but not destroying the flesh and bone. Another hit his shoulder, only inches from the pilot's face. He was too slow, their escape too late. They had taken Matteo, Ehri was missing, and he was going to die at any moment.

At least he would fight to the last breath.

He rolled over onto his back, positioning the pilot on top of him and bringing his Dread rifle from the water to rest it in front. He pulled the trigger, aiming wildly at the soldiers on the side of the river, fighting back until the last. He smiled when he saw one go down. He laughed when he saw another fall.

He froze when he realized he wasn't the one shooting them.

The mech was.

8

DONOVAN LOWERED HIS BODY, TRYING to find the bottom of the river with his feet. He kept his eyes on the scene ahead of him the entire time, watching in awe and confusion as the mech on the south side of the bank decimated the Dread clones on the north side, tearing them apart with heavy projectile rounds.

"Dios mío," he heard Diaz say behind him, as she caught sight of what was happening.

He started swimming toward the shore as the last of the soldiers vanished beneath the onslaught. A Dread fighter streaked overhead, sending streams of plasma into the mech. It burned into the machine's armor, making deep scores but not taking it down. The mech pivoted to track it, missiles suddenly launching from hidden compartments on its shoulders. They streaked behind the fighter like a swarm of angry insects, exploding prematurely as the fighter pilot released some kind of chaff to distract them. A second Dread fighter appeared overhead, also targeting the mech.

The mech moved almost gracefully, sliding down the decline toward the water, shifting to fire at the newcomer. Plasma beams and projectiles crossed over one another, leaving the mech down an arm and the fighter without the rounded wing on its left side. It vanished behind the trees, the thunder of its crash and a cloud of smoke appearing seconds later.

"What the hell is going on?" Diaz said, reaching him.

"I don't know. Help me get the pilot closer to the shore."

Donovan and Diaz pulled the pilot further to the side of the river, where grasses overhung the water and gave them somewhere to hide while the battle continued to unfold. The mech had made its way into the water, moving toward the center and submerged to its knees. The first Dread fighter was circling back, coming in for another strafing run.

"It's wide open out there," Diaz said.

Donovan didn't respond. She was right. The mech pilot had left the cover of the trees and made the machine a massive target.

He watched in fascination as the two Dread weapons faced off. The fighter continued its trajectory, heading right at the mech while the mech responded in kind, raising its remaining arm and unleashing a barrage of missiles to go with projectiles and plasma bolts. Firepower met firepower, each machine generating small explosions as the attack caused extensive damage to both. The fighter passed fifty meters over the mech before spinning out of control, veering hard to the left and smashing into the trees. The mech groaned, pushed back by the assault, before flopping backward and slamming into the water.

Donovan turned his head away as the resulting wave crashed over them. Once it had passed, everything fell into silence.

He stared at the carnage upstream, barely able to breathe. His heart thudded in his chest, while his mind worked to make sense of what had just happened. Why had the mech pilot decided to defend them instead of killing them? It didn't make any sense.

A minute passed. Then another. Everything remained quiet. No other fighters flew over. No other mechs arrived on the scene. It was the closest thing to a miracle Donovan had ever seen.

"We're still alive, amigo," Diaz said, her face telling him she was as shocked and pleased as he was. "Someone up there is looking out for us."

"I guess so." He put his hand to the pilot's neck, feeling the steady pulse below his fingers. "For all of us."

"Not all," Diaz said.

Donovan flinched. He shouldn't have said that. "Diaz, you know-"

"Forget it. I know what you meant. It isn't your fault. We need to head downstream. We may not be alone here for long."

"Ehri's gone."

"I know. I'm sorry."

"You are?"

"Why not? I know you like her. I'd be an asshole not to care if you lose someone important to you, even if I'm not as fond of them. Or if I'm jealous of them."

"Jealous?"

"You know how I feel, D. We don't need to rehash, especially now. We need to get the hell out of here, stay alive and do something with these weapons. We can't count on St. Martin to come back and save us, not when he's got a Dread starship on his ass."

"The Dread ship didn't leave," Donovan said. It was large enough that they had seen it hanging in a synchronous orbit above the Dread fortress before the trees had blocked their view.

"Not yet. It will, or it would have come back down."

"Yeah, you're right. Hopefully, General St. Martin and his son will make it back, but we need to be able to handle ourselves either way." Donovan shifted his grip on the pilot. "Let's head another kilometer or two down the river, and then we can set up a camp for the night. I can barely think straight."

"Yes, sir," Diaz said, climbing out of the water, and then reaching out.

Donovan shifted the pilot's weight, turning him over to Diaz so she could pull him out by his shoulders. He hoped they weren't doing lasting damage to the man with as rough as they had been forced to be with him.

He planted his arms on the side of the river and lifted, pulling himself up and out. He paused on his hands and knees, a sudden feeling of nausea nearly overwhelming him. He was exhausted beyond any limits.

He dry heaved then, coughing and sputtering. Diaz lowered the pilot gently to the ground, and then came to his side, rubbing his back as he continued to choke.

"It's okay, D," she said. "Relax. You'll be okay."

Donovan nodded. He would. He had to. He coughed again, and then turned his head to the side, back toward the fallen mech. The front of it looked different now. The enclosure near the shoulders was open, revealing part of the internals. It was composed of wires and some kind of organic compound coated in a layer of gel that pulsed with light.

Someone was in the water, swimming toward them.

"Diaz," Donovan said. He had two of the Dread rifles hanging from his body, and she took one and lifted it from him, aiming it at the approaching figure. "Don't shoot."

She grunted in response. He wasn't sure if she was going to listen or not.

The figure was ten meters away when it stopped swimming and stood in the waist deep water.

Donovan fell back onto his rear, the tension draining from him, the exhaustion making him dizzy.

"I don't know how you did it," he said, "but I'm glad you did."

Ehri's face was covered in a layer of grime, her hair had been singed, her left arm was cut and bleeding, and she had another wound across her abdomen. Despite all of that, she was alive, her expression serious as she approached them.

"I've bought us some time, Major," she said. "Let us not waste it."

9

GABRIEL STOOD IN FRONT OF the hatch leading down into logistics, staring at the cold metal. It was the only thing remaining between him and Lieutenant Daphne O'Dea. The only remaining barrier before he would have to be the one to deliver the bad news.

"I'm sorry, Daphne," he whispered to himself. "Soon didn't make it back."

He wasn't sure how she would react when he said it for real. She was a soldier, and she had fallen in love with the pilot and married him knowing that he would likely die somewhere near Earth. She might be coldly accepting of his fate. She might fall apart. He needed to be ready for either reaction. The silver lining was that there was a chance, a small chance, that Soon wasn't dead. He was landing the starfighter, not crashing it.

He heard a noise behind him and glanced over his shoulder. A tech crossed the corridor behind him, pushing a heavy cart of tools. Two hours had passed since they had come out of slipspace, somehow still alive. Two hours since Reza had informed them that they were essentially trapped out in the middle of nowhere, right after they had kicked the hornet's nest and sent the Dread searching for them.

It was a truth that didn't sit well with him, or with anyone on the bridge who knew about it. Calawan was only fifty light years from Earth, close enough that if the Dread wanted to find it, they would be able to find it. Nobody had any doubts about that. Meanwhile, the only chance they had of defending the settlement was resting in a makeshift laboratory near the hangar, waiting for Reza and Guy Larone to be able to take a break from calculating possible stream positions to take a look at it instead.

Meanwhile, the Magellan was almost twenty generations away from the planet, and away from Earth, unless those calculations bore quick fruit. Plus, with the damage to the fluid systems, the starship only had three months of potable water. It sounded like a lot, but Gabriel knew it wasn't.

He put his hand to his chest, feeling his mother's cross beneath his shirt. He traced the lines of it, tentatively asking for strength. For all that had gone right in retrieving the weapon, so much had gone wrong immediately after.

He knew he would have to go and see his father soon. He wasn't going to make the mistake of abandoning him again. He just couldn't deal with all of the conflicting emotions that went along with it right now.

He tapped on the control panel beside the hatch. It slid open slowly, groaning as it did. The ship hadn't been in the best shape when they took it. The Dread's attack had only made it worse. There were dozens of doors within the ship that wouldn't open at all, and enough damage it would take their crews weeks to get to it.

Lieutenant O'Dea was standing in the middle of the large cargo area, holding a tablet in her hands and shouting to a dozen crew members as they dug through bins of replacement parts, bolts, and screws. The Magellan had been expected to break down during her journey to the stars, and so had come with a supply of pieces to keep her running. That supply had dwindled over time and seeing the way the crew dug into it signaled to Gabriel that it was running thin.

He had wondered if news of Soon's fate had leaked from the bridge ahead of him. He could tell by the way Daphne was working that it probably hadn't. He was proud of the crew for the level of professionalism they had shown. Most had spent their entire lives groomed to occupy Delta Station, to practice war but not to live it. They were holding up well.

"No, we need six of the inverse capacitors," she was saying as he approached her.

"We only have four, ma'am," one of the crew members said.

She shook her head. "We need six. See if you can find them in one of the other bins."

"Lieutenant O'Dea," Gabriel said.

She looked over at him. Her face immediately froze, paling and falling flat in a moment's time. He should have realized he wouldn't need to say anything. It should have been Soon coming to see her, not him.

"No," she whispered, blinking a few times.

"I think I found one," the crew member said. "Why didn't we get a decent inventory before we stole her?" He laughed for a second before looking back at Daphne and Gabriel.

"Sergeant Keene, is it?" Gabriel said.

"Yes, sir," Keene replied.

"Take over for Lieutenant O'Dea. I need to speak with her privately."

Keene nodded curtly, his whole demeanor shifting.

"Gabriel," Daphne said softly.

"Come on," Gabriel said, leading her from the large room.

He got her out into the side corridor where he came in from and tapped the door control. It groaned again and didn't close.

"Damn door," he cursed, his own control slipping at the mishap. Soon was his friend, too.

"What happened?" she asked, the tears beginning to run from her eyes.

"We were taking heavy fire from Dread Bats. Heavy fire. He was hit. He didn't have enough power left to make it out of orbit. He saved my life, Daphne. He distracted the Dread, gave us the time we needed to make it back out. He's a hero." Gabriel felt the wetness in the corners of his own eyes.

Daphne responded with a small smile. "I bet he made a joke while he was crashing."

"He didn't crash. He had enough control to land the fighter. There's a good chance he's still alive."

"If the Dread didn't capture him. Or kill him."

"Yes. He wanted me to tell you how much he loves you."

"Thanks, Gabriel. I already know that."

"I don't think we should give up on him. The rebels on Earth captured some of the Dread's weapons. They're able to fight back. The tides of war may be turning."

"What about us? What are we doing?"

"Trying to get back into the fight. Our slip away from Earth didn't go as well as it could have, but we'll recover. Reza's a genius, and for as much as I hate Guy Larone, he's got a good head on his shoulders when he wants to."

"We're going back to Earth, though, right?"

"Not right away, but yes, we'll be going back."

"You got the enemy weapon? Do you think we can use it?"

"They'll figure it out. They have to."

She took a deep breath, straightening up and wiping her eyes. "I was always worried he would die making a run. Knowing he has a chance, that's all I need. Don't ever talk to me like he's gone, Gabriel. Until someone proves otherwise, Soon is alive on Earth, helping the rebels take the fight back to the Dread."

"Okay," Gabriel said, wiping his eyes. "We'll save him. We'll save all of them."

"I know that, too. You and your father, you're cut from the same cloth. Neither one of you will be able to die before we're living peacefully on Earth again."

"I hope you're right about that," Gabriel said, his thoughts turning to Theodore again. "Are you going to be okay?"

"I won't lie and tell you that I'm one hundred percent. I'd rather have Soon here with me, and I'm going to miss the hell out of him. I'll survive, just like he will."

"I can bring Wallace over if that helps. So you don't have to be alone."

Daphne laughed at that, stepping into Gabriel and wrapping her arms around him. He returned the embrace, holding her in silence for a minute and letting her decide when to pull away.

"I don't need his hair all over my bed," she said. "But maybe I'll stop by and take him for a run."

"Anytime."

Daphne straightened her uniform, and then flattened her hair and wiped her eyes one last time. She looked back in at her team, pretending to be busy while they kept an eye on her.

"I'll tell them what happened," she said. "We're stronger together than we are alone."

Gabriel nodded. He knew it was true.

Now he just had to convince his father of that.

10

SERGEANT DIALLO WAS STANDING OUTSIDE Theodore's quarters when Gabriel arrived. She had a stern look on her face, one that suggested at her strict loyalty and stricter orders not to let anyone past.

"Colonel Choi was already here," she said as Gabriel approached. "She didn't get past me, and neither will you, Captain. General's orders."

"I'm not here as an officer," Gabriel said. "I'm here as a son."

Diallo shook her head. "I'm sorry, Gabriel. He doesn't want to see anyone."

"I know. That's why I came."

"He knew you would. So did I. He specifically told me not to let you in."

"And you're going to listen to him?"

She bit her lip. "Please don't make me choose. I promised your father I would follow him. If I renege on that, he'll never forgive me."

Gabriel thought about it. He appreciated the woman's loyalty to Theodore, even if it was getting in the way of his mission. "Okay. I won't ask you to choose. Can you just pass a message to him for me?"

"That I can do."

Gabriel paused. He wasn't sure it was a card he wanted to use, but what choice did he have? His father had holed himself up in his quarters, feeling sorry for himself instead of taking charge. It was an embarrassing response to his moment of failure. A response that Gabriel wasn't going to let him get away with.

"Tell him I have news about my mother. About Juliet. He doesn't get to know what it is unless he lets me in."

"Do you really have news?" she asked.

"Yes."

"Do you swear?"

"I very rarely lie, Sergeant, and only when it's important."

She raised her eyebrow.

Gabriel smiled. "I promise."

"Fine. I'll tell him. Step back a little. I don't want you trying to sucker me."

"Would I do that?"

"I think if it were important."

Gabriel took a few steps back, putting his hands behind him for good measure. Sergeant Diallo smiled and then opened the hatch to Theodore's quarters. Gabriel looked past her. His father wasn't sitting out in the open. It was more likely that he was in that bathroom sick, or in bed, tired.

She vanished inside, the hatch closing smoothly behind her. Of course, that one would be in good working order. Gabriel leaned back against the bulkhead to wait, keeping his arms folded behind his back.

He didn't have to stand there for long.

"He said he'll see you," Diallo said as the hatch opened. "Provided, as he says, 'you keep your coonass opinions of my fitness for duty to your damn self.'"

Gabriel smiled. At least there was still some sass in his old man. "You know I won't," he said.

"I know," she replied, stepping aside to let him in. "Be gentle with him, sir. He isn't feeling well."

"He's my father, Sergeant. First and foremost. I want to help him."

"Yes, sir."

Gabriel entered the living space, closing the hatch behind him. He could smell the vomit in the air, and he noticed the stain of it still on the floor.

"You come to tell me I'm a screw-up?" Theodore St. Martin asked, moving into the room. He was wearing his full dress uniform, crisp and tight. "You come to tell me I don't deserve to lead these fine men and women?"

"Dad," Gabriel said.

"We ain't stupid, son. Neither one of us. We both know what happened out there, and we both know the cause."

He pulled something from his pocket. The remainder of his pills. He tossed them to Gabriel, who caught them smoothly.

"I ain't hiding from my responsibility in here, Gabe. I'm getting my ass clean. Two hours ain't much so far, but I need to be stronger. I need to deal with the pain. Those people are counting on me. They're trusting me to take care of them, the way I did all those years ago. To get them away from harm." His voice cracked as he said it, his emotions threatening to break through the resolve of a General.

He paused, turning away so Gabriel couldn't see his face. It was just as well. Gabriel had never seen his father like this, and it was waging war on his composure, too.

"They still believe in you," Gabriel said. "They don't blame you for this. You did the best you could."

Theodore's head whipped back. "Best I could? No, I did not do the best I could. I gave in to the demon of pain. I let my weakness get the better of me, and I damn near got us all killed. If you hadn't been so quick up to the bridge, we'd all be one with the Atlantic Ocean right about now." He walked over to the sofa and sat down. "I blanked, son. Completely blanked. Couldn't think a lick. All I could see was your mom and me on the beach in Hawaii. What a time that was. No Dread, no war. No outpost in the middle of a sea of nowhere."

"Because of these," Gabriel said, shaking the bottle. "When you don't take them, you get sick."

"I'd rather be floating in my own vomit than losing my head when it's needed the most. Oh, don't get me wrong, son. I want them. I really want them. I'm damn near ready to tear your head off to get another hit. I ain't going to do it. I have a responsibility to these people. They're following me because I promised to give them everything I had to take back what's ours. You got us the gun. You gave us that chance. I need to hold up my end."

"I'm not arguing with that as a soldier," Gabriel said. "As a son, I don't want to see you in pain."

"I appreciate that. I do. There ain't no way around it. Not this time. I'm going to hurt. I'm going to hurt bad for the next few days. You want to help me? Don't tell anyone."

"Why not?"

"Ain't none of their business for one. It will be more effective when I reappear clean and sober for another."

"Okay. You know our situation?"

"Diallo passed the info along to me, yeah. Up shit's creek and we ain't got a paddle."

"Huh?"

"I guess you're too young for that one. Point is, we ended up in a bad way thanks to me. Now, the only reason I let you in here is because you know something about your mother. Vivian tried to use that line to get in here too, but I wanted to hear about it direct."

Gabriel clenched his jaw. He had been holding onto the slim hope his father would forget. As if that would ever happen.

"It isn't good news," he said.

"Fifty years," Theodore replied. "I wanted it to be. I was hoping she was with him. General Rodriguez. I wanted it so bad." He leaned forward, putting his head in his hands. At first, Gabriel thought he was going to cry, but then he rubbed his face and sat back up. "It was all wishful thinking, wasn't it? Selfish, wishful thinking. God's always had a plan for my Juliet. I wish it had included me for all of my days, but that ain't His way, is it?"

"I don't know," Gabriel said.

"I do. You don't get to choose when to believe and when not to believe. That ain't faith. I have to believe there's a reason she was taken from me. So, what did you learn?"

Gabriel sat down next to his father, turning toward him. "The resistance soldiers that gave me the weapon. There was a woman with them. She was human, but clearly not human."

"One of their clones?"

"Yes. I never met mom, but that picture of her that you always projected onto the wall of our apartment, that's etched into my brain. I don't even need to think about it to call it up. The woman, she was the spitting image. An exact duplicate."

"They cloned Juliet?"

"It seems that way."

"So they caught up to her, and they took her?"

"I think so."

Gabriel expected his father to fall apart again. To take the news hard, like he and Colonel Choi had both believed he would. Instead, he started to laugh. A hard, deep laugh.

"What's so funny?" Gabriel asked, as his father leaned forward, beginning to cough from the effort.

"They made copies of your mom," Theodore said. "Do you have any idea what that means?"

"It means she was captured. It means she's most likely dead."

"She was always most likely dead, son, as much as I hate to admit it. No, I'm laughing because it means that those couillons have no idea what kind of reckoning they've brought down on themselves. None at all. A spirit like Juliet's can't be quelled forever. They're going to learn that the hard way if they haven't learned it already.

"It's like I said, son. God has a plan, and it's a doozy."

11

TEA'VA SHIFTED SLIGHTLY IN THE confines of the gi'shah, the suspension gel of the cockpit cold and damp against his more sensitive, more human-like flesh. For older drumhr, the koo'lek was a necessary ingredient, as it was filled with nutrients, hormones, and chemicals that would make the pilot a more efficient fighting machine. For them, it would remove waste and add back needed fluids, as well as act as a transmitter to the bek'hai's every thought, transferring electrical signals into activity that would pass to the organic control system of the gi'shah. For him, it did little more than cling to his body, attempting to fulfill its design and failing miserably. Instead, he had to wear a cap and suit composed of the gori'shah, microscopic symbiotic organisms that were often grown to maturity woven into their more recently developed clothing.

It was the gori'shah that would enable the transfer for him. This made flying the craft less efficient for him than was for the others, and was one of the reasons he had given chase to the Heil'shur. He had wanted to prove that his more genetically advanced form strengths were greater than its current weaknesses.

He had failed.

It didn't matter. The Domo'dahm had listened to his plea. Had allowed him another chance. While the other pur'dahm ridiculed him, the Domo'dahm believed in him and his future. If only Rorn'el didn't insist on his mating with the Mothers, the situation would have been perfect.

He saw the Ishur growing nearer through a tiny transparent slit at the head of the gi'shah, slightly distorted by the fluid he had to look through. A thought sent the fighter into a slight vector change, decreasing thrust and angling for the ship's hangar.

"My bek'hai splice was second to Kan'ek," Gr'el said through their communication system. His voice was muddled by the transfer from the koo'lek to the gori'shah, to Tea'va's ears. "He commanded the Ishur during the invasion."

"Was it your splice who allowed the human ship to escape?" Tea'va replied.

"Drek," Gr'el cursed, speaking in bek'hai. "The human ship evaded the entire fleet. It makes no less of any of the bek'hai involved. Must you always be so abrasive?"

"It was an innocent question," Tea'va said.

"The Ishur has a growing history of failure," Gr'el said. "Perhaps that is why the Domo'dahm allowed you to command it?"

Tea'va felt his upper lip curl at the remark. He didn't respond to it. Rorn'el would be receiving reports from Gr'el about his performance. He knew he should be working to be friendly with the pur'dahm, not taunting him about his heritage.

"We will change the Ishur's fortunes together," Tea'va said. "When we destroy the humans, we will both gain rank in the eyes of the Domo'dahm."

"Yes, we will," Gr'el agreed.

Tea'va didn't speak again after the exchange. He watched the Ishur as it drowned out the entire viewport of the gi'shah. The hangar was little more than a thin line of white light along the huge lek'shah surface. It took nearly two hundred cycles to produce enough of the material to build a star fortress. He had heard it would take even longer now. Apparently, the Earth's atmosphere was not as favorable to the production process.

Gr'el was already a problem. He would become a bigger problem as time passed. Both were jockeying for position to take over the bek'hai when the Domo'dahm's years were up. This would be the best chance either of them had to make a lasting impression that could bring the bek'hai under their control. Not only would he have to outmaneuver the humans, he would need to outmatch Gr'el as well.

He was certain the Domo'dahm was fully aware of this. Rorn'el was affording him the chance to either prove himself or die.

He would make sure he wasn't the one who died.

He scowled at the thought, the expression forcing his crooked lips open, allowing the gel to seep in through the cracks. He sputtered, forcing it back out and refocusing his efforts to keep his mouth on the breathing apparatus.

Disgusting.

He shifted his attention back to the approaching hangar. The white lights had expanded, showing a depth to the space as it sank back into the fortress. It took little effort for him to line the gi'shah up with the pattern, and even less for him to guide the fighter through an atmospheric filter and into the cavernous space. Dozens of gi'shah rested in organized patterns along the floor of the hangar, along with a few of the larger ek'shah, more heavily armored and less maneuverable craft that were intended primarily for close combat. They had been sent out sparingly in the years since they had arrived on Earth.

The lights directed him to the proper position on the hangar floor. Tea'va turned the gi'shah sharply as it sank in the artificial gravity, bringing it to the ground with a soft thud. He watched through the viewport as a team of five human clones rushed over, pushing an apparatus with a large, empty bin ahead of them. They reached the fighter, and a moment later he heard a thud and pop, and then the gel began to drain from the cockpit.

Tea'va shivered slightly as it was released, though the gori'shah suit helped keep his thinner skin warmer. As soon as the gel was down to his ankles, he removed the cap, signaling the cockpit hatch to open. It rotated up on a hinge, revealing the rest of the hangar to him. A smaller pur'dahm was waiting nearby, his long fingers, thicker, scalier skin, and lack of expression showing him as a less successful splice.

"Pur'dahm Tea'va," the bek'hai said, lowering his head in submission. "The crew of the Ishur is prepared to enter your servitude."

Tea'va could imagine how difficult the statement was for the pur'dahm. As the now former commander of the Ishur, Ilk'ash had not only been demoted but also relegated to the third position in the command cell.

"Authority accepted," Tea'va said, raising his head in response. The body language was more important than the words. He took three steps toward the other pur'dahm before turning to wait for Gr'el.

He was already approaching. He lowered his head to Tea'va, just enough to be proper. "Gr'el dur Lok'ash is prepared to enter your servitude."

"Authority accepted," Tea'va repeated, raising his head. He was more careful this time, adjusting only enough to finish the ritual but not embarrass the pur'dahm. "Ilk'ash, take us to the bridge."

"Of course, Dahm Tea'va. Follow me."

Tea'va fell in line behind Ilk'ash and Gr'el, forcing himself to hold his mouth closed, or else risk upsetting Gr'el with a satisfied smirk. He was almost happy the Heil'shur had gotten away.

With greater risk came greater reward.

12

"TELL ME ABOUT YOUR PURSUIT of the human starship," Tea'va said.

He had positioned himself in the center of the bridge, in a seat on a pedestal intended for something much larger than he was. While many aspects of the bek'hai fortresses had been adjusted for the drumhr, there were reminders of their prior evolution still mingled in the details.

Tea'va didn't know why this seat had yet to be replaced. He didn't care. It was comfortable enough, even if it did make him look small.

Ilk'ash was at the command station below and to his left, his hands resting in more of the koo'lek gel so that he could monitor the ship's systems. He looked uncomfortable in the spot, unused to being forced into such activity. As a commander, he would never have been involved with managing the fortress himself.

The bek'hai withdrew his hands, the gel slipping off and back into the semi-circular receptacle in front of him. He then stood and turned to face Tea'va. Even standing, his head barely reached up to Tea'va's feet.

"The Domo'dahm ordered us to prepare the Ishur for launch immediately after the starship arrived inside of our domain," Ilk'ash said. "Most of the lor'hai were already present and carrying about their tasks. Many of the drumhr were not in a stage of warning. Why would they be, when there has been no outside threat for over fifty cycles? Under these circumstances, I am proud of how quickly we were able to put the Ishur into space."

"You should be proud," Gr'el said. "I am willing to wager that the Un fortress is not as well-prepared to launch."

"Go on," Tea'va said. "I'm more interested in how a human ship with no weapons managed to get away from you."

Ilk'ash's head snapped up, his eyes angry. He immediately lowered it again, though Tea'va could picture him glowering into the floor. He had to be careful with Gr'el. He didn't care what Ilk'ash thought of him.

"Their armor absorbed a number of direct plasma hits," Ilk'ash said. "It is thicker than the others we destroyed during the invasion. At least, that is what my science team tells me."

"Why didn't you fire any missiles at them?" Tea'va said.

"The Domo'dahm ordered me not to. He didn't want to waste them. He didn't know they had bolstered their armor either."

"And how did they escape?" Tea'va asked. He didn't need to. He already knew the answer. He had seen the human starship plummeting toward the planet. He had seen the way it shimmered and shifted, trying to gain purchase in the slipstream.

Then he had seen it disappear.

"It entered the slipstream, Domo Tea'va," Ilk'ash replied softly.

"Inside of the defenses?"

"Yes, Domo."

"I have never heard of such a thing."

"Neither had I," Ilk'ash said, looking up again. "If I had not seen it, I wouldn't believe it. They used the slipstream to escape."

"Why didn't you follow?"

"We couldn't."

"Why not?"

"We could not calculate the slipstream coordinates in time. We also-"

"You couldn't calculate the coordinates? A human calculated the coordinates."

Ilk'ash's head lowered a second time, dropping almost to his shoulders.

"The humans had time to prepare-"

"I saw the ship come down," Tea'va said, interrupting a second time. "They did not prepare to join the slipstream. I am certain of it. Who is the dahm in charge of the science team on the Ishur?"

"Lor'dahm Zoelle, Dahm Tea'va."

Tea'va felt his anger growing hotter. "A clone?"

"Yes, Dahm."

"One of the un'hai?"

"Yes, Dahm. Shall I call her to the bridge?"

"No. I will deal with that one later."

He paused, thinking. Should he be so bold, so soon? He glanced down at Gr'el. The pur'dahm was looking straight ahead, maintaining decorum. What would the Domo'dahm think if he followed his instinct?

"What did the Domo'dahm think of your failure?" he asked.

"Failure? Dahm, it wasn't my fault. My crew did the best they could. Lor'dahm Zoelle is an accomplished mathematician and astronomer."

"You didn't answer my question."

"He gave the Ishur to you, Tea'va," Ilk'ash said, dropping his title. "That is the answer."

"Your level of respect is even with your level of preparedness, Ilk'ash," Tea'va said. "I don't know how you managed to earn command of the Ishur in the first place, but it is clear to me that your usefulness has come to an end. If you have any pride in you at all, you will turn yourself in for retirement immediately."

Ilk'ash looked up again, angrier than before. Gr'el turned slightly, just enough that he could see Tea'va, but he didn't speak.

Tea'va knew the Domo'dahm would hear of this. He welcomed it.

"Do you have something to say?" he asked.

"Drek. Druk'shur," Ilk'ash cursed. "I will kill you."

He reached out, ready to climb the pedestal to attack. Tea'va didn't move. He didn't give up the exterior of calm. He had to make a statement immediately.

"Gr'el," he said.

The pur'dahm stood, drawing a plasma knife from his uniform and shoving it into Ilk'ash's side with one quick, smooth motion. The drumhr gurgled, still reaching up. Gr'el stabbed him again. He stopped the advance, falling first to his knees, and then onto his side, dead.

Tea'va locked eyes with Gr'el. Neither was surprised by the actions of the other. Both knew that Tea'va couldn't just assume control.

He had to take it.

13

THEY BARELY SPOKE FOR ANOTHER hour as they fled downriver, away from the carnage and the destroyed mech. Of course, Donovan had questions. So many questions. How the hell had Ehri gotten to the other side of the river bank? How had she gained control of the mech? How did she even know how to pilot the thing?

She was supposed to be a scientist. Maybe she had trained with a pur'dahm Hunter. Maybe she knew how to fight. This was more than knowing how to fight. It seemed like there was nothing she couldn't do.

Had Juliet St. Martin been the same way? It was her husband who had gotten the colony ship away from Earth during the invasion, somehow managing to avoid the plasma fire of the bek'hai's massive fortresses.

Were the other clones like Ehri just as gifted? Was the difference that they didn't know it?

"We should stop here," Donovan said.

They were in the midst of some thick vegetation that offered strong cover from all directions. The river was rough beside them, pouring over a patch of rocks and debris that kicked a fine mist over the area, keeping it damp.

"Diaz, can you help me with him?" He was too tired to lower the pilot to the ground without the risk of dropping him.

"I can help you," Ehri said.

"I've got it, Mary Sue," Diaz said, moving in front of her. "You don't have to do everything for us."

Donovan opened his mouth to rebut her and then decided against it. They could handle their differences themselves, and if Diaz was pissed and jealous, that was her own problem.

She helped him lower the pilot to the ground. Donovan reached down and felt his pulse. It was still steady.

"I don't know why he's been out for so long," Diaz said quietly. "I thought the bek'hai magic band-aid was supposed to heal him?"

Donovan smiled at that one. "Are you okay, Lieutenant?" he said, reminding her they still had a job to do.

"I'm feeling a little uncertain about Ehri. Every time we think we know her, she makes us look stupid again."

"I can hear you, Lieutenant Diaz," Ehri said.

"See," Diaz whispered.

Donovan stood, surveying both of them. "I think we're all exhausted and on edge, and it's getting the best of us. Before we wind up ripping one another's throats out, maybe you can debrief us on exactly what happened back there?"

"Of course, Major," Ehri said. "There isn't much to tell. I heard the mech approaching across the river, so I broke off from you, crossed at a ford a few hundred meters further upstream, and came at the mech from behind."

"If there was a ford so close, why weren't you directing us to it?" Diaz asked.

"Because of the mech. If it had reached us together, we would all be dead right now."

Donovan couldn't argue with that. "You made it ahead of us in a hurry."

"As with my hearing, most of my abilities are augmented. As you know, the bek'hai have a long history of genetic manipulation. Consider that they have been able to combine human DNA with their own in only fifty years. There are thousands of years of study and science behind those capabilities."

"Yet they couldn't prevent themselves from almost going extinct?"

"A series of tragic mistakes. Humans are not immune to the same."

"Why aren't the soldier clones powered up like you are?" Diaz asked.

"The Children of the Un'hai are special. You could say favored."

"Un'hai?" Donovan said. "Juliet St. Martin?"

"Yes."

"Your Domo'dahm must have been seriously in love with Juliet," Diaz said.

"He was. As much as any bek'hai is capable of love."

"What about the mech? You never told me you could pilot one of those things."

"I told you I know how to fight. That includes usage of all of the bek'hai weapons of war. I know the workings of the gi'shah, though they are not equipped to be piloted by clones."

"Gi'shah?"

"The starfighters. Your forces call them Bats. They currently require a symbiotic interface which makes them incompatible with the lor'hai. The mechs; however, were created for this planet, and with both clone and drumhr usage in mind."

"What about real human usage?" Diaz asked.

"It is likely that you could be taught, but the controls have the same lockout as the rifles normally do."

"We've gotten around that problem once," Donovan said. "Maybe we can do it again?"

"Getting ahead of yourself a bit, Major?" Diaz said. "We've got bigger problems right now."

"Affirmative," Donovan said. "How far off course are we from returning to base?"

"Forty kilometers or so," Ehri said. "It will be dangerous to go back there."

"I know, but we have to. If any of the children survived, if my mother survived. They're going to need someone to try to get them out." He held up the bek'hai rifle. "We're the best chance they've got."

"We may be the only chance they've got," Diaz said. "We don't leave people behind. We can't just make new ones."

Ehri didn't react to the barb. She shifted her attention to the pilot at their feet. His eyes had opened at some point during the conversation.

"He's awake," she said.

Donovan looked down at the pilot. He was staring at them, watching them. His breathing was calm.

"My name is Major Donovan Peters," Donovan said, leaning down to greet him. "I'm glad you're finally awake. Welcome to Earth."

14

"Captain Soon Kim," the pilot said. His voice was soft. Tired. "New Earth Alliance." He smiled weakly, lifting his arm to salute. "I've never been to Earth before." He breathed in. "I've never breathed fresh air. I've never been outside! It's incredible."

Donovan still felt odd returning the Captain's salute. His own rank wasn't a real thing. Not compared to a man who had spent his whole life training to be a soldier. At the same time, he knew the planet. Captain Soon didn't.

"I wish we were meeting under better circumstances, Captain," Donovan said. "I wish I was welcoming you home. You and all of your people."

"Me, too. Do you know? Did Captain St. Martin make it out?"

"He did," Ehri said.

Soon smiled. "We did it. I can't believe we did it." He tried to push himself up, groaning and laying back down. "Must have hit my head. Hard."

"You have a wound to your abdomen as well," Ehri said. "It will heal quickly, but it will help if you stay still."

"We had to carry you quite a way," Donovan said. "It didn't help. We didn't have a choice."

"I'm sure you didn't."

"Diaz, can you get Captain Kim some water?"

"Yes, sir," Diaz replied, heading off toward the river.

"That's Lieutenant Renata Diaz," Donovan said. "This is Ehri."

"Just Ehri?" Soon said.

"I'm a lor'hai," Ehri replied. "A bek'hai clone."

"Bek'hai? You mean the enemy?"

Donovan expected Soon would be afraid. He wasn't.

"She helped us get the weapons," Donovan said. "She's on our side."

Soon stared at her in silence for a moment. "You look familiar." His face changed when he placed her. "General St. Martin has a picture of his wife, Juliet. I've seen it a thousand times. Even with the grime on your face, I would know it anywhere."

"Yes," Ehri said. "I am aware of Juliet St. Martin."

"Did Gabriel see you?"

"He did," Donovan said, remembering the look on Captain St. Martin's face when he saw the spitting image of his mother. "He was shocked, to say the least."

"I can imagine."

Diaz returned with the water, held in a large leaf. She kneeled next to Soon, helping him drink.

"Thank you," Soon said. "I've never tasted anything like it."

"You're welcome, Captain."

"We have a lot of catching up to do," Soon said. "A lot you need to tell me. A lot I need to tell you."

"You should rest, Captain," Ehri said. "You likely have a concussion. We're fortunate you didn't die with as much as we put you through."

"There's no time to rest," Soon said. "Not now. If the enemy wasn't taking us seriously before, we both know they are now, or they wouldn't have launched a ship to chase the Magellan."

"I can't argue with that," Donovan said. "We're headed back to the rebel base. It was attacked by the bek'hai, but there's a chance there may be some survivors."

Weapons Of War

"How have you managed it all these years, Major?" Soon said. "Being down here with them? Being hunted?"

Donovan remembered what it had taken for him and his mother to get to Mexico. To make it to the missile silo they had called home up until yesterday. "As much as you're enjoying the taste of the water and the smell of the air, I think we'd feel equally grateful to be at peace, to have some measure of safety and security. To be out there, instead of down here."

"Not me," Diaz said. "Somebody has to fight. Somebody has to keep it all going."

"You don't want peace?" Ehri asked.

"Of course, I do. Peace on Earth. No more bek'hai. That's why we're all here, right?"

"General St. Martin swore he would come back," Soon said. "For as long as I've been alive, he promised we would find a way to fight the enemy, and when we did, we would. He's an incredible man, the General. You're right, Lieutenant. Somebody has to keep it all going. We have a key. We just need to figure out how to use it. Our scientist, Reza, he's a genius. If anyone can reverse-engineer the enemy tech, it's him. The Magellan will be back. I can promise you that. If we can keep the enemy on their toes, if we can soften them up until the General returns, that's what we need to do."

"That's what we will do," Donovan said. "We already sent a message to our headquarters in New York, to General Parker. The rest of the resistance will be organizing as we speak, preparing to fight back. Some of our people must have escaped. Once we regroup, we can make plans to begin to counter the bek'hai."

Soon grunted in agreement, his eyes shifting over to Ehri. "Where do you fit into all of this?"

"I convinced my Domo'dahm, my leader, to allow me to study humans up close. To join them before he completed his goal of ending the resistance. I learned of your ways. Your freedoms. Your ability to choose. I don't want to destroy my people. The lor'hai, the clones, are all like you. We are fully human, even if we are copies. The others don't choose freedom because they don't know what it is. They don't know it is a choice. I hope that by helping you, I will be able to give them a choice, and in doing so, will force the Domo'dahm and the drumhr to make a choice before all of our blood is shed."

"I appreciate the idealism," Soon said. "I hope you have a chance to practice it. For my part, I'm not keen on letting the aliens off the hook so easily. Not the ones who are in charge, anyway."

"I understand," Ehri said. "I have pledged my loyalty to Major Peters. I will follow his orders as they are given. At the same time, I trust in the compassion of humanity, as much as anything else."

"You should try to rest a little," Diaz said. "We need to keep quiet, anyway. The bek'hai have excellent hearing." She looked over at Ehri when she said it.

"Sensors," Donovan said. "Heat. Motion. Sound. There are ways to avoid all of them, and we'll teach you. For now, enjoy the chance to sleep under the stars for once, instead of among them. Enjoy the sound of flowing water. Wind. Air."

Soon grunted again. "I'd rather be back up there with my wife, to be honest. But I'll take what I can get. I hope I get to share this with her one day."

"I hope so too, Captain. I hope so, too."

15

GABRIEL WAS ON HIS WAY to the bridge when he nearly collided with Guy Larone. The astronomer was on his way out of the main conference room, a concerned look crossing his otherwise sour expression.

"Pardon me, Captain," he said, his eyes betraying his almost cordial words.

Gabriel didn't have a chance to reply. The scientist continued past him, storming down the corridor.

Reza, Sarah, and Colonel Choi followed close behind, more calm in their demeanor. More focused. Reza smiled when he saw Gabriel.

"Captain St. Martin," he said. "How is your father?"

"I don't know," Gabriel lied. "He won't let anyone in to see him."

"Not even you?" Sarah asked.

"No. Believe me, I tried."

He glanced at Colonel Choi. Her face suggested she didn't quite believe him. That was okay. As long as he didn't say anything, he was keeping his father's promise.

It had been nearly twenty-four hours since he had spoken to Theodore. He had done as his old man had asked, retreating to his own concerns while his father succumbed to the pains of withdrawal from the meds. He could picture Theodore in the bathroom, spitting up everything he tried to put down, cursing against the agony he was surely feeling in the stumps of his legs by now. The thought made him want to rush to his father's side, to do something for him.

Instead, he had been headed up to the bridge to take a shift. The Magellan was doing little more than traveling in the general direction of home at STL speed, balancing her acceleration with the overall load on the reactors. That didn't mean he couldn't give Lieutenant Bale a little R&R time.

"What happened to Guy?" he asked, pointing at the man's back, nearly vanished in the dimness of the ship's lighting. Repair crews were still working on getting power regulation back up to spec.

"He's unhappy," Sarah said. "What else is new."

"About being stuck out here?" Gabriel asked.

Guy's wife rolled her eyes. "About pretty much everything. I've tried to get him to see the light in all of this, but all he wants to do is complain about how we could have been on our way to the New Earth by now."

"The one that only half of us would have reached?" Choi said.

Sarah looked at the floor. "Yes, ma'am. We were all trying to find a viable solution for our future. It was never personal."

"When you're intentionally letting people die, it's always personal," Choi said. "But personal feelings aren't what's important right now. Captain, Reza and Sarah have been working on the slipstream problem."

"And?" Gabriel asked.

"We've calculated that the stream that brought us here is likely still active," Reza said. "What we think happened is that the gravitational field of the Earth pushed us forward on it, onto the leading edge."

"Normally, a starship can't join the edge of a stream because the nacelles need more purchase in subspace," Sarah said. "The result is that we were cast off by the stream when it reached its terminus."

"Cast off?"

"Like the ocean tides on Earth," Colonel Choi said. "We washed up on the shore."

"I don't completely understand that," Gabriel said.

"The important part is that we've been able to reconcile our position with the edge of the slipstream," Reza said. "We're outside of mapped space, but our sensors have picked up a solar system approximately two thousand AU from here. We believe we can pick up a slipstream there."

"That's good news," Gabriel said, doing the math in his head. Somewhere between twenty and thirty days. It was more than he had hoped for, but it was better than being stuck for months. "I would think Guy would have been excited about getting out of here."

"You would think that, wouldn't you?" Sarah said.

"He thinks we've doomed the entire colony," Choi said. "We showed the Dread that we're willing to fight back and made them angry, and now they're going to come looking for us."

"That part is probably true," Gabriel said. "He does realize the Dread don't know where the colony is, and that space is a big place? Plus, we have the plasma rifle."

"We've been tied up figuring out where the Magellan is," Reza said. "Now that we have a course to set, we'll start working on the rifle."

"That's where Guy was headed," Sarah said. "He wanted to examine the device before Reza got to it. I think he's feeling a little jealous."

Gabriel noticed the way Sarah looked at Reza when she said it. It wasn't any of his business, but it appeared that Guy might have a reason to be angry.

Reza seemed oblivious to the older woman's attention. "Colonel, Captain, even if we do discover the method the Dread use to defeat their own shields, how are we going to weaponize it? The Magellan doesn't have any offensive capability."

"We'll get to that when we have to," Colonel Choi replied. "With any luck, we'll have to figure that out very soon."

"Yes, ma'am," Reza said. "If you'll excuse me, I'm going to head down to the mess, and then join Guy in the hold."

"Reza, do you mind if I join you?" Sarah asked.

He shrugged. "Sure, if you want."

"Colonel," Sarah said. "Captain." She smiled at them both, and then headed off alongside Reza.

Both Gabriel and Colonel Choi watched them depart for a moment. Then Choi turned to him.

"You saw your father, didn't you?"

"No," Gabriel said.

"You can't lie to me," Choi said. "You spent nine months in my womb, remember?"

"Then don't push," Gabriel said.

Choi nodded. "Understood. Should I be worried?"

"About my father? No. About Guy Larone? Maybe. Did you see the way Sarah was making eyes at Reza?"

"I did. She's old enough to be his mother."

"Thankfully, Reza is too focused on his work to notice. For now. I'm willing to bet Guy has noticed."

"You think he'll do something irrational?"

"If his wife starts cheating on him on top of all of the other embarrassments he's already endured? His ego is getting crushed. I don't know if he can take it."

"Those embarrassments are of his own doing."

"I know. You're in charge while Theodore is missing in action, Colonel, but I recommend not giving him unfettered access to the most powerful weapon on the ship."

"Agreed. I'll send Hafizi down to the hold, ostensibly to keep an eye on the weapon, not on Guy."

"Yes, ma'am."

"Where are you headed, Captain?"

"I was going to relieve Lieutenant Bale. I've had time to rest and recover. She hasn't."

"Bale is off-duty," Choi said. "Maggie is handling flight control at the moment. It isn't as if we're in any imminent danger."

"There's no chance the Dread fortress followed us?"

"No. According to Reza, their ship's design would make it unable to reach slip speed inside of the atmosphere. Even if they followed the same stream, their wave calculations would be completely different, as would their speed. They would be weeks out of sync, and considering how much there is out there, the odds of crossing paths with them are infinitesimally low."

Gabriel smiled. "You sound just like Reza."

"I'm not surprised. I was quoting him. In any case, Captain, take advantage of the time you have. I suspect we'll all have plenty to do soon enough."

16

THEODORE ST. MARTIN CLUNG TO the edge of the sink, dropping his head over the waste disposal. His stomach gurgled, and then he coughed, choking up small amounts of bile. It was all that was left in his system, ravaged and purged over the last twenty-four hours at his cold stop of the pain meds that had made him weak.

It was nothing compared to the pain in his legs. Without the chemicals coursing through his bloodstream, the burning and itching sensations had returned with full force, leaving him barely able to prop himself up to vomit. He had never felt physical pain like it before.

At the same time, he had known mental anguish ten times worse. He could recall it like it was yesterday. The day they reached Ursa Majoris. The first time he had a minute to himself, time to think about his Juliet.

It was another pain to add to the rest of the stack. Juliet had been captured and cloned. His Juliet, his love, his angel. She was dead, sure as shit. She was gone. But her face would always be there to remind him. To distract him. He accepted that she was with God. That didn't make it hurt less. Everybody had a degree of selfishness in him. That was his.

There were strategic implications, too. Could he fire on an enemy position when he knew he would be destroying her likeness, enemy or not? Could he do harm to a creature made from her DNA, who might share some of the qualities and quirks that he had loved so much?

He knew he might have to. He knew he had to be ready for that.

One thing at a time. The withdrawal was kicking his ass right now. There would be time for the tough choices to do that later.

He coughed again, his hand slipping on the edge of the sink. He cursed, turning his shoulder so it would hit the shelf, cursing again at another new pain, and falling onto the floor.

"General, are you okay?" he heard Diallo say. He appreciated the loyalty of the damnable woman, but she made him feel like an infant sometimes.

"Just dandy, Sergeant," he replied. "Fell on my ass again. At least it makes it harder for it to get kicked."

He rolled over and leaned back against the metal cabinet, gritting his teeth. The pain was intense. He wondered if Vivian had felt this way when she delivered Gabriel? He had been there with her. He had watched it happen. She was a trooper. The most loyal friend he had. Only Gabriel was more loyal.

He reached up, wiping some cold sweat from his forehead. He had refused medical attention, but Diallo said stopping the medication the way he did would leave him this way for forty-eight hours. Two days. He could manage two days. It was a small price to pay for almost killing everyone on board, and ending their side of the war. A small absolution. He had been stupid for taking the pills in the first place.

Forty-eight hours. It was making him feel old. Hell, he was old. He had no business still being alive, and he knew it. Stupidity had caused him to crash into that BIS. Arrogance. Maybe there had been a systems failure, but he shouldn't have been out there to begin with. He should have been above such things. Getting older was hard. To lose your reflexes, your eyesight, your legs. Getting older meant more and more loss, either within you, around you, or yourself altogether. He was the Old Gator. He had a responsibility.

He closed his eyes, focusing on his breathing. Medication or meditation. That was the only way forward. He couldn't command with the full brunt of the pain, no matter how tough he tried to be. The nerves were damaged, sending constant signals of panic and fury to his brain.

Minutes passed. Tears began to roll from his eyes. He couldn't do it. He couldn't conquer this demon. No matter how much he wanted to. Its pull was too strong.

He took the bottle of pills from his pocket and looked at it. His lip curled in pathetic sadness, his heart thumping rapidly. Why did things have to be so hard for him? Why did God challenge him this way? He had played it strong for Gabriel. Didn't let him see how hard this really was, and how hard he knew it would be.

He opened the top and looked into the bottle. His legs were throbbing. Burning. Stabbing. He thought of Juliet. She would have been so calm, so cool and collected. She would have helped him through the meditation. She would have been patient.

He shifted, turning the bottle over into the waste disposal, taking away his choices. He had to do it. For her memory. For Gabriel. For all of the souls on his ship.

For himself.

He heard her voice in his head as he focused on his breath again. "In through the nose. Hold. Out through the mouth. Five. Seven. Five."

He repeated it over and over as he did it. He didn't know for how long. He only knew there was a point that he stopped thinking about his legs. He stopped thinking about the pain. He stopped thinking about everything.

Everything except Juliet. What would she want him to do about the clones? About the Dread?

Save the planet. Be compassionate. He was a military man. Compassion was hard to do.

If he had the chance, he would try.

For her.

First, he needed the chance. He needed to survive this.

Forty-eight hours.

He opened his eyes, pulling out his watch. An hour had passed.

Only twenty-two to go.

17

"HOW COULD ANYONE BE ALIVE out there?" Diaz said.

Donovan peered across the remains of the city from their vantage point at the base of the mountain. There had been few enough buildings still upright, and many had been brought to the ground by Dread mech and fighter attacks. Some of the areas were still smoldering, sending plumes of smoke into the sky. There were bodies visible on the ground, soldiers mostly, men and women who Donovan had served with and in some cases called friends.

"I'm sorry," Soon said, standing beside him. The bek'hai bandage had served its purpose, healing the gash in his side fast and well. His head was better but not perfect. He refused Donovan's offer of a rifle they had captured, telling him that he wouldn't know which of the three duplicates he should shoot at.

"The children were hidden," Donovan said, refusing to give up on their people. "They could still be down there. Others might have come back, too."

"We should be quick," Diaz said. "Get in, look for survivors, get out."

"Agreed," Donovan said. "Soon, can you handle it?"

"Don't worry about me, Major. Take care of yourself and your people."

Donovan pointed to the mass of mud they had carried from the river. It was a heavy burden to manage, but he knew they would need it. They set about covering themselves in the mud.

"You have the signals down?" Donovan asked.

"Yes, sir," Soon replied.

Donovan slopped the wet earth into his hair and over his face. The others did the same. Once they were damp, he led them down and out to the open road. There was no sign of Dread soldiers, mechs, or fighters, though they had heard them flying overhead overnight.

"Have they stopped giving chase?" Donovan asked.

They had seen the fortress floating in orbit when daylight had come. They had watched two of the starfighters fly up to it, and a short time later it had left. They all knew it was following the Magellan.

"A trap?" Soon asked. "Maybe they're waiting for us in the base?"

"No," Ehri said. "The bek'hai don't fight like that. They won't hide underground. I believe this is a sign of respect. The Domo'dahm is allowing you to return to your home."

"How nice of him," Diaz said.

"Of course, they will be monitoring the area. He'll want to know when you do return. They will probably give you a small head start before following."

"Is it us he respects?" Donovan asked. "Or you?"

"We destroyed a mechanized armor and a fighter, as well as a squad of Hunters. It is all of us, Major. We have earned our way here."

"Do you think he'd be willing to give me my brother back?" Diaz asked.

"Your brother is very intelligent and very handsome. I believe he will become a pur'hai."

"Pur'hai?"

"A template for cloning. It is the easiest life a human can have among the bek'hai if that is any consolation."

"It isn't," Diaz said.

"Okay, quiet time," Donovan said. "We need to get across the open area to that rubble as fast as possible. Soon, if you want to stay here, we can rendezvous back at this spot."

"I can run. My head can wait."

Donovan nodded. "Let's move."

They charged across the field at a sprint. Donovan kept his eyes on the sky, watching for signs of incoming fighters. Diaz scanned the ground, while Ehri and Soon took up the rear. Soon was slower than Donovan would have liked, but he managed to stay on his feet and running until he caught up to them at a blown-out wall.

"I should have spent more time in the gym," Soon whispered, breathing hard.

"You made it; that's all that matters," Ehri replied, also keeping her voice low.

Donovan put his finger to his lips. Then he moved to the corner of the building and tracked his vision across the street. He knew Wilcox as soon as he saw her, laying on her back with a gaping wound in her chest.

He felt a pang of sadness and forced himself to swallow it. He had to worry about the ones who might still be alive. He used hand gestures to lead them around the corner, making a zig-zag pattern from cover to cover through the city.

They paused when a distant rumble sounded.

"Diaz, can you get eyes on whatever is making that noise?" Donovan said.

Diaz nodded, running across the street and scaling a pile of debris. The rumbling remained distant until it faded completely. Diaz returned a moment later.

"Some kind of Dread ship," she said.

"What did it look like?" Ehri asked.

"Long, narrow. Lots of spikes or points or something."

"A transport. Which direction was it headed?"

"Northeast."

"What does it mean?" Donovan asked.

"I'm not sure," Ehri said. "The transport can hold up to one thousand soldiers, both clones and drumhr. The Domo'dahm may be seeking to accelerate his conquest of the resistance now that we have threatened the status quo."

Donovan tried not to think about how many humans that single ship was going to be responsible for killing. It was harder to do when a second rumble echoed across the sky, matching the first. A third followed a moment later.

"I'm afraid that escalation is the most likely cause," Ehri said.

"There's nothing we can about that right now," Donovan said.

He brought them the remaining distance to the pile of rubble that had once hidden the silo. It had been blasted aside, leaving a gaping hole that revealed the depth of the missile tube. There were no bodies at the bottom. He hoped that meant the Dread had decided not to go down.

"Diaz, I need you stay up here to keep watch."

"Me?" Diaz said, reacting to the request. "Why me? Why not Ehri?"

"Diaz," Donovan barked softly. "That's an order, Lieutenant."

She stared at him for a moment before shaking her head. "Order? The military is gone, amigo. We're nothing but a pair of kids who are in way over our heads. That was my home, too."

Donovan felt himself getting angry. She was choosing a lousy time to be difficult. "Ehri, stay and keep watch with Diaz. Soon and I will go down."

"Yes, Major," Ehri said. Diaz scowled but knew better than to complain again.

"What do you say, Captain?" Donovan asked.

"Lead the way," Soon replied.

18

"YOUR LIEUTENANT SEEMS TO BE a bit of a spitfire," Soon said as they descended the silo.

"Renata? She wears her heart on her sleeve. Sometimes that's a good thing. Sometimes it isn't. That's why I left her up there. After losing her brother, she might not react well to finding everyone else dead or gone. I need her rational."

"A good assessment of the situation. You trust her to be alone with the clone?"

"Ehri can take care of herself."

"I meant, do you trust the clone?"

"Yes. With my life." He remembered the kiss he had shared with Ehri. There hadn't been any time to explore that any further. Maybe one day. "She saved our lives, and yours."

"I don't mean to be ungrateful, Major. We know so little about the situation down here. So little about them. We're raised knowing that they stole our home and killed billions of our people. That alone is enough to inspire hate and mistrust."

"It isn't any different down here. But it's harder to hate something once you know it personally. Once you can relate to it."

"That is true."

"And believe me, I won't hesitate to kill any of the Dread that I have to in order to get our planet back. What Ehri says about freeing the clones is all well and good, but it isn't my top priority."

"I'm glad to hear that, Major."

They reached the base of the silo. The heavy lead door that was supposed to protect them was hanging open; the locks sawed off by a plasma beam.

"So much for them not coming down here," Donovan said, feeling his stomach drop. He didn't want to lose his mother. Not after everything they had endured.

He had a second Dread rifle slung over his shoulder. He lifted it and handed it to Soon. "Ehri said they won't ambush us down here, but just in case she's wrong. Shoot at all of them if you have to."

Soon took the rifle, running his hand along it. "I can't believe I can kill them with this. I've never killed anything before."

"Remember that it's them or us. Don't let it be us."

"Yes, sir."

Donovan stared at the half-open doorway for a moment. His heart was racing, his nerves tense. He breathed out heavily and then made his way into the base.

He clenched his teeth at the sight of Captain Reyes crumpled in the corner, his neck clearly broken. A woman's body was a few feet back, her neck bruised. Choked to death. She looked like she had been trying to run.

"Brutal," Soon said, the sadness in his voice tangible.

"More than it had to be," Donovan agreed.

They kept going, moving through the long corridor that connected the silo with the living area. There were no other bodies in it. There were also no scorch marks or bullet fragments. He realized why when he reached the end.

The few who had remained inside the base had barricaded the door. Then they had tried to escape through it. The Dread had come at them from behind, somehow finding another way in. Had the bek'hai discovered the path they had taken out?

He felt his heart jump. His mother was supposed to take the children that way. Had she tried? Had they found her? He was tempted to rush to the hidden passage behind General Rodriguez's office. He didn't. He had to be careful and do things right.

There were six corpses right at the barricade, all of them killed with blunt force trauma, thrown or crushed or beaten. It was an ugly way to die. An unnecessary way to die. Why had the Dread done it? What did they have to gain through the violence?

Ehri said the Domo'dahm respected them, but he didn't see that. He saw the Dread Leader taunting them, teasing them, showing them how weak and small and unimportant humans were. Not even important enough to waste plasma energy on.

They worked their way through the halls. Donovan kept his ears open for signs of activity. There was no sound. The silo was a tomb.

He finally reached the General's office. The door was hanging open slightly, the base's lights revealing little. Donovan could barely breathe, his body was so tense, his heart racing so fast. In the back of his mind, he knew what he was going to find. He knew she was going to be dead. That they were all going to be dead.

"I can check it if you want," Soon whispered.

Donovan was tempted. He shook his head. "I have to."

"Okay."

He led with the front of the rifle, using it to push the door open the rest of the way. His heart sunk to see that the door to the passage was open, though there were no bodies directly inside. He started toward it.

A gunshot sounded from somewhere deeper inside the base.

It was followed by three more.

19

DONOVAN STARED AT THE OPENING to the passage for a few seconds before turning. Someone was in here, alive, and they were shooting at something.

"Come on," he said, rushing past Soon and down the corridor.

"Where?" Soon said.

Donovan wasn't sure. The shots were muffled, only obvious because of the overall silence of the base. It had sounded like they came from further down.

He reached the steps, pausing before opening the door. He needed more. Another sound. The base was too big to find the source quickly without it.

It was probably too late already.

He closed his eyes. Silence. He would have to guess. Someone had been alive in here. Who might it be?

He entered the stairwell, descending as fast as he could, Soon close behind him. He reached the second floor, stopping at the nursery and peering in through the small window. Empty. He hurried down the hallway, heading for the infirmary.

A large shape turned the corner ahead of him. For a split-second, he thought it was a bek'hai Hunter in powered armor, it was so big. He almost fired without thinking.

The shape gained focus. A man, muscular, with dark skin and big eyes. He was bleeding from his shoulder, and had a pistol in his hand.

A Dread weapon.

Donovan threw himself to the side, shoving Soon with his shoulder at the same time. The clone's attack missed, the plasma strike going wide. Donovan stumbled back the other direction, keeping the clone's attention. It tracked him calmly, taking the time to aim.

A bolt from the other side of the corridor caught it in the chest. It grunted but didn't fall, finally taking the shot.

It hit the wall right next to Donovan's head, the aim thrown just enough by Soon's attack. That was the only shot it was able to fire, as four more bolts burned into it in rapid succession. The clone fell face down and didn't move.

"Thanks," Donovan said, looking over at Soon.

The pilot was shaking, his eyes stuck on the dead clone, his weapon still raised and ready to shoot again.

"Damn," Soon said, swallowing hard. He lowered the rifle. "They look just like us."

"They are us. Copies of us. Stay alert. There may be more." Donovan approached the clone.

It was wearing a rough spun green shirt and pants, similar to the simple fatigues the resistance soldiers usually wore. It was barefoot too, intended to look like a rebel fighter. It was no one that Donovan recognized.

"So much for not ambushing us down here," he said. Ehri had been wrong about the Domo'dahm's intentions.

Soon scanned the corridor, keeping the rifle ready. He had passed the most important test with flying colors, even if it had left him unsteady.

Donovan reached under the clone, grabbing the pistol and examining it. He hadn't seen such a small plasma weapon before. It didn't seem as powerful as the rifle, but it was more than enough to kill a human, and likely easy to conceal. Of course, it was locked.

"Somebody shot him," Soon said.

"It was coming from the infirmary," Donovan said. It was leaving, which meant whoever had shot it was most likely dead. He hoped not.

They hurried to the area, finding the medical equipment in disarray, the exam table on its side. There was blood on the ground, the clone's fresh blood. There was a second spread of still wet blood on the back wall, the pattern disrupted by a now-closed door.

"Who's in there?" Donovan said, trying to keep his voice low. He approached the door cautiously. "Doctor Iwu?"

He heard motion behind the door. He knocked softly.

"Doctor Iwu? Is that you? It's Donovan Peters."

The door clicked and opened. Doctor Iwu was standing behind it, holding General Rodriguez's gun in her hand.

"Donovan? You're alive." Her face hardened. "I need your help."

She lowered the gun, turning on her heel and heading back. Donovan followed behind her.

General Rodriguez was laying across her desk, his shirt torn off, his stomach bleeding beneath a heavy bandage.

"General?" Donovan said.

Rodriguez's head turned slowly. He smiled when he saw Donovan. "Donovan. Thank God."

"Donovan, I need you to keep pressure on the wound," Iwu said, pushing past him. "Excuse me," she said to Soon, who filed into the room.

"What's going on?" Donovan said. He turned around, watching Iwu search the cabinets for tools.

"The plasma bolt tore through his internals," Iwu said. "Either we sew them back together and pray, or he dies." She found what she was looking for and headed back into the room. "Did you kill the Dread soldier?"

"Yes," Donovan said. "General, where's everyone else?"

"I don't know," Rodriguez said, his voice barely more than a whisper. It was obvious he was having trouble breathing.

"Keep pressure here," Iwu said, pointing. She laid the tools out on the desk next to the General. Donovan did as she said. "You." Iwu looked at Soon. "When I ask for bandages, they're over there."

Soon found them. "Yes, ma'am."

"They were supposed to double back," Rodriguez continued. "Nobody came."

"I came," Iwu said.

"How long?" Donovan asked.

"Three hours. After the Dread cleared out."

"Except it wasn't clear," Donovan said. "The clone."

"It was clear," Iwu said, taking one of the tools and lifting the bandage. "There's too much blood." She was angry.

"It followed me back here," Rodriguez said. "I thought I had lost them. An entire squad of clones, plus that one. I've never seen a clone like that before." It took him ten breaths to say it, and he growled in pain when he was done.

"Me neither," Donovan said.

"Can you stop talking?" Iwu said to Rodriguez. "It makes it worse."

"It thought I was dead," Rodriguez said. "That's why it left. It didn't know the Doc was here."

"I said shut up," Iwu said. "You're going to die."

"Where's the rest of the squad?" Donovan asked.

"Don't know. You didn't see them?"

Donovan glanced over at Soon, who nodded and left the room.

"Who is that?" Rodriguez said. Iwu had moved back into the exam room, searching for something.

"Captain Soon Kim. He's a pilot from the space force. His fighter crashed. We saved him."

"You accomplished your mission?"

"Yes, sir."

"Suction. I need suction, damn it," Iwu said from the other room.

"I'm going to die, Major. There's nothing she can do about it now, even if she's too pig-headed not to try."

"Are they all dead?" Donovan asked. "The other resistance soldiers?"

"They didn't come back, except for you. They better be." He tried to laugh. It turned into a gurgling cough. Iwu came back into the room.

"Christian, you need to stop talking," Iwu said.

"Forget it, Nailah," Rodriguez said. "Even if you patch me, I can't move like this. You need to get out of here."

"I can't just leave you."

"You have to. It isn't safe. Donovan, I'm sorry. Your mom is probably dead. It's my fault. It was a bad plan."

Donovan ignored the pang of sadness. He didn't want to hear Rodriguez tell him what he already knew. "It wasn't, General. We did the best we could. We got the weapon to General St. Martin. That's the best we could have hoped for."

"It is. Thanks to you, Diaz, and Matteo. Thank you, Donovan."

"Major," Soon said, rushing into the room. "We've got company."

"Nailah, you have to go with them."

Doc Iwu looked pained, but she nodded. "You're a good man, Christian."

"You're a good woman. That's why I want you to stay alive."

She leaned down, kissing him on the mouth. "I always wanted to do that," she said.

"You should have said so sooner. Give me my gun."

She handed him his gun. He lifted himself to his feet, using the desk to stay up.

"Go. Donovan, try to make your way back to the States. There's a resistance base in Texas. At least, there was as of a few weeks ago. Austin. Look for the broken angel. The access code is one forty-three, twelve. It's a long way, but I know you can make it. Get the weapon to them in case the Gator doesn't make it back."

"Yes, sir," Donovan said.

"Major," Soon said.

"Goodbye, General," Donovan said.

"Adios, Donovan," Rodriguez replied. "Take care of yourself."

Donovan took Iwu's arm, pulling her gently out of the room, joining Soon and heading out into the hallway. He could hear the motion now. It sounded like the soldiers were headed their way.

"Go that way," Rodriguez said, stumbling through the door behind them, barely able to stand. "I'll keep them busy."

Donovan didn't argue. He kept moving. He heard Rodriguez speaking behind him as he turned the corner.

"In your unfailing love, silence my enemies; destroy all my foes, for I am your servant."

They were on the stairs when the gunshots sounded again.

20

THEY RETURNED TO THE FIRST level of the base. The shooting stopped by the time they reached the stairs, and they paused to listen. It was silent for a few moments before the enemy footsteps could be heard once more.

"He didn't get all of them," Soon said.

"We should get out of here," Iwu said. "That's what he wanted."

"Did you check the passage?" Donovan asked her.

"What passage?"

"The one in the General's office."

"No. I didn't know there was one."

"Then I'm not leaving. I need to know."

Rodriguez told him his mother was likely dead, and he knew it was true. Why did he have to go back to look for himself? What was the reason?

He had already lost Matteo. He wouldn't abandon her. Not if there was any chance she was alive. That was the reason. That was what he told himself.

"He died to get us out," Iwu said.

"He was going to die anyway," Donovan said. "We'll have a better defensive position from the General's office. And an escape route."

"Donovan," Diaz said, appearing from the corridor on their left.

He whipped his head around, his heart jumping. He had been so focused on listening to the Dread on the stairs he hadn't heard her coming. Stupid.

Ehri appeared beside her a moment later.

"We destroyed a squad of clone soldiers trying to get into the base," Ehri said. She froze for a second. "There are more already here?"

"Yes. They followed General Rodriguez back. I guess the Domo'dahm didn't want him to get away."

"Where is the General?"

"Dead," Iwu said.

"The Domo'dahm isn't behind this. One of the pur'dahm perhaps, trying to make a good impression. Ulr'ek or Dur'rek, I bet. If the pur'dahm could capture the General and interrogate him for information about the other resistance leaders, it would allow him to move up a cell."

"So it was a trap?" Soon said.

"Yes, but not for us. Even so, we must leave this area."

"We will. I need to finish what I started here. I need to know if she's dead or not."

"I understand."

"We've got the numbers. We should take care of this group. Soon, you and Diaz take position over there. Ehri, Doc Iwu, and I will wait there. We'll catch them in a crossfire when they come out of the stairwell."

"Yes, sir," Soon and Diaz said, backing up into the corridor.

Donovan retreated to the side, along the same wall as the stairs, positioning himself in front of Doctor Iwu.

Then they waited.

The three remaining Dread clones reached the top of the stairwell a minute later, moving out onto the floor without noticing the gathered rebel soldiers right away. By the time they did, it was too late. Bolts from both sides tore into them, dropping them in the space of a single breath.

"Nice work," Donovan said, stepping over the dead clones. "I guess it would have been too much to ask for the pur'dahm behind this to do the dirty work."

"Neither of those pur'dahm are Hunters," Ehri said. "They are strategists. Politicians."

"This is a game to them?"

"In the sense that they are jockeying for position within a traditional ranking system, perhaps. There is nothing jovial about it."

They returned to Rodriguez's office. Donovan felt the same fear and anxiety bubbling up a second time as he entered the room. Until he saw her, there was a chance she had gotten away. He needed to know.

He circled the desk, reaching the open passage. He didn't hesitate, pushing it open wider so he could fit through and allow more light to filter in.

Nothing. There was nothing. Where were they?

He looked back at the others. They were waiting for him to make a decision. Should they follow the passage and keep seeking his mother and the children, or should they head back out through the silo? There were no guarantees either way, but the silo was definitely the shorter escape route.

Diaz had lost Matteo and kept going. She hadn't insisted that they find him, as much as he was sure she wanted to. She knew that wasn't the world they lived in. He knew it, too. He didn't have to like it.

He did have to accept it.

All of these people were looking for him to lead them and to keep their small part of the resistance going. They had gotten the weapon to General St. Martin. Now their job was to get the ground forces ready. They had to rendezvous with the rebels in Austin and reconnect with the larger forces, before the bek'hai turned those forces into scattered remains like they had done here.

Maybe Ehri understood why he wanted to find his mother. That didn't mean it was the right decision. Not now.

"It's time to go," he said, leaving the passage and heading back the way they had come.

21

"LOR'DAHM ZOELLE," TEA'VA SAID, LOOKING down at the clone from his position on the command dais.

"Dahm Tea'va," Zoelle said, lowering her head to her chest. "I am at your service."

"Ilk'ash spoke very highly of you before I had him retired."

Tea'va watched the clone carefully, studying her reaction to the news. She flinched slightly but otherwise remained in place.

"I would be honored to prove my worth to you, Dahm."

Tea'va almost smiled at the response. It nearly sounded sincere.

"Tell me, Lor'dahm. Were you practicing copulation with Ilk'ash?"

"Dahm?" she raised her head only slightly, maintaining respect. "I do not know what this means?"

"Were you ever unclothed with him?"

"No, Dahm. Why would I do such a thing?"

Tea'va stood. He was pleased with her response. She didn't know that had she answered differently, he would have killed her as well. "Why, indeed?" He made his way from the dais, reaching the level of the deck and standing in front of her. "Look at my face."

Zoelle raised her head, looking up at him. Tea'va had never been this close to an un'hai before. He stared at her features. Her soft, pale skin, her blue eyes. She had a smell of Earth. Flowers and spices. Did the humans think she was a pretty thing?

He didn't.

"Ilk'ash also told me that you were unable to calculate the human starship's slip trajectory in time to follow. You and your team. Is this correct?"

She didn't buckle under the statement. "Yes, Dahm."

"Why not?"

"We failed, Dahm. We were not prepared."

Tea'va smiled. She didn't react to his crooked grin either. "Your honesty is refreshing."

"The Lore of the Bek'hai demands honesty from a lor'hai, Dahm."

It was true that their laws put this burden on clones. It was also true that few enough of them followed it. Especially the un'hai. Even after fifty years of modification, they remained willful.

"Have you since calculated the trajectory?" Tea'va asked. It was intended to be the last question he had that would decide whether or not he replaced her, but he had already decided. He would keep this one. She was properly obedient, even if her team was not adequately intelligent.

"We have, Dahm. The slipstream has a powerful course through the planet. Once the gravitational effects are factored in, the wave will have carried them approximately six hundred light years from this location, if they rode it to its terminus. Based on the calculated wave velocity and the distortion of the accelerated stream, there is a ninety-eight percent likelihood that they did."

"They will have gone beyond the limits of the stream's ability to carry them. Are there other streams they can join to vector away, or can we follow?"

"We can follow, Dahm Tea'va. Most of the way."

"Most?" he shouted, losing control of his temper. He clenched his jaw. "Most?" he repeated more quietly. He noticed Gr'el was watching him with intense interest. Tea'va knew the pur'dahm would seize any sign of weakness he could find. He had to get his emotions under control.

"As you know, the slipstream wave strength is variable. We would be required to remain stationary for six Earth days to join a stream that is of equivalent power."

"We can't afford to wait six days," Tea'va said. "How close can we get?"

"Within one hundred light years, Dahm," Zoelle said, remaining calm.

Tea'va nearly shouted again. He held his tongue.

"That distance might as well be six hundred light years," he said.

"Perhaps we should consider a different approach?" Gr'el said.

Tea'va didn't want to listen to his Si'dahm. It would look bad to the Domo'dahm if he didn't entertain the pur'dahm's words.

"What do you suggest?"

"We seek out the human settlement," Gr'el said. "We know from our scans of the smaller craft we destroyed that they have a limited range. I am certain with the help of the complete science cell we can limit the possible locations. We can destroy the remaining colony, and then wait for the starship to return."

"And what if they don't return?" Tea'va asked. "What if they choose to go back to Earth?"

"Why would they do that? They may have escaped with our technology, but they would still need to be able to integrate it with their ship. One ship, against all of ours."

"One ship that has escaped us twice already. The Heil'shur, who has evaded our defenses over fifty times. Do not underestimate them, Gr'el. That is why they got away to begin with."

"One hundred light years, Tea'va. You cannot argue with pure mathematics."

"If I might, Si'dahm," Zoelle said.

"Go ahead," Tea'va said, not waiting for Gr'el to answer her.

"I have already plotted a course that will bring us close to our most accurate estimate of their position, a system we have charted as Pol'tik. We believe this is where their slipstream typically fades."

"How many streams?" Gr'el asked.

"Fourteen."

"Fourteen?" the pur'dahm replied in disbelief. "It isn't possible for you to accurately calculate the relative positions of fourteen streams."

"Of course, the timing is not perfect, Si'dahm, due to the variable nature of the waves, but I have chosen a course that remains highly stable. The risk is minimal."

"Would you be willing to put your life on it?" Gr'el asked.

Zoelle didn't look at him. She looked at Tea'va instead, keeping her eyes locked on his. There was no fear in them, only confidence.

"We were not prepared before, Dahm. We are prepared now."

"What is the time in slipspace?"

"Four hundred thirty-two to four-hundred eighty hours."

"Dahm Tea'va, you can't," Gr'el said. "Both the lor'hai and the drumhr will become sick."

"Do you want to advance in the cell, Gr'el?"

"Yes."

"With risk comes reward. We will either return to the Domo'dahm as victors, or we will not return at all."

Gr'el lowered his head, surprising Tea'va with the strength of his submission. The pur'dahm understood the game better than he had even thought. "Yes, Dahm."

"Enter the calculations, Lor'dahm Zoelle. We will depart as soon as they are verified."

"Yes, Dahm Tea'va."

"You are dismissed."

Zoelle lowered her head to him, spinning on her heel at the same time and heading for the exit. The lor'hai that composed the rest of the bridge crew watched her from the corner of their eyes. Tea'va could see their interest there. Their longing. It was revolting. He decided he would meet her in private next time, so he wouldn't have to look at it. Nor would he have to deal with Gr'el's opinions.

"Dahm Tea'va," Gr'el said. "A word?"

"Yes, Si'dahm?" Tea'va said.

"I too would like to move up in the cell, and destroying the humans will be the impetus that will allow this to occur. As you are well aware, I am currently behind Orish'ek to replace Rorn'el on his retirement. I'm certain you also understand what that makes you and me."

Tea'va did understand. It was a delicate game they played. If they succeeded, Orish'ek would be out of the picture, but as commander of the Ishur, it would be Tea'va who took his place, leaving Gr'el still in the second position. At the same time, Gr'el couldn't sabotage the mission, or he would lose his place altogether. It meant that his Si'dahm would be plotting against him, even as they were working together. The pur'dahm was being gracious in warning him of his intentions, though Tea'va didn't need the warning.

"As I said, Gr'el. With risk comes reward. One of us will gain Rorn'el's position when he retires. The other will be dead."

22

"My GREAT-GRANDFATHER GREW UP here," Diaz said, her eyes scanning the scattered ruins of the city.

"San Luis Potosi," Ehri said. "Population four million at the time of the invasion."

"Your invasion," Diaz said.

"Not hers," Donovan replied. "The bek'hai. Ehri didn't exist before they arrived. It's ignorant to blame someone for something they didn't do."

Diaz glared at Donovan. Ehri raised her hand, playing peacemaker. "It is human nature, Major. Racial inequality persisted for centuries because of the sins of your forefathers. Besides, I'm willing to accept the derision."

"You shouldn't have to deal with derision," Donovan said, glaring back at Diaz. "Especially from your allies."

He didn't blame Diaz for her mood. They were all in poor spirits, after having spent the last twenty days on the road from Mexico. It was a grueling journey, slowed by their need to travel on foot, slowed even more by the frequent flyovers the Dread were making in an attempt to locate them. They had covered a little over four hundred kilometers in that time. It was a snail's pace as far as a Donovan was concerned, and it left him worried on a daily basis that the war would be over and lost before they ever arrived at the resistance base in Austin.

If there was still a resistance base to arrive at.

The pace was only one of their problems. The weather hadn't been favorable, the onset of summer leading into rising temperatures, high humidity, and an overabundance of mosquitos. They were fortunate malaria, and other insect-borne illnesses had been stamped out years ago. The loss of so many humans had given nature a chance to rebound, and the mosquito population was no different. While the Dread clothing made most of their bodies immune, their hands, necks, and faces were still exposed and had been fed upon freely. The summer weather had also brought the rain, daily thunderstorms and downpours that benefitted them by making them difficult for the Dread to track, but also left them constantly damp.

They had reached the outskirts of the city the night before, waiting until the sun had ridden high before moving into the ruins. It meant dealing with the heat, but that was better than dealing with the Dread, who they had found tended to avoid the direct sunlight when they could. Ehri had said the intensity would degrade their armor faster, reducing its effective lifespan from two thousand years to closer to eighteen hundred. Donovan had thought she was joking at first. She had reminded him to try not to think like a human. For a race the age of the bek'hai, such things were worth consideration.

While potable water had been easy to capture thanks to the heavy rains, food had been a different story. They had hurried away from the silo without pausing to take any of the stockpiled food, though Diaz had insisted on pausing at the Collection to locate the teddy bear her father had given her when she was only three years old. The plasma rifles they carried were useless for hunting, which had meant spending time every day foraging as best they could, or in some cases going hungry. None of them had been carrying a lot of extra weight when they had started the walk. Now they were all as lean as they could be.

"Where did he live?" Soon asked.

"My great-grandfather?" Diaz replied.

"Yes."

"Near the city center, close to the Barrio de San Sebastian. He died in the invasion. My mother told me he urged her father to get her away from the city when the news reports of the Dread ships started coming in. He practically threw them out himself." She smiled at the memory. "I wouldn't be here today if it weren't for him."

"It's still hard to look at," Soon said.

"It doesn't get easier," Donovan replied. "You tell yourself that you get used to it, but you don't. Our world isn't supposed to look like this."

Soon stared at the city. His initial wonder and intrigue over the planet had faded within the first few days, replaced with the cold, hard reality of not only what had occurred, but also how it was still affecting them all today. He had nearly come to tears as they had walked along the side of the highway, where hundreds of old cars had come to a final rest and the wild around them had started to cover it over. Some of the cars had bodies in them. Few carried any food. There had been so little time to try to escape, and the Dread had seen to it that they hadn't.

Donovan had talked to the pilot at length about that reality and how it compared to life at the human settlement on Calawan. They had wound up both agreeing they would rather be there than here, where freedom was a constant, daily battle, and usually meant little more than bare survival.

They had talked about other things as well, and most importantly about General St. Martin and his son, Gabriel. Soon had nothing but praises for both of the men, and firm conviction that not only would they return, but when they did the Dread would be truly challenged for the first time since their arrival. Soon had told him that the New Earth Alliance had a fighting force at their settlement, one that had been raised to wage war against the Dread. Once they could arm them properly, it would only be a matter of time.

"There's no use crying about it," Diaz said, moving ahead of them. "Don't get sad. Get even."

She hopped over a small, half crumbled wall, vanishing behind the uneven ground. The tip of her rifle appeared a moment later, signaling that she had expected the drop.

"This way," she said.

Donovan motioned for the rest of them to follow. For all Diaz's talk, she seemed to be taking their current situation the hardest. She had always been tough, but she had also managed to maintain some edge of softness, a genuine heart that beamed through the hardened exterior. Donovan had watched that light fade into a constant, desperate anger. She wanted to reach Austin. She wanted to get the weapons in the hands of someone who might be able to decipher them from the ground. She didn't want to depend on anyone else. Not General St. Martin, and not even him.

She had lost too much and was hurting too much. The more he tried to get her alone, to get her to open up, the more she withdrew. She said she didn't blame him for Matteo. That might have been true in the first few days. He knew that was bullshit, now. They had known one another all of their lives and had always shared a connection through her brother. Now that he was gone, the connection was gone.

It would have been harder to take if he didn't have Ehri.

As much as he tried to deny it, as much as he wanted to make it about the mission, and about the war, he couldn't help the feelings that were prompted whenever he was near her. Whether they were talking about human or bek'hai society, or simply sitting in silence, her very existence grew more important to him every day. He often found himself ruminating on the kiss they had shared back in the silo. When he had done it, he had thought that it was because he wanted to win her over to their side, and maybe he had. Now he wanted to do it again for the emotional value and connection. To show her how he felt.

Love? That might have been taking things a little too far. He had a definite crush on her. It was a strange feeling, one that made him both excited and uncomfortable. She was a replica of General St. Martin's wife. That fact alone made it strange. He also didn't know if she felt the same way. He was certain they were friends, but beyond that? She had never treated him in a way that suggested anything more. Was it because she didn't know anything about it? Or was it because those feelings just weren't there? It was maddening for him to think about, and at the same time, he wasn't going to make any romantic move on her.

They had enough problems.

They scaled the wall, dropping down into a narrow alley. Donovan turned when he reached the bottom, reaching back and helping Doc Iwu down. She was doing her best to hold her own, but she was older than the rest of them by at least twenty years, a child during the invasion. She struggled to keep up at times, though she had done so with the same poise and dignity that came so naturally to her.

"Thank you," she said, reaching the ground.

"Of course," Donovan replied.

Diaz was on point, her hand up to keep them stationary in the alley. Donovan could see by the way her head was darting back and forth that she was trying to find a route through the rubble. Their goal was to locate a market or a shelter, or some other building that may have been holding canned food and hope that it hadn't already been picked clean.

They had to be careful. The Dread weren't the only concern. There were plenty of random groups of humans who would rather prey on one another than wage war against the common enemy. General Rodriguez had always referred to them as jackals.

Diaz signaled for them to wait and then took off at a run, crossing an open area and ducking back into another narrow alley. She turned around when she reached it, looking back at them. Then she motioned them to get down.

Donovan dropped with the others, ducking into the shadows as a Dread fighter streaked over the position. The flybys were common in the morning and evening. They had been rare at this time of day.

It wasn't a good sign.

Seconds passed. Donovan finally stood and motioned to the others to do the same. Diaz was on her feet on the other side. She waited a few seconds before signaling them to cross.

Donovan stayed in the rear, covering them as they passed the wider passage. They made it across without incident and then ducked a minute later when another Dread fighter went over.

"Do you think they spotted us?" he whispered to Ehri.

"I don't think so. They're moving too fast."

"D, look," Diaz said, pointing toward the sky.

A Dread transport had appeared behind the fighters. It was moving much slower, and coming in low enough that Donovan could make out the ripples of the armor that covered it.

"You're sure they haven't seen us?" Donovan asked.

"As sure as I can be," Ehri replied.

"Major," Iwu said. "Something's moving over there."

Donovan crawled to Iwu. She was near the corner of the rubble, also on her stomach. He watched as two people ran across the open area. They were dressed in rags and filthy. Scavengers.

The transport shifted direction, turning slightly toward them. Plasma cannons released rounds of bolts that decimated the area, raising a cloud of smoke, dust, and debris. The transport continued, disrupting the rising cloud as it passed and allowing Donovan to catch a glimpse of the scavengers.

They were both dead.

"There must be a small settlement here," Diaz said, joining him. "They'll have already picked the markets and pantries clean, but at least we can use the cover to get through the city."

Donovan looked back at her. "We should help them."

"Are you loco? There's five of us against an entire transport of them, plus two fighters."

Donovan considered, and then slid back to where Ehri was positioned. "If we can get to that transport, would you be able to fly it?"

"If it has been modified for lor'hai use, yes. Not all of the transports have."

"How can you tell?"

"If the transport only contains clones, it is likely that I can fly it. Otherwise, there is a good chance it has a drumhr pilot."

Shouts echoed in the distance, along with sporadic gunfire. Donovan had to make a decision. Escape the city on foot, knowing it would take them at least another sixty days to reach Austin, or make a play for the transport.

"I say we go for it," Soon said, unprompted. "We're already beaten and hungry, and if we manage to win?"

"If we manage to win, we'll piss off the Domo'dahm more than he is already," Donovan said. "That might be a mistake."

"He sent an entire transport to kill the people here," Ehri said. "Listen."

Donovan did. The gunfire was random, and already decreasing in volume.

"They aren't soldiers. They aren't fighters. He's destroying them anyway. He wants to kill every last one of us."

"Us?" Donovan said, surprised by the remarks.

Ehri froze for a moment, having surprised herself. Then she nodded.

"This is our war, Major. Let us fight."

23

DONOVAN CROSSED OVER A SMALLER pile of debris, turning the corner, leading with the end of the Dread rifle. The shouting and screams were louder now. Closer. They had closed the gap between the fighting and their original position, though the Dread transport was still out of sight.

He looked back at Soon, using the hand gestures he had taught the pilot to direct him around a separate pile of rubble. Then he glanced over at Ehri, pressed against a solitary standing wall to his left. He saw a Dread clone ahead of her, facing away from them. He signaled her a warning.

A soft whistle beyond his line of sight gave him Diaz's position. He had sent her to find the transport and report back if she saw any of the bek'hai, an indication that they might not be able to use the vehicle. Not that it would stop them from attacking. It was almost too late for that.

A clone came around the corner, shooting at something Donovan couldn't see. He was cautious with his power levels, taking the few seconds to aim before pulling the trigger and sending a bolt into the clone's abdomen. The enemy soldier fell.

Now it was too late.

Ehri broke around the corner, taking the clone by surprise. She didn't shoot him, using the rifle as a club instead. She hit him hard in the jaw, knocking him over. She fell on top of him, letting her weapon fall to her side and freeing her hands. She shifted on him, twisting his head with enough force that Donovan heard the crack of his neck. She grabbed her rifle and sprang back to her feet, signaling the all clear to him a second later.

It wasn't clear on the other side. An entire squad of clones had appeared ahead of Soon. One of them must have spotted him, because he was crouched behind the rubble, staying clear of the incoming plasma fire.

Donovan gestured to Ehri, and they made their way around the position, getting a better angle of attack on the soldiers. They fired in tandem, efficiently dropping them one at a time. Soon stood when the shooting stopped, giving them the thumbs up.

Diaz whistled again. Donovan ran to Soon's side.

"Head back to Doc Iwu, help her through this mess," he said.

"Yes, sir," Soon replied, falling back. "Thanks for the save."

"Anytime."

Donovan and Ehri went forward in the direction of Diaz's signal. He didn't know how she managed to evade the enemy so well, but he was glad for it.

A scream close to their left forced them off course. Donovan made his way past a somewhat intact building, spotting the scavengers before he saw the soldiers. They were trying to hide between two old cars, the plasma fire keeping them pinned down and frightened.

The soldiers never saw him or Ehri coming. Two plasma bolts dropped them, freeing the scavengers.

One of them was too scared to move right away. The other stood.

"Who are you?" she asked.

"The resistance," Donovan replied.

"The resistance is gone," the woman said.

"Who told you that?"

"Our leader, Murphy. He said that the base in Mexico City was wiped out and that the Dread are sending their armies after the rest. He said even the peaceful settlements and the jackals weren't safe. That's why we were trying to hide here. We thought we could escape their attention." The woman paused. "That's one of their weapons, isn't it?"

"Yes. Whatever you heard, it's wrong. The resistance isn't over."

"There were rumors someone had gotten their hands on Dread weapons, and that they were killing the bastards. I guess that's you." She smiled. "It may be too little, too late, I'm afraid."

"We're not going to let it be. Do you know where the rest of your people are?"

"That way," she said, pointing in the same direction as Diaz. "We had a few guns; maybe we'll take some of the clones with us. We can't do anything about the others, though."

"Others? Did you see the Dread?"

"I saw one. He killed my husband. He went that way."

"You might be safest to stay here for a while."

"What's your name, son?"

"Major Donovan Peters, ma'am."

"I'll pray for you, Major Peters. For as much time as I have left on this Earth. God bless you."

Donovan nodded, breaking off to join Ehri. She was standing behind another building, watching the field ahead of them.

"It looks like they've pinned down a small force over there," she said, pointing at a small zone where a group of scavengers and clones were trading fire. "Diaz is positioned over there." She pointed behind the clones, toward a thirty-foot pile of debris that had once been a skyscraper. "I think the transport is behind it."

"The woman told me she saw a bek'hai. We might be out of luck."

"What do you want to do?"

"What can we do? We've already committed. We'll try to make it to the transport and hope for the best."

"What about the others?"

Donovan knew she meant the scavengers. There was a good chance that helping them would bring the remaining bulk of the bek'hai clones to their position.

Donovan shifted as Soon and Iwu came up behind them, joining them at the wall.

"We got three of them," Soon said.

"Not before they killed two more civilians," Iwu said.

"They're all going to die like that," Soon said, noticing the firefight.

"You want to stop it, Captain?" Donovan asked.

"Yes, sir."

"Okay. Circle to that corner. Ehri, wait here with Doc Iwu. I'll head to the left and try to get to their flank."

Diaz whistled again. It was a sharper tone. She was asking them to hurry.

"Forget that," he said. "There's no time to get fancy. Conserve your ammo, watch out for friendlies. Follow my lead."

Donovan closed his eyes for a moment. The woman had blessed him.

He hoped it helped.

24

HE MOVED OUT FROM BEHIND the wall, sprinting towards an old car thirty meters away. The others followed behind him, joining him in the race.

One of the Dread clones must have noticed them, because a plasma bolt burned past his head a moment later, followed by two more. Then the return volleys began, Soon and Ehri returning fire, disrupting the attack and giving him a chance to reach cover.

They crouched behind it, the Dread offensive now split between them and the scavengers.

"I think I hit one," Soon said, pressed against the car beside him.

"We can't stay here," Ehri said. "Move."

She grabbed Donovan's arm, pulling him away from the car. Why? They would die as soon as they left cover.

Soon and Iwu followed them without question. Bolts cut the air around them, and then a heavy stream of burning energy blasted into the car, the Dread fighter streaking past as it finished its run, leaving the wreck in smoldering slag. Donovan looked back to the clones. One fell. Then another. To his left, the scavengers were breaking cover, going on the offensive.

"They're rallying," he said, stopping his retreat. They were open, too open, but they might not get another chance. He started shooting back at the Dread, careful not to waste the bolts he had remaining. He hit one, and then a second. He looked up. The fighter was circling back, coming in for another run. It would cut them apart.

"We need cover," he said.

Ehri noticed the fighter. "There isn't any."

"Back toward the scavengers."

He led them toward the human position, tracing the outskirts of the battlefield. Bullets and plasma bolts were filling the air with obstacles. There was nothing they could do but run.

They reached the line, where dirty men and women fired at the Dread with century-old pistols and rifles. They were surprised by the newcomers, but they didn't stop attacking.

The fighter streaked over, plasma cannon firing and slamming into the center of the human militia. Screams and shouts followed, along with smoke and debris.

"This isn't working out for us," Donovan said.

"I need to reach the transport," Ehri said.

"What if you can't fly it?"

"Then we're dead anyway."

Donovan frantically scanned the line of scavengers. There were only a dozen of them left, standing resolved in front of a stairwell.

That was why they hadn't run. They were defending something. Children, if he had to guess.

"Murphy," he shouted. "I'm looking for Murphy."

One of the men turned his haggard face in Donovan's direction. Donovan ran over to him.

"I need cover fire. A lot of it. From here to that corridor over there. Can you do it?"

"Who the hell do you think you are?" Murphy asked. He was a big man with tattooed arms and a thick beard.

"I know you have children down there," Donovan said. "Maybe women, too. Lay down some cover fire, and we may all be able to survive this."

Murphy didn't look convinced. He shouted to the scavengers anyway. "Keep them covered. Keep it clear."

Donovan retreated to the others. "Ehri, let's go."

She stood, following him as he ran across the open field.

Bolts whizzed past them once more, diminishing as Murphy and the scavengers organized their fire. Soon joined them, sending plasma digging into the enemy position.

Donovan's heart was racing, his legs burning as he streaked across the field with Ehri beside him. The sprint seemed effortless to her, legs moving steady and strong to keep pace.

He heard the fighter coming, swooping in behind them. Ehri heard it too. They fell forward, pausing their run, tumbling on the ground as the plasma beam slammed into the ground ahead of them, close enough that he could feel the ionized heat of it. He rolled to a stop, wasting no time pushing himself up. Ehri did the same, falling in beside him. They were almost to the narrow corridor between the buildings.

Somehow, they were still alive.

They reached the wall, breaking free of the firefight, hurrying to the other end of the decimated building. The front of the transport became visible as they did, angled slightly toward them. It reminded him of a hornet with its sleek, angry face.

There were no soldiers near the transport that he could see. It looked as if it had been landed and abandoned, the entire contingent of the soldiers disembarking into the fray.

"We made it," he said through heavy breath, too excited about the outcome to stay silent. Ehri was pacing ahead of him, rushing to the open platform into the vehicle with an abandon that surprised him.

Humans were dying, and she wanted to stop it.

"Lor'el shur!"

The shout from behind them broke Donovan's train of thought, and caused Ehri to pull up to a fast stop in front of him.

They turned to face the source at the same time.

An armored pur'dahm, cradling something in his arms. He threw it to the ground as they looked his way.

Donovan couldn't breathe.
It was Diaz.

25

"LOR'EL SHUR," THE BEK'HAI REPEATED, his helmeted head turning from Ehri to Donovan. "Come back with me, un'hai," he said to Ehri in thick, growling English. "No more humans have to die today."

Donovan stared at the body on the ground in front of the pur'dahm. Diaz's limbs were twisted unnaturally; her head limp on a broken neck. His entire body was numb and tingling. His mind was nearly blank.

He had known Diaz almost their entire lives. She had gone from annoying kid sister, to valued Lieutenant, to what, exactly? He didn't know. Ehri had come along, and everything had been happening so fast.

It didn't matter now. She wasn't just dead. She was broken. Treated like a toy and used as an example by the Dread Warrior.

Ehri was making her way back toward the bek'hai. Her face was stone, but her eyes betrayed her anger. She and Diaz had never gotten along, but to Donovan they had been more like bickering sisters. They shared a level of respect if nothing else.

"Come with you? I'll kill you, Til'ek," she said.

"Ehri, no," Donovan said.

She froze next to him. "What?"

Donovan swallowed his nerves, taking a few steps in the pur'dahm's direction. He hoped he understood the customs.

"Call off your soldiers, Til'ek," he said. "We can settle this here and now."

The bek'hai seemed amused. "Hesh dur bek?"

Ehri had taught him those words. An honor fight. A duel.

"Yes."

"I will crush you."

"Hand to hand in your armor, you will. Will you fight on my terms?"

"Name them."

"Ehri, did you ever watch streams from the twentieth century? Westerns?"

"Westerns?"

"Gunfights? Two people at opposite ends of a street, ready to draw their weapons?" He had seen an old stream of it once. He knew people settled their differences that way centuries ago. It was the most fair fight he could have with the Dread pur'dahm.

She considered for a moment and then nodded. "Yes, I do remember something like that, once."

"Can you describe it to that asshole in his language, so we're clear?"

"Of course."

Ehri barked at the pur'dahm in the bek'hai's guttural language, describing how it worked. Donovan noticed that the sounds of violence had paused in the distance. Til'ek must have ordered his troops to stand down.

Donovan's eyes fell back to Diaz's body. He felt the anger welling up. It was his fault she was dead. He shouldn't have let her go off on her own, but she had always been so good at evading the enemy. He wouldn't fail again.

"When I am victorious, your people will be forfeit to me," Til'ek said. "And you will return to the Domo'dahm and explain yourself."

"If I win, your forces will retreat from this area," Donovan said. "On foot."

"You want the ship? I piloted it here, lor'hai. You cannot use it."

The words were a blow. Ehri's face showed her frustration for an instant before returning to calm. Donovan fought hard to keep his emotions from becoming apparent. Even if he won, they were still going to be on foot. Maybe they could at least salvage something from the vehicle.

"On foot," he repeated. "And these people are to be spared."

"I do not have the power to promise that. Only the Domo'dahm can spare your people, and he chooses not to. I can offer three days."

Donovan glanced at Ehri. She nodded. He was telling the truth.

"Agreed."

The pur'dahm bowed his head slightly. Donovan knew it was a show of respect. He did the same. Then they approached one another, for a moment standing face to face. The bek'hai was shorter than him without the armor, slightly taller with it.

They didn't speak, turning back-to-back. Then they walked away from one another, fifty steps each before turning around again.

Donovan held the Dread rifle at his side, staring across the distance to Til'ek. The Dread was holding his weapon almost casually. He was arrogant. He didn't believe a human could outmatch him at anything.

Donovan would make sure it was his undoing.

They faced off, motionless and silent. Donovan caught movement in the corner of his eye. The Dread clones, the scavengers, Soon and Doc Iwu had all come to witness this. He couldn't see Iwu's face when she noticed Diaz's body. He didn't dare lose his concentration.

Til'ek twitched, his rifle rising from his hip.

Time seemed to stop.

Donovan began lifting his weapon. He could hear every heartbeat in his ears, sense every molecule of air against his face, smell every scent of death and blood and burning. It all happened so fast, and yet so slow. He got the rifle up in one hand. The pur'dahm did the same.

He squeezed the trigger, the plasma bolt rocketing across the distance. Til'ek had yet to take his shot.

The Dread saw the bolt coming. He fired back in desperation, his bolt going wide as Donovan's blast hit him square in the chest. The plasma pierced his armor, burning a hole through it and his flesh. He didn't seem to understand the rules. He stumbled, trying to get his rifle up and shoot again, sending a bolt into the ground ahead of Donovan. A second bolt from Donovan's right it the pur'dahm in the face. Ehri. The body tumbled to the dirt.

Silence. Til'ek's corpse rested a few meters from Diaz. Donovan let himself breathe, the tears springing up as soon as the moment had passed. The scavengers and the bek'hai clones all remained in place, shocked and confused.

"Yes," he heard Soon shout from his left.

The pilot's voice shattered the tense aftermath. The scavengers raised their rifles, aiming them at the clones. The clones didn't fight back.

At once, they all turned and began to walk away.

Donovan ran to Diaz, crouching down next to her. The teddy bear she had salvaged from the silo was hanging by its neck from her belt. He reached down and took it, holding it tight in his hand while he let the tears come. He hadn't cried for his mother like this, but then, he had never seen her body.

Ehri stepped up next to him, putting her hand on his shoulder.

"The bek'hai have no death rituals," she said awkwardly. "Death just is. I'm sorry."

"We'll help you bury her," Murphy said. "It's the least we can do."

"You have three days," Donovan said, looking up at him. "That's all I could get you."

"It will have to be enough. We've been running from them for years. It's getting harder, but we do what we have to. You saved our lives here. You saved my daughter's life."

"And my son's," one of the other scavenger said.

"And ours." Donovan recognized the woman that had been trapped behind the car.

"Ehri, check the transport," Donovan said. "See if there's anything we can use. Unsecured weapons, hopefully."

"Yes, sir," Ehri said, moving away.

Soon and Iwu made their way to him.

"I'm sorry," Soon said.

"So am I," Iwu said.

"We won today," Soon added. "Thanks to you, and to her. These people are alive because of us."

Donovan smiled. In this world, the best any of them could hope for was not to die for nothing.

Diaz hadn't.

26

Tea'va shuddered slightly as the Ishur came off of the last of the fourteen slipspace waves, the universe coming back into focus through the viewport. At first, all he saw was empty space and a few stars through eyes blurred by too much time in the void. They regained themselves within seconds, and he turned his head to survey the crew beneath him.

Gr'el seemed to be the next least affected. He leaned forward at his station, shaking slightly, before sitting back and looking around. The clones were faring the worst. Some sat motionless. Others vomited onto the floor.

One fell from his chair, dead.

Fourteen. It had to be a record. Just remembering the sequence of returning to realspace, accelerating to the next point, and joining the slipstream again made Tea'va feel dizzy once more.

He had to stop thinking about it.

He stood up, fighting off the instability of his legs. It was as if his body had yet to return to the same spacetime, and was moving out of sync with his mind. He leaned against the side of the dais as he descended.

"Gr'el, you have the bridge," he said as he passed the pur'dahm.

"Yes, Dahm," Gr'el replied.

"Get a report on the health of the lor'hai. Begin scanning the system for signs of the human ship."

"Yes, Dahm."

Tea'va made his way from the bridge. The days in slipspace had given him an appropriate amount of time to adapt to being in command. He had calmed a bit as a result, feeling more confident and less defensive. The crew knew who was in charge. Even Gr'el grudgingly accepted it for now. He was certain his Si'dahm was plotting against him, but Gr'el had not even tried to be subtle about that. It was all part of the game, and his responsibility to see it coming.

Zoelle had been valuable in that regard. He had found an ally in the un'hai, one who was eager to please him. He had confided in her about Gr'el's position, and she had quietly organized a network of spies to watch the Si'dahm and ensure he was not creating a faction of his own. So far he wasn't, but it was still early.

As much as he had wanted to hate the clone before they had met, he had become quite fond of her. He had no interest in her body, or in trying to breed with her. Rather, he appreciated her analytical mind and her genuine intellect and ability to reason through challenging problems. He had gone to her to discuss his position in the cell on more than one occasion, and she had provided discourse that he had always been lacking.

When the human ship was destroyed, and he returned to Earth to take the bek'hai from the Domo'dahm, he would do it with Zoelle as his heil'bek. He was certain that with her input, there was nothing that he couldn't accomplish.

At the same time, there was a part of him that was disgusted with the thought. He had come into being with the idea that he didn't need anybody to help him do anything. He would rise to power on his own, under his own strength, and when he ruled the bek'hai he would do it his way and his way only.

How had this creature, a lor'hai, changed his perspective so quickly?

Had this same fate befallen the Domo'dahm? Was that why the original un'hai had become so revered?

He would have to be careful, and work harder to keep his emotions in check. It was one thing to value the opinion of the un'hai. It was another to rush into giving her such control.

She was waiting for him in his quarters when he reached them. He hadn't requested her presence, and for a moment he was angry that she had been so presumptuous. Maybe it was better to retire her now and avoid complications later? But she had plotted this course, a complex masterpiece of mathematics, and gotten them to the Pol'tik system ahead of the human ship. Surely, that kind of performance deserved a little forgiveness.

"Zoelle," Tea'va said, remaining calm. "Why have you come to see me?"

She was standing near the viewport, looking out at the newly refocused stars. Her gori'shah covered the length of her arms and neck and fell to the heels of her feet. It was also loose around her chest, making her gender less apparent. It was a more conservative look than the last time he had seen her. He approved.

"Dahm Tea'va," she said, turning and sweeping her head low in a strong sign of servitude. "My apologies for intruding. I would not if it were not important."

"What is your concern?" Tea'va asked.

"I have been studying the effects of the compounded slipspace maneuvers on the health of the crew, both drumhr and lor'hai, to help educate future needs to follow a similar trajectory."

"And what did you discover?"

"Forty percent of the drumhr are sick beyond operating capacity. It is a higher number than I had hoped, but it is still within range of my calculations. Interestingly, Var'ek, like yourself, did not suffer any ill effect from the travel."

"I would not say that I have not felt unwell. You also appear to have escaped unharmed."

"I have been too consumed with my work to tell one spacetime from another." She smiled at that. Tea'va cocked his head in curiosity, and the smile vanished. "The lor'hai did not fare as well, Dahm. Ninety-five percent are unable to perform their duties, and two percent of them did not survive the trip. By my estimates, it will take four days before the crew is well enough to be back at full operational capability."

"I already know the lor'hai are weak," Tea'va said. "While you overassessed their capability, I assumed what you have just stated as true. I am not surprised."

"With your permission, Dahm, I urge caution in the next few days. With our numbers at their current levels, we would be hard-pressed to mount a serious offensive should the human starship arrive."

"Caution?" Tea'va said. That statement started to make him angry. "Their ship has no weapons. Once we have caught up to them, we can destroy them at our leisure. I trust you won't let them slip away again?"

"No, Dahm. I will not. Even so, I ask that you consider that the humans may have succeeded in reverse-engineering our technology and that they may have already produced one or more weapons capable of damaging the lek'shah. Also, there is the matter of the slipspace variability in this system that could become a detriment, for as much as we have used it as an asset."

"You overestimate them as you overestimated the lor'hai. They have not had enough time to determine the properties of the weapon so soon. In fact, I don't believe they will ever comprehend the nature of the technology. Their methods and understanding are too primitive to make the proper logical assumptions."

"I disagree, Dahm Tea'va," Zoelle said, keeping her head low as she did. "The humans caught us off-guard, both in their ability to escape with the weapon and in their ability to escape from Earth. They have proven to be unpredictable and resourceful, and I believe that makes them dangerous."

Tea'va stared at Zoelle. "You almost sound as though you admire them."

"I am intrigued by their actions, as any scientifically minded clone would be. I wish only to serve you, Dahm, and offer you my opinion, as you have specifically requested it in the past. You have shared your political ambitions with me, and I would like to see you achieve them."

"Those are the right words. I am curious about your motivation."

"When you have power, I will have power. It is as simple as that."

"I did not believe the lor'hai hungered for such things. You are less. You will always be less."

They were sharp words, but they drew no reaction from her. "Within the right contexts, with the right pur'dahm as Domo'dahm, I believe I can be more."

They were both silent for a moment while Tea'va considered her words. If she had been any other lor'hai, he would have dismissed them already. He did value her opinions, her honesty, and her subservience.

"I will think on what you have said. Go now. I require time in the regeneration chamber."

Zoelle swept herself low again. "Yes, Dahm. Thank you, Dahm."

She was heading for the exit when Gr'el's voice pierced the room.

"Dahm Tea'va, my apologies for the disruption, but our scans have returned an anomaly near the edge of the system. I believe we have found them."

114

27

TEA'VA HURRIED FROM HIS QUARTERS with Zoelle trailing a few meters behind him. His legs were still unsteady from the slipspace travel, his excitement growing at their immediate success. The un'hai behind him had made it possible, and if power were what she was after, he would be sure to reward her for that.

"Where are they?" he asked as he gained the bridge. The crew was supposed to stand and lower their heads in deference, and some tried, but many were too unwell to react quickly enough.

Gr'el brought up a star map, a holographic view of the system that hung in the center of the bridge. The Ishur was obvious near one side of the system. A purple shape hung at the other side. The anomaly.

"It may not be the humans, Dahm," Zoelle said. "Only an unexpected mass within the system, based on our prior mappings and projections."

"What else would it be?" Gr'el asked. "The Azera?"

"Not this far from their home world," Tea'va said. "It has to be the humans." He glanced at Zoelle. "Or do you have another guess?"

"No, Dahm."

She wouldn't dare repeat what she had said to him in his quarters in front of Gr'el and the crew. Even so, her reaction forced him to consider it.

The lor'hai were sick and even the drumhr were at half-strength. At the moment the Ishur was barely able to stay operational. If the enemy had managed to harness the technology to damage the ship's armor, they would be on much more equal footing in a fight.

If they had conquered the technology. The plasma weapons were deceptively simple things, and the most important components were at nano-scale. Did the human ship even possess the means to see that deeply into the internals?

He doubted it.

"How quickly can we intercept?"

"Six hours, Dahm," Gr'el said.

"Zoelle, what will the state of the crew be in that time?"

"Not optimal, Dahm. A ten percent improvement, if that."

Tea'va could tell by her expression that she was trying to warn him subtly against moving forward once more. Some part of her believed the humans were capable of creating a weapon, and that the Heil'shur would be skilled enough to use it to destroy them. He didn't understand how that could be.

"We cannot let them slip away again," Gr'el said. "We must move forward now before they can reach a stream."

"If they run, we can follow," Zoelle said.

"Why is this lor'hai on the bridge, Tea'va?" Gr'el replied. "I do not recall you requesting her here, and I certainly did not."

Tea'va felt the fury rising within him. Gr'el wanted to make him look like a fool.

"If I did not want her here, she would not be here," he growled.

He didn't have the option of heeding her words now. It would make him look weak. Not that he was going to, anyway.

"Set a course for the anomaly at full thrust. Gr'el, order the Gi'shah Dahm to assess his drumhr and prepare the combat ready. Also, get an assessment of how many plasma batteries we have the crew to operate. We will devise our strategy based on our operational efficiencies."

"Yes, Dahm" Gr'el said.

"Zoelle, you are dismissed. Scientists have no place in war."

She bowed low, the subtle change in her face telling him she didn't approve.

Fortunately, the decision wasn't hers.

He stared at the purple blob in the middle of the display. His crew was sick from the many slips it had taken to reach the system, but it was a risk that was already bearing results. He hadn't come this far to back away once the humans came into his sights.

"Prepare for battle."

28

GABRIEL WAS GETTING WORRIED.

TWENTY days had passed since the Magellan had dropped back into realspace.

Twenty days since his father had vanished from the bridge, retreating to his quarters to battle his addiction to the pain medication and to battle his ability to handle the pain.

Twenty days out of twenty-two that would see them reaching the planetary system where they could finally rejoin a slipstream and make their way back home.

His father had yet to make a public appearance. He had remained in hiding, secured behind the barrier of Diallo and Hafizi, who refused to let anyone into the quarters, not even to make sure Theodore was still alive. They insisted that he was. That was all the information they would give, even to him.

He had made a promise to his father that he would keep quiet, but it was getting harder to do with each passing day. There were whispers among the crew that his father had lost his mind, deteriorated to the point that he couldn't lead them, or had flat-out given up on the mission and abandoned them completely. Fortunately, that was the rumor that was least believed. Most felt he was in bad shape, an unfortunate casualty of war.

Even Gabriel was beginning to think that way.

The other thing that had him worried was Guy and Reza's lack of progress on the weapon they had recovered. In the first week, the pair had spent eighteen out of every twenty-four hours down in the laboratory, trying to crack the mystery of the device. It had proven to be harder than they had expected. By the second week, that time had been reduced to twelve hours. Now nearing the end of their third week, Colonel Choi had sent Gabriel to find Reza, who hadn't made an appearance in the lab in three days.

Gabriel wished General St. Martin would return to the bridge to pull them together. Sometimes, he even prayed that he would. A pall was being cast over the ship, despite the repair crews getting most of the damage shored up, despite their proximity to a slipstream that would finally get them back into the fight. The entire mission, the entire war, was beginning to come unglued by inaction, the cracks forming at the seams. He knew Theodore could fix them with one round of sharp commands cracked off in his signature Cajun accent.

But he also couldn't rely on it.

It was a hard thing for him to accept. His father had always been so dependable. He felt sick at the idea that this was a fight the General couldn't win. That after years of promises that he would get the planet back, he would fall apart over something as small as a pill. It was such a human thing, and he had never seen his father as human.

Reza's quarters weren't far from the central hub. He had been given a larger berthing than some of the other crew members, to allow him space and privacy and the ability to think without distraction. Gabriel had spoken to Miranda before heading down, trying to determine where Reza had been for the last three days. As part of operations, she was supposed to know where every crew member was when they were on duty. She had told him that the scientist had been spotted in the mess a few times each day, often with Sarah Larone at the table with him.

It was a worrying development for Gabriel. Guy was smart, but he was also a hothead, and if anything was happening between Reza and Sarah, it had the potential to explode. In a closed environment like theirs, it only took one detonation to cause a chain reaction of bad morale.

And morale was already down. They couldn't afford to let it get any worse.

He reached the scientist's door and banged the side of his fist against it. He knew the control pad was non-functional. Reza had rigged something to get himself in and out, and most of the time that was good enough.

Nobody answered.

"Maggie, connect me to Spaceman Locke," Gabriel said, asking the ship's computer to patch him into her station.

"Yes, Captain," it replied, the voice seeming to come from everywhere.

"Captain St. Martin," Miranda said. "How can I help you?"

"I'm at Reza's door, but nobody is answering. Can you verify he's in there?"

"Give me a minute, sir," Miranda replied.

He knocked again while he waited for her to get back to him, again receiving no response.

"I asked around. He isn't in the mess or the lab. Nobody has seen him in a while."

Gabriel wished the doors on the Magellan were a little less thick. "What about Sarah?" he asked, unhappy that he even needed to question.

"One minute, sir."

Gabriel waited again while she pinged the senior officers, asking after Sarah Larone's whereabouts.

"She hasn't been seen in awhile either, sir," Miranda said. "Guy said that if you do find her, he would appreciate a minute alone with his wife so they can talk."

"How did he sound when he said that?"

"Angrier than usual."

"I don't have a good feeling about this."

"No, sir."

"Have you tried to contact Reza?"

"Yes, sir. His comm is set to private."

"Sarah?"

"The same."

"Bad to worse."

"Do you think they're messing around behind Guy's back, sir?"

"Messing around? Yes. Behind his back? Not nearly far enough."

Gabriel sighed. Colonel Choi was doing the best she could, but she didn't want to get involved in people's private lives. His father would have never let this become an issue. He blamed himself for not doing more himself. Reza and Sarah were civilians, but they were on a ship at war, and they had a duty to conduct themselves with more tact.

"Maggie, connect me to Reza Mokri, please," Gabriel said.

"Reza Mokri has set his communication status to private," Maggie said.

"Command override," Gabriel said. "Captain Gabriel St. Martin. Reason: mission critical communication."

"Override accepted."

"Reza," Gabriel said. "It's Gabriel. I'm standing outside your door. You have ten seconds to open it before I get a tech to open it for me. I'm not usually a violent man, but if I have to do that, I will be."

29

He stood facing the door, tapping his foot to count off the seconds. He had reached five when the door slid open.

Reza had a pair of pants on without a shirt. His wild hair was even more wild than usual. He caught a glimpse of Sarah Larone in the background, sitting in bed with the blankets covering her.

"Gabriel," Reza said.

Gabriel grabbed him by the arm, tugging him from the room.

Reza hit hard against the bulkhead, his door closing behind him. Gabriel didn't want to be violent. He didn't want to be angry. He was angrier because of that.

"You do recall that we're at war, do you not Mr. Mokri?" he said, getting up in Reza's face.

"Gabriel? I... uh..."

"It's Captain St. Martin," Gabriel snapped.

"Uh... Yes, okay," Reza replied, still stunned.

"Yes, what?" Gabriel shouted.

"Yes, sir," Reza said.

Gabriel let him go, backing up a step and pointing a finger at him. "I don't want you to say a damn thing. I don't want to hear any excuses. What you do with your free time is your own business, as long as it doesn't impact the operations of this ship."

He paused, giving Reza a chance to try to speak. The scientist remained pressed against the wall, his eyes frightened.

"Number one, you don't have any free time on this ship. Number two, what you're doing with what you don't have is impacting our operations beyond my capacity to understand how you think it could possibly be acceptable."

"Colonel Choi," Reza started to say.

"Colonel Choi was giving you a chance to use some of your intelligence to figure things out for yourself. Apparently, you're incapable of doing that when there's a woman added to the equation. A woman who is married, I might add. A woman who also helped get you tossed into prison, by the way."

"Sarah's not like that. She was just trying to-"

"Trying to what? Save half the settlement? And suddenly that's okay for you, too?"

"Uh... No... Gab- Captain St. Martin, sir. Please. I can explain."

"I don't want you to explain. I don't want either of you to explain. I don't care if she came on to you, or you came on to her. I don't care if she's misunderstood, or you're misunderstood. I don't care if the two of you having sex with one another helps one, or the both of you think better." He paused. "Unless you can tell me that you have a solution to our problem with the Dread weapon that resulted from your romantic interlude?"

"Uh." Reza looked at the floor. "No, sir."

"Do you think that Guy is stupid? Do you think he has no idea what's going on with you two? I have three scientists on this ship. Three scientists that are supposed to be reverse-engineering an enemy weapon so that we can get our planet back from the Dread, which in my estimation is a little more important than a few minutes, hours, or days of physical pleasure. Now those three scientists are going to be impossible to get to work together with any kind of cohesive effectiveness. Do you get where I'm going, Mr. Mokri?"

"Yes, sir. I wasn't thinking-"

"I know you weren't thinking. Neither of you were thinking. If you were thinking, maybe you would have solved the damn problem already, instead of making a bigger one."

Reza swallowed hard. "I'll get back to the lab. I'll put in extra time. I promise."

"I'm not about to work with this little piece of shit," Guy said.

Gabriel turned to look at Guy, who had approached unnoticed in the middle of his tirade. Guy looked almost as haggard as Reza, though it was likely from stress and lack of sleep. The scientist's hands were balled into fists, his face beet red.

"I'd like nothing more than to beat the living snot out of him and you, Captain St. Martin. This is your fault. You and your father. We don't belong out here, trying to win an unwinnable war. The weapon? All it has served to do is prove it. I've scanned the entire thing in and virtually disassembled every component. There is nothing about it that offers any clue as to why it can defeat the Dread armor when nothing else can. You've hindered our chances to reach the New Earth with this folly, and if that wasn't enough, you've destroyed my marriage as well."

Gabriel barely heard any of the other words that Guy had spewed. Nothing? There was nothing? He had seen the Dread plasma rifle pierce the Dread armor. There was something. There had to be. Why had the scientist been unable to find it?

"There has to be a difference," Reza said. "You aren't looking at it right. But then, you don't look at anything right, do you? You think everything and everyone is against you. Even your wife."

Guy's face contorted in anger, and he lunged for Reza. "Don't you dare say a thing about my wife," he snarled.

Gabriel stepped between them, pushing Guy back. He ducked aside as Guy took a swing at him, dodging it before punching the scientist hard in the gut.

Guy doubled over; the wind knocked out of him. Then he started to sob.

"I wanted to get us off that damned rock," he said. "To give humankind a chance to start over, to grow and expand. Why does that make me the bad guy? I don't want others to die, but there was no other way to make it work. Sarah said she understood. She supported me. And then we came here, and she turned on me so quickly. She came over to that crusty old man's side without a second thought. She betrayed me once, and now she's betrayed me again. What did I do to deserve that?"

Gabriel looked at Guy, finding himself almost sympathizing with him. The anger was fading from him quickly. He needed to get both Guy and Reza back on track, their attention refocused on the Dread technology.

Reza's door opened again, and Sarah came out, fully dressed. She glanced at Gabriel and then looked away, embarrassed.

Guy looked up at her, his eyes red, tears on his face. Her expression turned more distraught when she saw it.

"The weapon is useless, Captain," Guy said softly. "The Dread are too advanced. We don't have the means to break down what they've done into something we can use. I'm sorry. I've tried to play along, to be part of the solution. I tried to work it out. I failed. I'm sorry I failed."

Gabriel realized Guy was speaking to Sarah when he said that. Tears were beginning to flow from her eyes as well. He looked at Reza, who was slouched against the bulkhead, looking small.

"What do we do now?" Reza asked.

"You get dressed and get your ass down to the lab," Gabriel said. "I need to know if what Guy is saying is true. Guy, Sarah, whatever you need to figure out, figure it out. I need everyone operating-"

Gabriel was cut off as the lights began flashing around them, and a voice sounded from the speakers.

"Captain St. Martin to the bridge," Colonel Choi said. "All other crew to your stations immediately. This a red alert. I repeat, this is a red alert."

"What's happening?" Reza said.

Gabriel did his best to keep himself from tensing. "It means the enemy has been spotted."

30

"CAPTAIN, TAKE THE PILOT STATION please," Colonel Choi said, the moment Gabriel arrived on the bridge. Sarah and Guy weren't far behind, taking their places at their station without comment.

Reza had returned to his quarters to find some clothes.

"What's the situation, ma'am?" Gabriel asked on his way.

"Maggie, release steering controls," Choi said.

"Releasing," the computer replied.

"You know what Red Alert means, Captain," Choi said, glancing over at the Larones. She didn't look happy.

"Yes, ma'am."

Gabriel took his seat, bringing up the sensor view to see for himself. The shape of the Dread fortress was unmistakable. He checked the distance. It was still a good ten minutes away from their position. At least they had a little time to prepare.

"How did they find us?" Guy asked. His eyes were still red, but he had regained his composure and was pointedly ignoring his wife. He didn't even flinch when Reza finally made it to the bridge and joined them.

"They must have followed the stream," Reza said. "They knew which one we took, and they would have understood the likelihood that we were dropped at the terminus. The real question is, how did they get here so fast?"

"There were no streams from Earth to here," Sarah said. "They would have had to make multiple slips."

"That would make humans ill," Choi said. "Do you think it affects them the same way?"

"I don't know," Reza said.

"What should we do, Colonel?" Gabriel asked. He had control of the Magellan, but no idea what to do with it. He checked their surroundings. There was a small planet not far from them, but it would offer limited cover.

Then again, limited was better than none.

"Head for that planet," Choi said, sharing his thought. "We'll figure the rest out when we get there."

Gabriel took the controls, adjusting the main thrusters and vectoring thrust to begin to bring the Magellan around. He tensed when the Dread fortress released the first volley from its main plasma cannon, sending a huge stream of molten energy spewing toward them.

Gabriel deftly adjusted course and speed, rotating the Magellan and turning it belly up. The plasma continued past them, missing by a wide margin.

"They're trying to keep us from the planet," Miranda said from her station.

"Clearly," Choi agreed. "Captain St. Martin, we need to make it to the other side. It's our only chance to delay them."

"Yes, ma'am," Gabriel said. He was surprisingly calm, despite the fact that the Dread were closing in, and they still had no means to fight them.

He got the bow of the Magellan pointed toward the planet and drove the mains to full thrust. The direction put them moving away from the Dread fortress, exposing their rear and their engines. It was a dangerous thing to do, but they didn't have a choice. He put a hand to his chest, whispering a prayer and tapping the crucifix beneath his shirt. He needed his mother's divine intercession now more than ever.

A second plasma blast launched from the Dread ship. Gabriel followed it closely on his screen. He shifted the Magellan, rolling it and dipping like he would if he were in a fighter. The larger ship was slower to respond, the size making it less maneuverable. He cursed at it for being slow before breathing a sigh of relief as the plasma cleared the top of the ship by meters.

"Too close," he said.

"They're closing the distance," Reza said. "We can't outrun them."

"We'll make it," Gabriel said, monitoring the two distances.

A third plasma stream streaked toward them. Gabriel adjusted course, making every effort to avoid the attack. The Dread fortress was closer, the Magellan too slow to change position, or maybe the enemy had guessed their direction. The plasma skimmed the edge of the left QPG nacelle, tearing the side of it away in a shower of quickly snuffed out sparks.

"Damn it," Gabriel said out loud. He wasn't used to piloting a ship like this, and they were going to die because of it. He knew it, and by the hushed silence around him, he was sure the rest of them knew it too. "Where the hell is my father?"

"Locked and loaded, my boy," Theodore said, rolling onto the bridge. "Sorry I'm late, but I needed to pee first."

Gabriel felt the change in the air the moment he did, the feeling of tense desperation turning in an instant to one of true hope. He was amazed by the effect his father had with nothing more than his calm, confident presence.

"Colonel Choi, you are relieved of command," Theodore said. "If you don't mind stepping away from my chair?"

"Of course not, General," Choi said.

"Captain St. Martin, head on down to the hangar and get your fighter crew ready for launch. I'll take the reins from here."

Gabriel stood and turned around, setting his eyes on his father for the first time in three weeks. General St. Martin had done more than clean himself up. He had transformed himself. He was freshly washed and shaved, his hair tight against his scalp, his uniform crisp. There was no sign of pain as he lifted himself into the command chair. There was no sign of weakness.

"Don't just stand there staring at me like you see a ghost, Captain," Theodore said. "We've got couillons to confuse."

"Sir?" Gabriel said. "You want to launch the fighters?"

"Are you questioning my command?" Theodore yelled. "I know we can't hurt them, but that don't mean we ain't going to try. I bet it's the last thing in the world they expect."

"Yes, sir," Gabriel said, reaching the command chair. His father didn't look at him; his focus was already dedicated to evading the Dread attack. "It's good to have you back, sir."

He couldn't resist the urge to put his hand on his father's shoulder as he said it.

Theodore risked a glance over, a small smile creasing his face. "Thank you, Gabriel. It's good to see you, too. Now, let's show them what we're made of."

"Yes, sir."

31

"THIS IS CRAZY," LIEUTENANT BALE said over the comm. "Completely crazy. The General is missing for three weeks, and then he just shows up at the eleventh hour and takes command, and we follow him like he was never gone?"

Gabriel adjusted his seat in his fighter, flipping the switch to prep the thrusters. "Yes."

"And nobody is worried that maybe he's not all there?"

"I'll take my father flying the Magellan not all there over myself any day. Besides, did you get a look at him? I haven't seen him that fit in twenty years."

"Okay, but he's going to send us out there. That doesn't worry you? We can't hurt the Dread, Captain. What are we supposed to do? Wave at them as they blow us into space junk?"

"We're supposed to do whatever the General says. Are you going to stop whining, Bale, or are you going to mutiny? One way maybe you die a hero. The other way, you just die."

Bale fell silent. Gabriel could hear the snickers of the other two pilots on the comm. Gerhardt and Celia. They were both as green as any pilot could be, greener even then Lieutenant Bale. At least she had flown a combat mission before.

He was leading a squad of children on a suicide mission and asking them to be happy about it. The crazy thing was that he was happy about it. Happy to have his father back on the bridge. Happy to be doing something against the Dread.

"This is General St. Martin." Theodore's voice cut across their comm. "Get ready to launch on my mark. Timing is everything here, boys and girls, so don't dilly-dally."

"Yes, sir," Gabriel replied for them.

"What do you think he's doing?" Bale asked.

"We won't know until we get out there," Gabriel replied. "What I do know is that we aren't dead yet. That's a positive sign."

"Looks like your squadron's going to have some company out there, Captain," Miranda said. "Half a dozen Dread Bats are incoming. Watch your six."

Gabriel closed his eyes to calm the sudden rush of fear. They could avoid the Dread fortress' plasma fire as long as they didn't center themselves on the main cannon. Their fighters were another story.

What the heck was his father doing?

He jumped when the hangar began to open, individual bay doors moving aside at the same time. The oxygen had already been pumped out, and on his father's command, they would release the clamps holding them to Magellan and join the fray.

Gabriel's heart rate spiked. He had never been in combat in space before. Sure, he had trained for it, but this was the real thing.

He had survived on Earth. He would survive here.

"Stay tight," he said. "Cover each other out there."

"Yes, sir," his pilots replied.

He felt the fighter shift slightly as the clamps release.

"Now," Theodore shouted.

Gabriel fired his thrusters, launching from the hangar ahead of the others. He didn't check to see if they had followed. He was certain they had.

The fighter moved out into space. He found the Bats immediately, strafing the left side of the Magellan with their smaller plasma weapons, hitting the same nacelle that had been grazed by the fortress' plasma cannon.

Gabriel's heart sank when he realized why.

Without the nacelle, they couldn't escape.

He cursed himself silently for letting the enemy hit one of the most vulnerable parts of the ship. His father would never have made that mistake. Why couldn't he have shown up a little earlier? A minute, an hour, a day. Theodore had shown too much confidence in him.

It wasn't over yet.

He tracked the other targets. The Dread fortress was still behind the Magellan, but it was drawing closer. The Magellan was still moving toward the planet, vectoring in a random pattern to throw the enemy cannons.

He had to do something about the Bats.

"Form up, we need to hit them hard," he said.

"Sir?" Bale replied. "You want to attack?"

"We still have power left, and if they destroy the nacelle, we'll be trapped out here forever."

"Our weapons are useless," Gerhardt said.

"Are you questioning me, son?" Gabriel replied, barking like his old man.

"No, sir," the pilot replied meekly.

"Stay tight, concentrate your fire. The rounds still have force. At the very least we can push them off target and try to buy the General time for him to create a miracle."

"Yes, sir," they replied.

Gabriel led them back toward the nacelle, checking his levels. Each shot drained the battery that powered the starfighter. Would there be anywhere near enough available energy to do much of anything against the Dread?

He was going to find out.

A flash of light blinded him for a moment, the fortress' main cannon sending a burst of energy over the top of the Magellan. Gabriel would never know how his father did it, but he was thankful that he could.

"You need to get those sons of bitches off my shoulder," Theodore said. "Maggie's chewing my ear about critical damage."

"Yes, sir," Gabriel replied. "I'm about to engage."

"Good man."

Gabriel focused his eyes forward, tracking the closest of the Bats. Like the fortress, they were struggling to keep up with the many changes in direction Theodore was expertly affecting on the starship, their aim not always centered on the weakened area of the nacelle. Taking fire might not hurt them, but it would give them more of a distraction.

Was that his father's plan? Buy time to reach the planet, use it as a shield to swing around and escape to a stream? The Dread might be able to follow, but it would be difficult for them to know where the Magellan had dropped back into realspace. Or at least, they had to hope it would be. They had no idea of the extent of the enemy's capabilities when it came to space travel. The fact that they were hitting the nacelle suggested that even if they could track the ship, they didn't want to.

"Target the closest enemy ship, prepare to fire."

"Roger," the pilots replied.

Gabriel and his squadron swooped down on the Bats, coming at them from an off angle to try to evade detection. He was about to give the order to shoot when they suddenly veered away, breaking off the attack on the Magellan, spinning back to face the fighters.

"Break away, spread out," Gabriel said, caught by surprise as lances of plasma punctuated the space around him.

He rolled the fighter, adding a little extra to the underside vectoring thruster and pushing it out of plane from the incoming attack before streaking past. He flipped the fighter back when he neared the nacelle, returning to the fight.

"Sir, they broke off the attack," Gabriel said. "They're targeting the squadron."

"Ha! Better than I hoped," Theodore replied. "Keep them busy, Captain, we're almost there."

Gabriel looked out at the planet. They weren't that close to it yet.

Almost where?

He didn't have any more time to think about it. He threw the fighter into a wild swerve as one of the Bats dove in at him, plasma cannons sending bolts flying past him. He scanned for the rest of the squadron. They were outnumbered, but their fighters were smaller and more nimble. For the moment, they were managing to keep the Dread off them.

He knew from Earth that it wouldn't last. The pilots would adjust to their tactics and then begin to pick them apart.

"Bale, watch your tail," he said, avoiding the fire from the Bat behind him and coming up on Bale's position. "Bring him over to me; I'll try to knock him off course."

"Yes, sir," Bale replied, her voice calm. Regardless of how she had gotten into and through the Academy, she was proving to be a solid performer.

She shifted her vectors, rolling her fighter over and coming back his way. Her ship was a blur rocketing past him, and he opened fire, sending hundreds of ion blasts out at the chasing Bat.

He expected that the Bat would take the hit, lose its concentration, and break off for another approach.

Instead, he watched as his rounds tore into the dark skin of the alien craft, ripping through in a way he had never seen before. The shots pierced the hide, one of them hitting something that must have been important. A brief flash of a small internal explosion, and then the Bat went dark, floating away from the battle on its final trajectory.

Gabriel blasted past the dead ship, his mouth hanging open in silent shock. What the? It couldn't be, could it? Had Reza secretly solved the riddle and augmented the fighters to be able to defeat the Dread armor? And not tell anyone? That didn't make any sense.

Nothing else did either, but somehow it was true.

"Alpha Squadron, the Bats are vulnerable," Gabriel said, still in disbelief. "I repeat, they're vulnerable. If you can hit them, hit them hard."

"Captain, I hope you ain't playing a nasty trick on an Old Gator," Theodore said, hearing the report.

"No, sir," Gabriel replied. "I just disabled one of them. I'm as surprised as you."

"Well, this don't change my plans too much, but maybe just enough. Keep those couillons distracted; I'm about to put the fear of God into these bastards."

"Sir? Do you feel okay?"

"Trust me, Gabe. I feel better than I have in years. Mind over matter. Hang tight."

"Yes, sir."

Gabriel let himself smile as he shifted direction, heading back at one of the enemy fighters. They were more cautious now, backing further away from the Magellan and his squadron, spending more time on the defensive. Were they surprised by their vulnerability too?

He watched as Bale lit up, sending a stream of ions into a second Bat. He almost laughed when the rounds poured into the ship, creating the same scene as he had. A small flash and then it stopped reacting, floating away on a straight path.

"Try to keep up with me now, Captain," Theodore said.

Gabriel swung around the Bats, watching as the Magellan's main thrusters burned out. A moment later, vectoring thrusters fired from the bottom and the left of the ship, pushing it up and over. A moment after that he noticed that the hangar doors had sealed, and now were re-opening. Oxygen vented out as they did, adding a little more thrust.

The Magellan rose up, vertical to the fortress within seconds. It looked vulnerable, and the Dread believed it had to be. The main cannon belched plasma, spewing it forth in a stream that should have cut right through the center of the Magellan.

Except she was still rolling up and over, the rear rising and swinging out behind her. The plasma blast passed harmlessly beneath, and the ship came about, the bow facing directly toward the Dread starship.

Then the mains reignited, a ring of heat forming around each of the outputs, a jet of energy forming behind it. The engines could output massive thrust for a short amount of time to escape atmosphere and gravity. It would put a strain on the systems and drain their reserve energy stores almost completely. It was a desperate maneuver, but also a brilliant one.

"Form up," Gabriel said to his squadron. "We don't want to fall out of range."

"Roger."

They only had so much power themselves, and would need to use all of it to keep pace with the Magellan.

They streaked alongside the main action. Gabriel's eyes were peeled to the starship as it pointed itself directly at the fortress. Was his father planning to ram them? He might hurt the Dread ship, but he would kill himself and everyone around him at the same time.

Or was he daring the Dread to let him strike them? Was he testing their mettle and motivations?

The Magellan leaped at the Dread fortress, the long bow like a spear ahead of it. The Fortress responded immediately, changing direction, dropping down, not wasting any time trying to avoid it. Gabriel increased his thrust, accelerating ahead of the Magellan as the secondary burn faded out.

The Magellan crossed over the top of the fortress, shooting past it and heading toward the inner portion of the system. The Fortress remained behind it, working to change course, its forward velocity carrying it further and further away as it did. The Dread Bats peeled off, ceasing the chase and heading back to their ship.

"Score one for the Old Gator," Bale said, her voice bubbling through the comm.

"Roger that," Gabriel replied. "Let's head home."

32

GABRIEL OPENED THE FIGHTER'S COCKPIT, climbing out and standing on the floor of the hangar. The air was harder to breathe than before, the oxygen levels limited after Theodore's maneuver to get them past the Dread.

He had never been happier to be short of breath.

He left his bay, heading through the interlocks and into the connecting corridor, where Captain Sturges was already waiting for him, a big smile on his grizzled face.

"Nice flying, Captain," Sturges said.

"Maybe I'll see you out there next time?" Gabriel replied.

"Me? I'm old and slow. The BIS is more my speed." He clapped Gabriel on the shoulder. "Truly well done, Gabe."

Lieutenant Bale was the next pilot to appear in the corridor. She rushed over to Gabriel, wrapping her arms around him. "He did it. He really did it."

"I told you to have faith," Gabriel said, returning the embrace. He released her as Gerhardt and Celia joined them.

"Mission accomplished, sir," Celia said. Her hair was matted with her cold sweat.

"You both did well," Gabriel said. "You survived your first mission.

I'm proud of you both."

"Thank you, sir," they replied.

"I'm heading up to the bridge," Gabriel said. "Captain Sturges, can you take care of these brave souls for me?"

"Yes, sir," Sturges said. "Thank your father for me."

"Will do."

Gabriel hurried to the bridge, leaving his flight suit on and zipped. They might have escaped the Dread this time, but he was certain the enemy wasn't about to give up its pursuit. They had bought themselves some time, that was all.

It was as much as they could hope for.

"Hull integrity is good," Sergeant Abdullah was saying as Gabriel reached the bridge. "Decks are sealed and stable. All of the damage was isolated to the port-side QPG nacelle. I'm still collating the sensor readings and data outputs from the nacelle to get a full understanding of the damage."

"How does the old girl look from the outside, Captain?" Theodore asked without looking.

Gabriel moved to stand beside the General. "The plasma grazed the side of her, sir," he said. "There was quite a bit of visible damage, and the fighters were doing their best to add to it. It's my fault she got hit, sir."

"Nonsense," Theodore said. "You're the best damn pilot I've ever seen. Half this game is luck, and you got a little bit unlucky. It could just as easily have been me at the wheel."

Gabriel remained silent, not quite willing to accept Theodore's excuse.

"The important part is that we're still alive. We can still fight. Even better, you managed to shoot down one of their fighters."

"So did Bale, sir," Gabriel said.

"A damn fine job, Captain. The point being, they were vulnerable. That's data we can use, ain't that right, Mr. Mokri?"

"Yes, sir," Reza replied.

"Maggie, how's our distance from that big turd out there?"

"Ten thousand kilometers and holding," Maggie replied.

"Seems like they're backing off to regroup," Theodore said. "Ha! I don't think they were expecting that little game of chicken."

"We're lucky you didn't kill us all," Guy said.

"Damn right, Mr. Larone," Theodore replied. "Sometimes luck is all we have left to lean on. By the by, you've had three weeks with the Dread rifle. What have you got?"

Colonel Choi interrupted before Guy could respond. "Pardon me, sir, but I recommend tabling that discussion in the immediate. I think the entire crew might appreciate a word from you. We've been worried about you, General."

"I was worried about myself for a while there," Theodore said softly, his expression changing. He recovered a moment later. "Quite right, Colonel. Quite right." He leaned forward to tap his control pad.

"Sir," Abdullah said before he could. "The preliminary report is in. Maggie's initial assessment was accurate. The main power conduit to the nacelle is offline, and we lost thirty percent of the phase surface."

"That sounds bad," Reza said.

"It means we can't slip," Theodore replied. He paused while he considered. "Can we repair it?"

"The conduit if we can get a crew out to it. The phase surface is going to be a little more challenging. We don't have any paint on board."

"Can we slip without it?" Choi asked.

"Good question," Theodore said. "Mr. Mokri? Mrs. Larone?"

They glanced over at one another, clearly uncomfortable to be grouped together. Gabriel noticed his father's eyebrow raising as they did.

"Hmmm," he said, coughing lightly. "What do we have here?"

"Uh. It's. Uh. It's nothing, General," Reza said, looking at the floor, his face turning red.

"Ha! Funniest nothing I ever did see. I wasn't born yesterday, Mr. Mokri. We can deal with that later. Can one of you answer my question? Mr. Larone, do you want to take a stab at it?"

"Slipping a starship is usually based on a percentage of phase surface in comparison to overall size," Guy said before Reza could respond. "We would need to know the overall cubic size of the Magellan as well as the size of the QPG prepared surfaces. If she were constructed with some buffer, it's quite possible getting the conduit back online would be good enough."

"What if it's close?" Theodore said.

"What do you mean, General?" Guy replied.

"The math. What if it's close? What if we try to slip without enough surface?"

"Part of the ship will make it into slipspace," Reza said. "The other part won't."

"You'll tear the Magellan into pieces," Guy said.

"The surface damage is an estimate, sir," Sergeant Abdullah said. "We'd need a team to go out there and measure."

Theodore sat back in the command chair. He ran a hand across a clean-shaven chin. "Seems we're in a bit of a pickle then, don't it? I doubt that Dread ship out there is going to wait for us to make a few spacewalks and fix our nacelle. In fact, I suppose they're going to do whatever they can to prevent it."

He leaned forward on his arms, looking the crew over. He turned his head and looked at Gabriel before speaking again.

"Here's what we're going to do. I'm going to make a rousing speech ship-wide to get morale back under its own power. Then I'm going to pull Mr. Mokri, Mrs. Larone, Vivian, and Gabriel aside so someone can tell me what all is with the weird tension on my bridge. I have to tell you, I don't like it, and I ain't in favor. Mr. Larone, I expect to find you with the alien rifle after that. I want a full report on what you've learned about the thing, and I want you to give a bit of thought to why the Dread fighters might have been vulnerable right here when they have never been before. I feel like there's an obvious clue staring us in the face, and we're too trained to feel powerless to notice.

"Sergeant Abdullah, get me a plan on how we can get the team out to the nacelle for repairs without slowing down, and with the understanding that we may come under enemy attack at any moment."

"Yes, sir," Abdullah said.

"Gabriel, while I'm yapping, get a message down to Lieutenant Bale. I want two pilots riding the hot seat at all times, and since we're low on trained bodies, she's up first with Lieutenant Celia."

"Yes, sir," Gabriel said.

"Oh, and tell her she's promoted to First Lieutenant."

"Yes, sir."

"While I'm at it, congratulations, Major St. Martin."

Gabriel froze. "What?"

"You've earned it, Major."

"Sir, I appreciate it, but I can't."

"Why not? You worried about nepotism? Nobody's going to question you. You're the best damned pilot we've ever had. Besides, it's all academic at this point. You aren't getting paid, anyhow."

"The Magellan was hit under my stick," Gabriel argued.

"Blah, blah, Major. Remember what I said about luck? You ain't happy with that?"

Gabriel didn't answer fast enough.

"All in favor of Captain St. Martin's promotion, say 'aye,'" Theodore said.

"Aye," the bridge crew replied. Everyone except Guy Larone.

"Maggie, note it in the record. Second Lieutenant Sandra Bale is promoted to First Lieutenant. Captain Gabriel St. Martin is promoted to Major."

"Data recorded," the computer replied.

"There you go. It's done. Now skedaddle so we can get on with the important business."

Gabriel saluted. Theodore saluted back. Then Gabriel left the bridge. He considered contacting Bale through the comm but decided to go and find her instead. Why not break the news to her in person?

His father's voice boomed through the ship while he walked.

"This is General Theodore St. Martin. As you may or may not know, I was incapacitated up until recently. The loss of my legs was causing me a great deal of pain, and to help deal with that pain, I was taking medicine prescribed by the doctors back home.

That medicine was affecting my operational abilities, and in one instance affected my ability to make an important decision that almost cost the lives of each and every one of you. It was a failure that struck me right down to the core. A failure that I've sworn to myself to never be in the position to repeat.

I've been to hell and back over the last few weeks. The withdrawal from the pain medication was a challenge on its own, and damn near murderous in conjunction with the continuing pain in my limbs. There were times when I believed it was a fight I couldn't win."

Silence fell in the corridor. Gabriel could tell his father was choking up.

"I know there have been rumors that I've lost my touch and that I'm not the man I used to be. I'm gonna put those rumors to rest right now. I ain't the man I used to be. I've been to hell and back, and I'm better for it. I'm stronger; I'm smarter, and I'm more resolved than ever to see this thing through. We survived the first round against the Dread; and I know that together we'll survive the next round too.

"I know that I let you down, and I'm sorry. It ain't often a General apologizes to his troops, but I know there's power in humility. I know that we ain't just a collection of soldiers. We're a family, and we owe it to one another to do right and to be man enough to admit when we've done wrong. Again, to each and every one of you, I'm sorry.

"The enemy is at our door. They came knocking, and not only did we slam that door in their face, but we also broke their nose to boot. We showed them that just because we don't have any big, bad guns, that don't mean we're going to roll over and die. We showed them that we're made of tougher stuff, and if they want to wipe us out of the universe, they're going to have to earn it.

"I went to hell and back, and I was afraid. But I tell you, I ain't afraid anymore. Not with you, the good men and women who have joined me on this ship, on this mission to free our brothers and sisters back on Earth. I believe in you. I trust in you. I'm proud to have you with me. Let the Dread come. Let them try to break us, to destroy us, to knock our door down and finish us once and for all.

"I'll be here to stop them, and I know you'll be here with me. Together, we'll show these yellow-bellied couillons who we are. Together, we'll show them that they messed with the wrong damn race, and the wrong damn planet. Together, we'll break their armor, and then we'll break their spirits.

"Thank you, and God bless."

33

TEA'VA STARED SILENTLY THROUGH THE viewport of his bridge. The expansive outer edge of the Pol'tik system was spread out ahead of him.

The human starship wasn't there.

It was behind them, having executed a maneuver he wasn't expecting, a maneuver made possible by the druk Heil'shur.

He knew that it had been him out there, leading a squadron of the small human fighters against his gi'shah. He recognized the markings of the fighter, including the dark splotches where his plasma had singed the frame. How he wished he could have been out there with his pilots, hunting down the human who was causing him so much grief.

How he wished he had been able to send more than six of the gi'shah into the battle.

Zoelle had warned him against committing to a battle so soon after arriving in the system. She had tried to tell him that his ranks were too thin, his forces too weak from the travel. He had chosen to listen to Gr'el instead and push the attack. Despite his inability to field a full complement of fighters. Despite his inability to operate more than the main plasma cannon. Despite being beyond the flow of slipspace, and despite the weakened state of his crew slowing their reflexes and hurting their effectiveness.

She had tried to tell him not to underestimate the humans. He should have been more considerate. He should have remembered that they had the Heil'shur, instead of rushing to make a decision.

He looked down at Gr'el. His Si'dahm was setting navigation to get the ship turned around and back in pursuit of the humans. It was his fault this had happened, but Tea'va knew he would report back to the Domo'dahm and shift the blame to make him look weak and foolish.

Thanks to Gr'el, the humans had discovered that the lek'shah had a vulnerability. It would only be a matter of time before they realized what it was, and from there made the correct logical assumptions to form a theoretical basis on how the bek'hai armor was so impervious to their weapons. After that, it would only be a matter of time before they were able to duplicate the feat. He didn't need to hold humans in high regard to accept that they could figure out that much, at least. It was an elementary level of deductive reasoning.

He slammed his hand down on the side of his chair, causing a few of the lor'hai to jump. And it was all because of Gr'el and the Heil'shur. If the Heil'shur hadn't shot down one of the gi'shah, if Gr'el hadn't convinced him to attack straight away, they would be in a different situation now.

He wanted to end his Si'dahm, to retire him here and now. He knew he couldn't. The only way he could be rid of Gr'el was if he died in battle and the right evidence was available to prove as much. It would be a difficult scenario to orchestrate, but he decided that he would find a way, no matter what it took. Certainly, Zoelle would help him, and use her connections among the lor'hai to make it so. As Domo'dahm, he could reward all of them handsomely for their loyalty.

He got to his feet and began descending the command dais. At least the attack hadn't been a total failure. They had damaged the human starship's slip nacelle. He was certain it would be enough to keep them from leaving the Pol'tik system any time soon. It meant that he could afford to be patient for now, to give chase to the fleeing ship but keep his distance, to allow his crew to regain their strength before making a second attempt.

He would have to make that attempt before the humans could solve the equation, but he had time. A day or two at least to let his lor'hai and the drumhr recover their strength. The human ship had survived this time.

It wouldn't survive the next.

He left the bridge without a word. Gr'el was at least capable of staying behind the human ship, and he had delayed his time in the regeneration chamber for as long as he dared. He could feel his muscles weakening, his body beginning to reject itself. It had been weeks since he had used the chamber, a vast improvement over other drumhr who had to use it every few days.

He expected Zoelle to be waiting in his quarters again when he reached them. She wasn't. Instead, a plump Mother was standing at the door, clothed in a simple white dress that hung to her knees.

He was tempted to return to the bridge and stab Gr'el right then and there. He was taunting him, trying to get under his skin. Who else might have sent this creature to him?

"Dahm Tea'va," she said, lowering herself to her knees and bowing before him.

"Who sent you here?" Tea'va asked.

"Si'dahm Gr'el," she replied. "On behalf of Domo'dahm Rorn'el."

He was about to tell her to leave. The Domo'dahm? That gave him pause.

"Is that what Gr'el told you?"

"Yes, Dahm."

"How do you know he isn't lying?"

"It is not my place to judge the words of the Si'dahm, Dahm."

Tea'va paused. What if Gr'el wasn't lying? Certainly, he had sent a report to Rorn'el before the battle, and would send another soon. Had the Domo'dahm ordered this? Was he trying to ruin him and keep him from power?

No. The Domo'dahm had always supported him. Rorn'el knew that he was the superior pur'dahm. It was up to him to prove it.

Still, it was possible the Domo'dahm was trying to entice him with this thing. To test his willingness to please him by breeding.

He had no desire to please him.

"Stand up, Mother," Tea'va said.

The clone stood.

"Follow me."

The hatch to Tea'va's quarters slid open. He allowed the Mother to enter behind him as he approached his regeneration chamber and began tapping on the surface to program it.

He could see the Mother in the reflection as he did. One hand was reaching for the strap of her dress because she thought that was why he had brought her in. The other was reaching beneath. Disgusting.

He didn't want to see her human flesh or the ways she might try to entice him. He turned quickly, reaching out and grabbing her hand. She screeched in fear as he tightened his grip on her wrist, pulling her arms away from her body.

A plasma knife fell from her grip and clattered onto the floor.

Tea'va's eyes narrowed. What was this?

She lashed out at him, her foot catching him in the knee, buckling it and forcing him to fall. He loosened his grip on her to catch himself, and she slipped back, ducking down to grab the knife.

"Did Gr'el send you to kill me?" he asked, recovering and moving out of range of her reach. He didn't fear the clone now that the element of surprise had been lost. He was a pur'dahm, the ability to defend himself part of the implanted knowledge that he had been created with.

She didn't speak. She lunged forward with surprising speed, picking up the knife on the way. She swung it at him, forcing him to move to the side, nearly killed because he wasn't taking the threat seriously enough.

Why would he? Mothers weren't programmed to fight. They held only one purpose for being, one that had yet to be fulfilled.

At least, that was how it was supposed to be.

He got his arms up in time to block her next attack, batting the hand with the knife aside. She came at him ferociously; her lips split into a mad grin. He moved backward, circling the regeneration chamber.

"How did Gr'el do this?" Tea'va asked out loud. It was more than her ability to fight. She wasn't sick either. Unless...

She rushed him again, the knife darting toward his throat, his chest, his gut. He slapped each attack aside, a greater concern rising in the back of his mind.

Could it be? Was it possible? And right under his view?

The Mother lurched forward again. He caught her wrist this time, holding on and pushing her back. The force sent her to the floor, and he fell on top of her, the knife positioned between them.

If it were true, it wasn't a new plan. Perhaps he wasn't even the original target. If not, then who?

The Domo'dahm, of course. Tea'va almost laughed at the thought. He wasn't the only one with designs on breaking tradition, on stealing rulership instead of earning it through succession.

The Mother's arms were more powerful than normal, and in his weakened state, he found her strength almost equal to his. He struggled against her, pushing the knife down toward her ever so slowly. She didn't lose the grin while he did.

His anger flowed, and with one last burst of fury, he sank the plasma knife into her chest. The force buried it so deep his hand began to press into the wound. He released the knife, staring down at her while she died.

He got to his feet, still shaking with anger. Gr'el had forfeited his life by sending an assassin to kill him. He didn't care if the Domo'dahm found out. He didn't care if all of the bek'hai armies came to capture him. He had taken the game and made it personal. Was his disdain so great?

He stumbled away from the body toward the wall, opening the compartment that held his plasma gun. He needed to calm himself and be careful. If his hypothesis was correct, Gr'el had done more than betray him.

He had betrayed the Domo'dahm as well and created his own army of clones.

34

TEA'VA DIDN'T RUSH RIGHT TO the bridge to confront his Si'dahm. He also didn't report anything out of the ordinary regarding the Mother. Instead, he dressed her wound to prevent her from bleeding and then moved her body to his bed. He considered removing her clothing before positioning her to look as if she were sleeping, but couldn't bring himself to do it. He hated the thought that anyone should come upon her like this and guess at what he had done.

As if he were so weak.

When that was done, he dressed in a skin-tight gori'shah suit beneath his official robes, mounting the plasma gun in a holster there, within easy reach of his hand. He looked longingly at the regeneration chamber before leaving his quarters. He could survive a few more days without. The risk was too great to ignore.

Then he moved out into the corridor, scanning for others as he did. He didn't want to be seen if he could avoid it, especially by the lor'hai. He was no longer sure who he could trust.

Could he trust anyone?

He considered Zoelle. She had tried to help him. She had tried to warn him. If he hadn't pressed the attack, it would have been more difficult for

Gr'el to move forward with his plan. At the same time, he had entrusted her with relaying anything she heard about Gr'el's designs to him, and she had said nothing.

Did that make her a friend or a foe?

He couldn't assume anyone was a friend. He had been foolish enough already. He had to stop looking to others and tackle this concern on his own. First, he had to know if his theory was correct.

He made his way down the corridor to the nearest transport beam. Each of the massive Fortresses was a self-sufficient city unto itself, and as a result, the Ishur held a cloning factory buried deep within its bowels. Tea'va was headed there, entering the green light of the beam and sending himself almost instantly down to the lowest part of the vessel.

He stepped out and walked down one of the corridors leading out of the transport hub. He was cautious as he did, taking care to keep his steps soft, his attention on all of his surroundings. He was the Dahm of the ship, and would have command over anyone who saw him, but only if they were loyal.

Was anyone on the ship loyal?

He had always been mistrustful of the other drumhr. He knew they envied him for his ability to breathe freely in Earth's atmosphere, and for his greater ratio of flesh to bone. He knew they saw him as the future, a future the Domo'dahm claimed to support, even as they vied for the same scraps of power.

He had always hated the lor'hai as well. Especially the un'hai, until Zoelle. She was the first clone he had ever cared for at all. Now he couldn't help but wonder if she had been dishonest with him from the beginning. She had admitted her desire for power to him. Power she had claimed to want to earn from him. What if she were seeking the same from Gr'el instead? Or worse, at the same time? What if she were using them both?

It was as appealing in its deviousness as it was repulsive in its potential. Was a clone capable of such things? If any were, it would be her.

He hated the thought. He hated himself for thinking it, and her for being who and what she was. His anger continued to simmer as he crossed the expanse of the ship.

A group of lor'hai turned the corner ahead of him. He didn't react immediately but then ducked to the side, standing in the shadows along the wall with his head down, looking at his hands as if he were carrying something interesting. He kept his eyes high enough that he could watch the clones as they passed. They didn't so much as look at him. It was the proper action, as he had not addressed them either.

He continued once they were gone, increasing his pace. Gr'el would surely be questioning the fate of his assassin by now. He would likely be seeking a reason to visit Tea'va in his quarters. A reason to find him dead. A task from the Domo'dahm, perhaps? He would not expect that his Mother was still missing, and no answer was forthcoming from Tea'va, the entry to his space barred to the pur'dahm.

He neared the entrance to the facility. It was located in a tall, cavernous space within the ship, adjacent to the laboratories where drumhr and lor'hai science teams worked to improve the compatibility of the genetic splice and to improve the health of the bek'hai. As a starship at war, the Ishur's geneticist population was only a handful, and the cloning facility should have been in hibernation until they needed to bolster their numbers.

He could tell right away that it wasn't sleeping. The facility rose along the frame of the room like a rounded honeycomb, and light was escaping through the thinner areas in the flesh-like wall. The floor vibrated softly from the operation of a segregated power supply. Tea'va hadn't known the Ishur's cloning facility was on separate power. No wonder there had been no noticeable strain on their overall output.

A clone soldier was standing guard near the entrance. There would be no way for Tea'va to enter without passing him. It didn't matter. Now that he had confirmed his suspicion, he needed to shift his focus to the truth that was coming further into clarity.

Gr'el was creating clones behind his back. Zoelle had to know about it and had lied to him. His command and his life were both under threat.

He cursed his blindness to the whole thing as he turned around and headed back to the upper part of the ship. He had to hurry and rally the lor'hai and drumhr who would be loyal to their Dahm. He had to stop Gr'el before his was able to solidify his plans. The first wave of clones had no doubt been released after the Ishur had arrived in the Pol'tik system. That was why the Mother had been unaffected by the travel. It meant there were as many as two hundred of them on board, fresh and healthy and under Gr'el's control.

He growled under his breath. It was all falling apart so quickly, so easily. All of his plans were unraveling before he ever had the chance to execute them. Druk to the humans. Druk to Gr'el. Druk to the un'hai, to Zoelle, and to all of the lor'hai.

He touched the pin on his chest, opening a comm channel. The drumhr would be loyal to their Dahm. No amount of empty promises could buy their loyalty.

"This is Dahm Tea'va," he said. "Gi'shah Dahm Vel'ik, what is your status?"

He waited through the silence.

"Gi'shah Dahm Vel'ik, status report," he said.

Again, only silence.

He growled again as he reached the transport hub. He turned the corner, heading for the beam and the upper decks of the fortress. He froze when he saw two lor'hai soldiers standing over the body of a third clone. He recognized the dead one as a member of the original crew.

Was he too late?

He grabbed the weapon from beneath his robes, holding it behind him as he approached the clones.

"What is the meaning of this?" he asked.

The two clones didn't speak. They each raised a plasma gun toward him and then tumbled over as he shot them in the head.

He didn't step into the beam. He knew now that he was too late. Gr'el had likely made his move at the same time the Mother was attacking him. There was some small satisfaction that his traitorous commander would soon discover that he was still alive, but it was only a small sense.

Just like that, he had lost control of the Ishur.

35

Donovan didn't bury Diaz, despite Murphy's offer of help from the scavengers they had saved. He burned her instead, building a massive funeral pyre in the center of the destroyed city, right near the church, close to where her grandfather had once lived. He had a feeling she would want it that way, especially knowing that there was no way the bek'hai wouldn't see the smoke. He pictured the rising pillar as a gigantic middle finger, casting its opinion back toward the dark spots in the distance. Diaz would have approved of that.

The pur'dahm had promised three days, and Ehri had affirmed that the Dread would keep the promise. For whatever else they were or weren't, they did have an honor system that they held to, one that had survived tens of thousands of years.

He hadn't said anything when he lit the pyre. He simply stood and watched the flames rise up the vegetation until they had enveloped Diaz and started to burn her flesh. He had wanted to turn away then, but he didn't. She was more than Renata Diaz. She was all of the people who had died for their cause, and he wasn't going to disrespect them by looking away.

Ehri, Soon, and Iwu remained close for a long time. Soon took a seat on the ground after a while, his head beginning to bother him. The others helped him maintain the vigil for the three hours it took to begin to die down. Murphy joined them an hour in, trailed by his wife and daughter.

"What do we do now?" the leader of the scavengers asked him. Murphy couldn't have been more than a few years older than Donovan, but he looked so much older.

"Why are you asking me?" Donovan replied. He couldn't even keep his friends alive.

"You're with the resistance. I thought that you might have a plan."

"I had the beginning of a plan. It fell apart."

Murphy looked at the pyre. "Was she your wife?"

"A friend. Maybe she would have wanted to be if it weren't for the Dread."

"Do you think she would have been?"

"I don't know. It doesn't matter now."

"It always matters. It's the possibility that motivates us. The potential that keeps us going. If you cared about her, it will motivate you more to make the Dread pay."

Donovan let himself smile. "I already have more than enough for them to pay for. What about you?"

"Everyone here has lost something. It might surprise you to hear that some of the worst stories come from people who have had run-ins with jackals. They say they make the Dread look downright friendly sometimes."

"Is it that bad?"

"I don't know. What I do know is that it isn't safe out there. Not for anyone. We came this way hoping to steer clear of it. We thought this city would stay abandoned. We've only been here a week. The Dread didn't waste any time coming after us."

"They have orders to kill everyone who's left," Donovan said.

"I've heard Washington State. Well, what used to be Washington State, is getting hit hard. There was a pretty large settlement building up there. A peaceful settlement. I heard they had been bribing the local bek'hai contingent to let them alone."

"Bribing them with what?"

"Booze? Women? Who knows. I heard they don't like any of that stuff. I have no idea what could convince them to be compassionate."

Donovan glanced over at Ehri, who shrugged.

"Yeah, anyway," Murphy continued. "Like I said, it isn't safe out there. For anybody. Then you come along. You're fighting the bek'hai. You have their weapons. You killed that one as easy and cold as I've seen a man kill any living thing. There's safety in numbers, mister." He paused. "Where the hell are my manners? I don't even know your name." He stuck out his hand. "Murphy O'Han. This is my wife Linda, and our daughter Shea."

Donovan took it. "Major Donovan Peters. This is Ehri. Captain Soon Kim is sitting over there with Doctor Nailah Iwu."

"A doctor?" Linda said. "For real?"

"Yes. Why?"

"Linda's sister is back in the underground. She's got an infection."

"Do you think she can help?"

"She will if she can," Donovan said.

Linda took Shea by the hand and guided her away from them and to Doc Iwu.

"So I was saying," Murphy said. "It's clearly not safe for us here. Maybe not anywhere. If we want to survive, we have to stick together, right?"

"Or scatter too far apart to get caught," Donovan replied.

"Workable in theory, but impossible in practice. Us humans are too social. We'll bunch up again sooner or later."

Donovan knew that was true. "So you want to travel with us?"

"I don't know where you're going, but it has to be better than here."

"I can't guarantee that."

"I'm not looking for a guarantee. Look, I've got fifty people down in the underground, and another fifteen left that are willing and able to hold a firearm and stand and fight against the Dread. That's sixty-six of us that I'm doing my best to keep alive. I didn't ask for the position, but it's mine."

"I understand how that is."

"Then you know I have a responsibility to do what I think is best for these people. Judging by the fact that you bought us three days of peace by killing that ugly bastard, I think our best chance is with you."

Donovan stared at the flames while he thought about it. "The problem is that if I accept you, they become my responsibility. I have a war to fight. I can't afford to be tied down by civilians."

"I get that, Major," Murphy said. "I respect that. If you say yes, they stay my responsibility. I take care of them; you take care of yourself. Well, maybe you send a few shots our way if the Dread attack. I want to help you fight your war, not hurt it. Believe me; even you'll be safer with some more bodies around you. The Dread purge is making the jackals more desperate. They think stockpiling weapons and food and slaves is going to save them in the end. Idiots."

"Did you say slaves?"

Murphy shook his head. "You think the Dread are the only ones keeping slaves these days? Not so, Major. I've heard stories. The jackals are taking servants of their own, women and children mainly. You can guess what they're using them for."

"Even if we win the war, will there be anything left to salvage?" Donovan asked.

"There's a lot of good people out there, too. It's just that they're running scared, hiding most of the time. You have the training. You have the weapons. Maybe you can do something about it."

"We're trying," Donovan said. "It isn't easy."

"Nothing worth doing ever is. What do you say, Major? Let us tag along. We'll give you safety in numbers; you'll give us safety in your experience. It's a good deal for both of us."

Donovan looked at Ehri. She didn't say anything. This was his decision to make. Like Murphy, he had somehow wound up in charge.

"Do you promise to follow my orders?" Donovan asked.

"Yes, sir," Murphy replied. "I'll make sure the others do, too."

Donovan wasn't confident he was doing the right thing, but he put his hand out anyway. He couldn't abandon these people after he had managed to save them.

"Deal."

36

IT WAS EARLY MORNING WHEN Donovan finally left the pyre to smolder. Diaz's corpse was no longer visible beneath the ashen remains of the fuel that consumed it. Murphy had agreed to take care of the bones, and he and a few of his men had been busy digging the grave nearby.

"Major," Ehri said. She had remained by his side for hours, standing with him in silent support, though she had left a few times to check on the others.

"What is it?" Donovan asked.

"We should go and examine the transport. Til'ik honored your request and ordered his troops to abandon it as it was."

"Not the smartest idea, was it?"

"He didn't expect you to defeat him. I can only imagine the Domo'dahm's reaction when he learns what happened. He will probably end Til'ik's splice line completely."

"Have you seen Soon and Nailah?" Donovan asked.

"They're with the people in the underground. Doctor Iwu is treating whoever she can, and Soon is playing with the children."

"With his injury?"

"He's mostly telling them stories about space."

"Maybe we should go down there instead?"

Ehri smiled. "It is good you haven't lost your spirit, Major."

"I won't let them take everything from me," he replied. "Let's go see the transport."

They crossed the open area, back to where the Dread ship was still resting. Murphy's people had stayed away from it at his request, looking relieved that they didn't have to get too close. Donovan had become so accustomed to the enemy he had forgotten how most people feared them.

The transport was large, nearly twenty meters long and five meters wide, with an angry face and the scaly, irregular shape created by the armored shell. There was a ramp leading up to the side of the vessel, and Donovan and Ehri climbed it to make their way inside.

There were no seats in the vehicle, but there were ripples in the floor where the clones could place their feet. The front of the ship was open, the outside visible through a clear viewport.

"A restraining field holds the soldiers in place," Ehri said, pointing at the ripples. "It is the same field that prevents the vacuum of space from entering the bek'hai ships beyond the atmosphere. It also provides artificial gravity to the fortress, and allows a vessel like this to fly."

"How does it work?"

"Microburst Gravitomagnetism. A type of magnetic field. It is similar to the process used on human starships, only more refined."

"You mean more advanced?"

"The bek'hai are thousands of years older than the human race. There's nothing shameful about what your kind has accomplished."

"I never said I was ashamed."

Ehri brought him to the front of the ship. The pilot seat was human-scale and looked rather comfortable. It was the controls that gave Donovan pause.

"How does it work?" he asked, staring down at the two pools of blue gel positioned on either side of the chair. They were resting in cutouts of four-fingered hands that were twice the size of a human's.

"It is called Kool'ek. It is an organic, conductive gel that is used for direct communication from the nervous system of a bek'hai to the ship's control system. The pilot places their hands in the gel, and the link allows instantaneous bi-directional feedback. In a sense, the bek'hai becomes the ship."

"It doesn't work for humans?"

"No. We lack the chemistry to create the proper signals, as do the more advanced drumhr splices. There are workarounds that utilize the gori'shah as a go-between, but they reduce the overall effectiveness of the system. The kool'ek is being phased out as the bek'hai move closer to maintaining a balance of derived genetics, but until the majority of drumhr are converted, such technology will remain. It is unfortunate. If we could fly the transport, we would be at the resistance base within a few hours."

"Very unfortunate," Donovan said. "Can we do anything with the transport?"

"That is what we came to find out."

She headed to the rear of the ship again, finding a blank space on the rear wall and putting her hand to it. A seam appeared on the wall, and then it slid aside, revealing a storage compartment.

Donovan peered into the space. It was large enough for a person to stand in or pass through. There was a visible hatch at the rear, and storage racks aligned on either side. The racks were mostly empty, but not completely. Four plasma rifles remained, standing upright in a simple receptacle.

Ehri entered the compartment and lifted one of them. She smiled and passed it to Donovan. "Unsecured."

He took it and turned it on, and then nodded. "What's back there?" he asked.

"The power generators."

"How do they work?"

"You are very curious today."

"I'm being exposed to more and more of the bek'hai technology. I want to understand it."

"The generators on the transports are a simplified version of the system you saw inside the capital fortress. It is like your quantum phase generators in that it creates a pathway into slipspace, though in this case, it is the size of a pinhole. The system extracts the zero-point energy from the quantum state."

"Won't that cause problems with slipspace? Instability or something?"

"No. The amount of zero-point energy available is large enough to be considered infinite. The difficult part is in the extraction. The fortresses increase the size and output of the generators, and pair them with secondary systems that store excess energy for use when a slipspace link is unavailable."

"I always heard that slipspace is everywhere."

"Almost, but not quite. There are a number of dead zones throughout the universe. Most occur near supermassive black holes, but they aren't unheard of in random places. Even the bek'hai don't understand the exact nature of these regions."

"It's a hard concept for me to get my head around," Donovan said.

"It can be challenging," Ehri agreed. "The fact that you asked at all is an important first step."

Donovan smiled. "Thanks." He pointed at the rifles in the rack. "This gives us seven. I'll have Murphy hand out the extras to the most skilled shooters in his group."

"I think that's a good idea."

Donovan backed up into the center of the transport again, looking around at the inner part of the ship. Ehri joined him there a moment later.

"I noticed how angry you became when you saw the soldiers killing the scavengers," he said. "And how angry you became at Til'ik for what he did."

"Every moment of freedom brings me further from my life as a slave," Ehri said. "Every moment with you and the others helps me feel more human. I want to be accepted by you. To be one of you. I want to show the other lor'hai that they can be, too. I'm genetically human. My loyalty is to my kind. Humankind. The bek'hai made me, but that does not give them the right to own me."

"You are accepted and valued. I'm happy that you're with us. With me."

Donovan stood facing her, looking into her eyes. A brief thought crossed his mind that he should kiss her, but he dismissed it as an image of Diaz's lifeless body followed. He broke her gaze, looking around at the transport again.

"I have an idea," he said a moment later. "Tell me if you think this will work."

37

THEODORE AND COLONEL CHOI WERE already in the conference room when Gabriel arrived. They were talking softly to one another and fell silent when he entered the room.

"Captain St. Martin reporting, sir," Gabriel said.

Theodore raised his eyebrow.

"Major St. Martin, reporting," Gabriel corrected.

"That's better. At ease, Major. The rest of the required participants will be along in a moment."

Gabriel took a seat next to Colonel Choi.

"Did you give Lieutenant Bale the news?"

"Yes, sir. She said she promises she won't let you down."

"I'm not completely sure about that, but I guess we'll see how the stump shakes."

"Sir?"

"She's impulsive, and her moral character is weak. She's either going to clean up her act, or she's going to get herself killed, maybe along with us."

"Isn't that a bit of a risk?" Choi asked.

"Yup. Sometimes it's necessary. She has potential if she can grow up a little. Anyway, that's small potatoes compared to what all else is going on around this neck of the bayou. Vivian here's been filling me in on everything. I'm about as angry as a rattlesnake in an alligator's gullet."

"You look great, though," Gabriel said.

Theodore smiled. "I've been out of action too long. Way too long. Casting off that demon was something else. I spent three days in bed, barely able to move, it all hurt so much. Then I woke up on the fourth day and knew I had to make a decision to live or die. I promised your mother I would live a long time ago, so it wasn't really much of a decision."

"Yes, sir."

Sergeant Diallo entered the room, with Guy Larone behind him.

"Guy. Thanks for coming," Theodore said.

"I don't recall having a choice, General," Guy replied.

"But you didn't bitch too much. I'll take whatever victory I can get."

Guy surprised Gabriel, sitting down next to him. Diallo left the room, and Hafizi entered a moment later with Sarah Larone.

"General," she said, sitting opposite her husband.

"Where's Reza?" Gabriel asked.

"He'll be along shortly," Theodore replied. "I wanted to talk to Guy and Sarah without him first. Sergeant Hafizi, can you wait outside with Diallo, and keep anyone from getting too close."

"Yes, sir," Hafizi said, leaving the room.

Gabriel looked at his father. He knew what his request meant.

Theodore cleared his throat, rolled his chair back, and leaned up on his arms. He looked at Guy, and then at Sarah.

"I already chewed out Mr. Mokri," he said. "Be glad you didn't decide to sit in that chair. He had to go back to his quarters to get a new pair of pants. Thing is, Reza's just a kid. Responsible for his own actions, yes, which is why he got chewed, but still a kid. Mrs. Larone, you should have known better."

Sarah looked down at the table. "Yes, sir. I'm sorry-"

"Sorry?" Theodore said.

Gabriel cringed, knowing it was the wrong thing to say.

"You're sorry?"

"It was a mistake," she said.

"Are you taking powerful narcotics that affect your judgment, Mrs. Larone?" Theodore said.

"What? No, sir."

"Then how the hell do you get away with categorizing putting the integrity of this team and the overall chance of the mission's success as a damned mistake?" Theodore roared, so loudly even Colonel Choi flinched. "That weapon is the key to this war. This entire damned war, Mrs. Larone, but for some reason, you decided that playing house with a man half your age was more important. Somehow, you thought that was some kind of acceptable. Do you even have the smallest understanding of the effects your shortsighted, ill-advised actions have already had on our chances?"

"General, I-"

"It is well within my rights as the commander of this starship to have you tried and convicted of treason, Mrs. Larone. You and Mr. Mokri both. I don't want your damned reasons, and I don't want your damned excuses. It wasn't a mistake. It was stupid. Pure, unfiltered, unadulterated stupid."

Sarah kept her head down, staying silent.

"General," Guy said.

"Hold on a second, Mr. Larone. I'm not quite done."

"General, wait," Guy said again.

Theodore looked at him without speaking.

"I don't want you to yell at her," Guy said. "What's done is done. It won't change her decision, or put things back together."

"Entirely my point," Theodore said.

"It won't help, either. It isn't her fault, General. It's mine."

"Oh? How so?"

"I've spent the last few weeks acting like a child. Pouting at the situation we're in, instead of doing my part. I closed myself off, made myself unavailable." He looked at Sarah. "What else were you going to do?"

"Not be unfaithful," Theodore said. "That's the coward's way out."

"I don't want us to fight, General," Guy said. "What you said is right. The enemy is behind us, and we don't have a way to defend ourselves.

That first attack, that was nothing. It was a test."

"My thoughts, exactly. Do you have a theory as to why?"

"Slipspace sickness," Guy said. "Their human clones would have the same response to long slipstream travel as we do if we aren't careful."

"I like the way you're thinking right now, Mr. Larone. If your hypothesis is right, we probably have two, maybe three days to figure out how to either stop their next attack or escape before they can hit us."

"We can't fix the nacelle in three days," Colonel Choi said. "There is no escape."

"Then we need to figure out how to repel them," Theodore said. "I need your heads in the game. All three of you. Together."

Guy's jaw tensed. Gabriel waited for him to rebuff the request. He nodded instead. "This isn't about me, or Reza, or Sarah. I understand that now. I'm sorry, General. I'm sorry, Sarah. I won't cause any more grief. What I want won't matter if we're dead. What any of us want won't matter if we're dead."

"I'm glad you see it my way, Mr. Larone. To be frank, I don't care about your individual personal lives. I do care about this mission and the integrity of it. We need to put our heads down and worry about surviving the Dread, not acting like a bunch of children. Do you think you can do that? Mr. Larone? Mrs. Larone?"

"Yes, sir," Guy said.

"Yes, sir," Sarah said. Her cheeks were wet with her tears.

"Good. Gabriel, go tell Diallo to fetch Mr. Mokri for me."

"Yes, sir."

"Mr. Larone, I want you to show us everything you've got. Let's put our heads together and solve this thing."

38

REZA ENTERED THE MEETING ROOM with Sergeant Diallo. Diallo was holding the Dread rifle, while Reza was carrying his tablet, the same one that Gabriel had often seen him absorbed by back on Alpha Settlement. He was staring at it even now, a look of interested curiosity drawn across his face.

"Mr. Mokri," Theodore said loudly.

The scientist shuddered slightly at the sound of the General's voice, looking up from the screen while his face turned red.

"Uh. Yes. Yes, sir," he said. He surveyed the room, his eyes purposely passing over Sarah Larone faster than the others.

Gabriel watched Guy's face. The older man held it tight and expressionless. There was no doubt he was angry at Reza, but he was doing a good job sticking to his promise and keeping his emotions to himself.

"Do you have everything I requested, son?"

"Yes, sir," Reza said, a little more comfortably the second time.

He approached the table, sitting at the end of it away from everyone else. He placed his tablet on the counter, tapping it a few times to switch the display. A three-dimensional image of the Dread plasma rifle appeared suspended in the center of them.

"I think Guy should be the first one to go over this," Reza said. "He's done the most work on the weapon."

"Agreed," Theodore said. "Mr. Larone? You're up."

"Yes, General," Guy said, getting to his feet. "You didn't want to risk damaging the rifle, so we did the highest resolution three-dimensional scan and composition analysis possible with the equipment we have on board. It isn't quite to the level of what we can achieve back home, but as you can see we were able to get a decent visual composite breakdown of the weapon into the system. From this, I was able to learn to take the real weapon apart and put it back together in working order."

"Have you?" Colonel Choi asked.

"No, ma'am," Guy replied. "I didn't want to be solely responsible for it, and Reza has better eyes than I do. In any case, I have been working with the model since we began heading for this system." He leaned forward, expertly manipulating the image, breaking it apart into its component parts. "I've identified one hundred percent of the parts used in the manufacture of the weapon, and matched them up with equivalent human technology. While some of the Dread's manufacturing processes and production compounds are more advanced than our own, the basic function of the rifle is in line with our science."

"What does that mean in English, Mr. Larone?" Theodore asked.

"It means that I believe I understand exactly how the weapon works, based on what we've derived from the imaging. Except, clearly I don't understand how it works, because I have no idea how it can penetrate their armor, while our own weapons can't. There's nothing in the composition of the weapon that suggests it has any special properties that we can't replicate."

"So you don't know how it works?" Gabriel asked.

"I know exactly how it works, up to that point. But I have identified all of the components. There is nothing out of the ordinary that I can see."

"There has to be something, Mr. Larone," Theodore said.

"Yes, General. And it is that truth that has me frustrated. I know there must be something different about it, and yet I can't discern that difference."

"It might help to take the weapon apart, sir," Reza said.

"Is that right, Mr. Larone?"

"Yes, General. As I said, I did the best I could with the equipment we have. Seeing the real thing may reveal something I missed."

"Mr. Mokri, do you understand how to deconstruct the weapon?"

"I've been reviewing Guy's scans," Reza said. "I believe so."

"You ought to be certain, son. We only get one shot at this."

Reza bit his lower lip and then nodded. "I can do it, General."

"Good man," Theodore said. "What do you need?"

"My tools from the lab. I can go and get them."

"No. Stay put. Sergeant Diallo, would you mind?"

"Yes, sir," Diallo replied.

"They're on the bench," Reza said. "Just grab all of them."

"Of course, Mr. Mokri," Diallo said. He handed Reza the rifle and headed from the room.

Reza placed the weapon on the table, looking uncomfortable to touch it. "I don't like guns," he said.

"The reason I wanted you to stay was so that we could talk things through a little bit. The fact is, we got a big fat clue as to what all we should be looking for from our encounter with that Dread fortress that's hugging our ass back there."

"Their armor was vulnerable to our weapons," Gabriel said.

"Yes," Guy said. "I have been giving it some thought, as you requested General."

"And?" Theodore asked.

"There is one thing that is different from this encounter with the Dread, and all of our prior encounters with the Dread." He pointed at the schematic of the rifle. "Do you mind if I replace this for a moment?"

"Go on, Mr. Larone."

Guy put his tablet on the table, replacing the image of the gun with one of his own.

"This is a star map of the system we are currently skirting the edge of," he said. "It happens to be right on the corner of a slipspace dead zone, which is where we've been trapped for the last three weeks."

He tapped his pad, and a field of red mist appeared throughout the system beyond the Magellan.

"These are the slipstreams we've detected within the system. There are two dozen of them crisscrossing one another, but as you can see they all reach their terminus at an eerily similar location."

"Any idea why?" Gabriel asked.

"No. We don't understand what causes slipstreams to end, or slipspace to have what seem to be holes throughout. It could be caused by dimensional tears, but to be honest, we don't have the technology to make more than a random guess. What we do know is that slipspace is a dimension that runs parallel to our own, and it is filled with ripples in spacetime. Streams. Riding these streams allow us to travel faster than light by using quantum phasing to cross the boundary between dimensions and take advantage of these distortions."

"Astrophysics one-oh-three," Reza said. Guy almost glared at him but stopped himself short. Reza's face reddened again as he prepared for Theodore to bawl him out again.

"Go on," Theodore said, glaring at Reza.

"Those are the slipstreams," Guy said, pointing at the mist. Then he pointed at the green dot some distance away from it. "That's us."

"We're still in the dead zone," Choi said. "You're suggesting that the Dread armor uses slipspace?"

"I believe it is so, yes."

"You mean it's phased?" Gabriel asked, not quite believing it. "How can something static like metal rest permanently in another dimension?"

"I didn't say it was," Guy replied.

"The Dread armor is coated in phase paint," Reza said. "Yes. It could be. It doesn't have to be phased all the time, only when it detects something is about to strike it. It enters phase, and the threat is avoided."

"No," Theodore said. "Missiles would go right through if that were the case. They don't. They hit the armor, explode, and don't leave a scratch."

"And shooting it still exerts a force on the armor," Gabriel said. "That wouldn't happen if the ions were being phased into slipspace."

169

"True," Reza said, pausing to think.

"What if the phase were partial?" Sarah said, speaking for the first time.

"What do you mean?" Guy asked.

"Well, instead of trying to stop the entire attack, only part of it is deflected. For instance, a missile strikes the armor and detonates. The force still exists, but enough of it is absorbed into phase that it doesn't cause any damage. It just kind of pushes against the armor."

"An interesting thought," Guy said. "To take it one step further, what if there is another type of phase, or use for the properties of quantum phasing that humans have yet to discover? What if slipspace can be manipulated into realspace, similarly to how we manipulate this dimension into that one."

"You mean pull slipspace in?" Reza said. "Impossible."

"Is it?" Guy asked.

"There's no viable theory to suggest it. No math that can prove it, or an experiment that has shown it."

"They used to say the same damn thing about slipspace," Theodore said. "They said it didn't exist, and even if it did, we could never use it to go faster than light. They said it was all just made up sci-fi bullshit. Until it wasn't."

"The Dread are an advanced race," Gabriel said. "I don't think it's safe to dismiss the potential for them to do anything just because we haven't done it yet."

"Especially because we haven't done it yet," Choi agreed. "I'm sure many geneticists would have thought the cloning and gene manipulation the Dread use was also impossible. When we limit the capabilities of the universe to what we currently understand, we undermine the potential of it."

Diallo re-appeared in the room, holding a bag full of small tools. He dropped it on the table in front of Reza.

"Thank you, Sergeant," Theodore said.

"Yes, sir."

"As I was saying, General," Guy said. "What if slipspace could be pulled into this dimension? How would it work? What effects would it have? I don't know the answer, but what we do know is that the Dread armor absorbs damage without the kinetic force of the blow being deleted. Reduced perhaps, but not removed. We also know that it is dependent on slipspace to operate. Without it, the armor is still solid, but it is not even as solid as the metal plating on the Magellan's hull. Finally, we know that whatever allows the weapon to bypass the defenses operates at a scale we weren't able to pick up with our scanning equipment."

"It may be nano-scale," Sarah said.

"Well, then, what are you waiting for, Mr. Mokri?" Theodore asked. "Open her up and let's see what we can see."

39

"WHAT'S THE WORD FROM THE science team?" Miranda asked.

Gabriel stood just inside the doorway to her quarters, stroking Wallace's head. His father had ordered him to take a break from the research that was ongoing in the meeting room since he would need to relieve Lieutenant Bale from her shift on the hot seat within the next few hours. He was supposed to hit the sack, but the whole thing had left his mind whirling and unable to calm enough to fall asleep.

He had decided to find Wallace instead, heading first to Daphne's quarters, and then to Miranda's, which was where he had found the dog.

"They're picking the Dread weapon apart a piece at a time, and then running everything through a microscope. It's slow going."

"What about your father?"

Gabriel smiled. "You saw him on the bridge. When I went to see him, and he popped up and told me he wanted to steal the Magellan, I thought I was seeing the old Old Gator. Now I know I wasn't. The real General St. Martin is the one we saw a few hours ago."

"He's changed the entire complexion of the ship. The crew is working with purpose and energy again. Of course, surviving a skirmish with the Dread didn't hurt."

"No. It felt pretty good."

"I'm glad you're not still beating yourself up about the nacelle."

Gabriel grimaced. "Oh. Thanks for reminding me."

"Come on, Captain, you know I'm always on your side."

She was. She always had been. "Don't you mean Major?"

She laughed. "I'm teasing you again. Seriously, Gabriel, I'm glad you made it back in one piece. I was worried about you."

"I don't know what would have happened if the Dread hadn't been vulnerable. Bale was real close to getting cut down, and if one of us had gone down, I think the others would have followed pretty soon after."

"But they were vulnerable, she didn't get shot down, and you're all still here. That's the important thing."

"I know. It's hard not to worry sometimes. It's hard to stop thinking in general. The Dread fortress is still behind us, and we can't get away. It's not a question of if they'll try again, it's when. My father looks great, and he sounds great, but I'm still worried about him. When I saw that clone of my mother on Earth, I could barely breathe. I could barely think. It hit me like a meteor. How is he going to react if he ever comes face to face with one?"

"Do you think he'll fall apart?"

"No. But what if they're not friendly? What if it's trying to kill him? He might just stand there and take it."

"And risk all of our lives again? I doubt that."

"Maybe you're right. I hope you're right."

"What else is bothering you?"

He shook his head. He had been feeling the doubts for a while, but it was hard to admit to them. "What if it's all for nothing?" he asked, throwing it out there. If he couldn't tell Miranda about it, he couldn't tell anyone. "What if we got the weapon back, but we can't figure out how to use it? Everyone on Earth will die. Everyone in the settlement will die. We'll die. We're responsible for the continuation of the entire human race."

"And everyone on this ship is doing the best they can. It's the only thing we can do, right?"

"That doesn't make it easier to stop thinking about it. I feel responsible for these people. As much as my father does. Maybe more, since I'm the one who got us stuck here."

"Gabe-" Miranda started to say.

"I know, I know. I did my best. Anyway, I have to go try to get some rest, or I'm going to be running on fumes if the Dread attack. Thanks for listening, Randa."

"You know I always will."

Gabriel smiled. He didn't think about it much, but she was his best friend. Always there for him. Always loyal. When he had lost Jessica, he had felt like she had lost her, too. "I can't tell you how much I appreciate that, or how much I appreciate you."

"You just did."

She reached out for him. He stepped forward into her embrace, holding her for a minute before letting go. They stared at one another for a long moment.

"Look, I don't want to be overly forward, and I don't want you to get the wrong idea," Miranda said. "Maybe you just need some company to help you relax."

"You mean Wallace? I think he's happier with you."

"I mean human company," she replied. "Why don't you hang out here? We can watch a stream, and maybe having someone else around will help you stop thinking so much."

Gabriel considered for a moment. He couldn't think of a reason why he shouldn't.

"It's worth a shot," he said. "If you don't mind."

"I don't mind at all. I like having you around."

"In that case, what do you want to watch?"

"The selection is pretty slim, but there has to be something in there we've seen less than a thousand times."

Gabriel stepped away from the door, giving himself permission to smile. He had no idea what the future was going to bring, but for right now he would just relax and let it go. His father was back and better than ever, Reza and the Larones were working on deciphering the mystery of the Dread technology, and Miranda was, well, he wasn't completely certain what Miranda was. A friend for sure, but there was something else there, a new sensation tugging at his emotions and whispering that maybe she could be something more.

He let that thought fade away and took his position beside her on her bunk, facing her comm station. For now, he was content enough to share her presence.

Besides, they had a war to win.

40

"THERE," DONOVAN SHOUTED, POINTING AT a spot beneath the Dread transport. "That's where it's stuck."

Murphy ran back to where he was standing, coming up beside him and leaning over. "Damn it. I told Rosa to guide us further to the right. It's going to take time to get free."

Donovan surveyed the area around them. There was a line of brush ten meters deep on both sides of the road, along with a large old building set back a few hundred meters on their left. A side road led up to it, and a sign rested against a worn facade. "Parada de descanso," it read in faded white lettering on an orange background. Rest stop.

Ehri approached a moment later, running back from her position at the front of the group. She also dipped down to see what had happened.

"We'll need something to dig it out with," she said.

"Do you have a shovel?" Donovan asked.

"No," Murphy replied. "We were too busy collecting food, clothes, guns and ammunition. I never thought we would need a shovel."

"Ehri, how much time do we have left?" Soon said, circling from the other side of the transport.

"Approximately eight hours, Captain."

"We aren't going to make it to Monterrey before then."

Donovan stared down the length of the roadway at the tractor ahead of them, vibrating softly as it sat idle, its driver waiting for him to pass along his orders.

His original idea had been to try to rig the anti-gravity controller on the Dread transport such that they could get it to sit a few inches off the ground. At that point, it would offer little to no friction, and they would be able to attach a few ropes to it and pull it along, like a covered wagon from that same old western he had seen. Most of the group could be piled inside to ride in comfort while a few pulled and a few guarded, taking turns as needed throughout the day and night to make it as far as possible in relative safety before the hard-won days of peace came to an abrupt end.

Ehri thought it was a great idea, and had immediately gone to the rear of the vehicle to begin working with the zero point engine that powered it while he returned to Murphy to inform him of his plan. Within an hour, Ehri had come running to show him that she had gotten the transport jury-rigged to the point that the engine was running, and power had been diverted to the plates on the bottom of the craft. He and Murphy had watched as she got it floating nearly a foot off the ground. Then they had watched as it tumbled back to earth a few seconds later, victim of a secondary security system that prevented it from changing coordinates without a pilot at the helm.

Donovan had been discouraged and ready to give up. Murphy hadn't. He quickly organized the scavengers to find an alternative means of enacting a similar plan. It had taken nearly a full day to get all of the pieces in place, but by the end they had managed to slip the frame of an old semi-trailer beneath the transport, letting it bear the weight of the ship and giving it a line of wheels to roll on. They had also somehow located a huge farming machine an hour outside of the city, a behemoth of rolling alloy that was almost wider than the transport itself. It had been lost for years beneath the crops it had been built to collect, a buried treasure that the scavengers had been lucky to come across. It had taken a little engineering know-how to get the long-dead battery feeding from the transport's generator, but Ehri and Rosa, a seventy-eight-year-old survivor of the Dread invasion, had managed to get it done.

They had been making good time since then, covering more ground in the hours that followed than any of them could have managed in a week on foot. The travel had been easy once they reached the wider road, with the tractor able to roll down the center of the highway, pushing most of the remaining derelict cars out of its path with ease and trailing the transport behind it.

Then they had come across deep scars in the road left by the Dread attack decades earlier. The tractor had gone over them without a problem. The transport hadn't been as fortunate, the rearmost axle getting hung up on a thick pile of rubble. The obstruction hadn't immediately overloaded the cab, but they all knew it would thicken and multiply if they continued to push it until it both bogged down their makeshift wagon and left it impossible to dig out.

"What do you want to do?" Murphy asked. "We came down through Monterrey. I remember that rest stop. It's a good two hundred kilometers to decent protection from here."

"We can cover that ground easily in the Monster," Soon said, using the nickname for the machine they had created. "Once we get it unstuck."

"It will take five hours to reach Monterrey," Ehri said. "We have less than three to get it loose."

"Can you levitate the transport again?" Donovan asked.

"No, Major. As soon as we moved it away from its landing position, the security systems shut down access to the anti-gravity functions."

Donovan considered the situation. Their agreement would expire soon, and he was sure the Dread wouldn't waste any time sending a force to deal with them. The goal was to be out of sight when that happened, preferably somewhere underground with the transport safely hidden away. They were hopeful the Dread would sweep the area, find nothing, and then decide to pass them over. That would give them an opportunity to bring the Monster back out and make a run for the border, crossing over into what had once been the United States of America and making a beeline for Austin before they were discovered.

It wasn't a great plan, but it was the only thing they had. Except now a simple error in judgment had left them stuck, and he had to make a decision: Try to get the Monster moving again or abandon it and take their chances on foot.

It wasn't much of a decision. He didn't like their chances on foot, which was why they had gone through so much trouble to create the Monster in the first place. He knew there were jackals out there, and while they had recovered more of the alien rifles it wouldn't help them if they were ambushed or attacked by a human force with greater numbers. It gnawed at him that they even had to worry about it. Didn't humankind have enough to deal with? He hated that some people would rather sew chaos than save one another from it.

"You said you passed that building before," he said. "Did you go inside?"

"No, sir. We went past it in the middle of the night, as quick and quiet as we could. For all we know, that place is already occupied."

"Jackals?"

"Maybe. Or anyone else who might shoot first and ask questions later. We were trying not to lose anyone. The Dread didn't let that happen."

"We need to make an attempt to excavate the transport. Our only choice is to see if there's anything we can salvage inside that building that might help us dig out the wheels."

"Understood. I don't have a problem with that, Major. Not when I know Linda and Shea and the others can stay safe inside the Monster while we explore."

"We'll leave the Dread weapons with them. If there's any trouble, it won't help to give up the means to get to the others."

"Agreed," Murphy said.

Donovan turned to Ehri and Soon. "We'll exchange our rifles for traditional guns, and then go search that old building over there. We have one hour, and then we have to consider abandoning the Monster and going ahead on foot."

"Yes, sir," both Soon and Ehri said.

"What if we find other people in there?" Soon asked a moment later.

Donovan glanced at Murphy, who shrugged. It seemed like his group went through a lot of trouble to intentionally not find other people. He couldn't question the practice when they had managed to survive.

"If they're friendly, we give them a chance to join us. If they're hostile, we take them out."

Soon's face blanched at the idea, but he nodded. "I hope it doesn't come to that."

Donovan looked over at the building. It certainly appeared abandoned. "Me, too, Captain. Me, too."

41

THEY APPROACHED THE BUILDING CAUTIOUSLY, staying low in the surrounding brush for as long as they could before breaking the cover and running full-speed to the smooth metal wall closest to the entrance.

Donovan smiled when Soon reached the wall first, barely a step ahead of Ehri. A chance to rest in the Monster for a day had helped the pilot regain most of his former health, and he was showing himself to be a capable soldier.

Murphy reached the wall after Donovan, pausing against it and breathing hard. The leader of the scavengers had proven that he and his people were incredibly resourceful, but also not accustomed to fighting. They had always preferred to run and hide than to take a stand, though Donovan's growing reputation seemed to have emboldened them. He had insisted on coming along, certain that he could help them find something they could use to get the transport unstuck. Even so, his nerves were obviously frayed, his eyes wide and body shaking.

Donovan pushed back the thought of Diaz. She loved these kinds of missions and had always been at home exploring potentially dangerous areas. He wished they didn't have to do it without her.

"Ehri," he whispered, pointing to the wall on the other side of the entry.

It had been a pair of sliding glass doors once. Those doors were long shattered, replaced by piles of debris that siphoned anyone who wanted through to a tight spot in the center. There was no question someone had lived there at one time. The question was whether or not anyone was still inside.

She darted across the open space, coming to rest against the wall once more. The activity didn't draw any attention from inside.

"Cover me," Donovan said, slipping away from the wall and approaching the bottleneck. Dirty food containers rested on the floor at the base of the entrance, abandoned months, if not years, earlier.

He led with the antique handgun Murphy had provided him. It was sleek in appearance and fairly heavy, with a fourteen round magazine loaded and ready and two more in his pockets. It was the kind of weapon a Dread would laugh at. It could still kill a human without much effort.

He hoped it didn't come to that. He had killed Dread clones that were essentially human, but he had never hurt another free human being, and he had no desire to start.

He was halfway across the barrier when a noise to his left caused him to pause, dropping to a knee and aiming the weapon. Ehri appeared behind him a moment later, keeping him covered. A cat appeared in the darkness, hissing and running from them, out into the brush.

"Damn cat," Donovan said. "Scared the crap out of me."

"My apologies, Major, I should have warned you. I saw it from back there."

Donovan glanced back at Ehri. Her enhanced capabilities continued to surprise him. "Anything else up there I should know about?"

She smiled. "No, Major."

Donovan waved Murphy and Soon forward, and they finished passing through the barrier and into the building. It had originally been designed as a place for travelers to pause and eat, use the restroom, and maybe buy something. As a result, it was organized into corridors with storefronts lining them, selling everything from hats to t-shirts to medicine.

Moving through the space, they quickly discovered that most of it had already been picked clean by earlier passers-by. Even the cleaning robots had been disassembled, their interior parts salvaged for use in more valuable tools.

"I was hopeful," Donovan said as they walked along the final line of stores. "But this place is too close to the road to have stayed pristine."

"It was worth a shot," Murphy said. "We've only lost twenty minutes, and now we know for sure our ride is done. We'll have to go on foot from here on out."

"We'll never make it to Monterrey on foot before the treaty ends," Soon said. "We have eight hours."

"We'll think of something," Donovan said. If he had learned anything, it was never to give up. He looked at Ehri. "How far can the tractor take us once we disconnect the generator?"

"With everyone weighing it down? Twenty kilometers at most."

"That's twenty more than we'll cover otherwise. I hate to lose the security the transport offers, but we knew we might not be able to hold onto it forever."

"We're lucky we made it as far as we have," Murphy said. "It took us weeks to get down to San Luis, and we made it back here in one tenth of the time. Then again, I know for a fact there's a gang of jackals in Monterrey. We managed to slip past, but all the signs were there. It would have been nice to have some protection."

"If that's true, the Dread have probably attacked them by now," Donovan said. "They may be helping us by clearing the cities before we get to them."

"Wouldn't that be something?" Murphy said.

"In any case, standing here isn't going to get anything done," Donovan said. "Let's head back to the others. We need to get them ready to move on foot again. Can Jane walk?"

"Thanks to Doctor Iwu she can," Murphy said.

"Good." Donovan took two steps before pausing. "Where's Soon?"

Ehri and Murphy looked at one another, and then scanned the corridor.

"There," Ehri said a moment later. Soon had gone into one of the stores and was standing motionless in front of something.

"What's he doing?" Murphy asked.

Donovan couldn't tell. He headed over to the pilot, finding him flipping through a line of clothes sized for an infant.

"Captain?" Donovan said.

"What do you think of this, Major?" Soon asked, lifting one of the tiny outfits from the rack. It was green and black, with a small patch across the chest that said "Federacion Mexicana De Futbol Asoc., A.C."

"I don't think it will fit you," Donovan replied.

Soon smiled. "Sorry for wandering away, Major. It's just that my wife Daphne and I really want to have a baby. It's a little more complicated than that up there because we only have resources to support a limited population. We have to wait our turn. Down here? There's enough for everybody. I can't even tell you how much I'd love to have Daphne here with me, and to dress the future Soon Junior in this thing."

Donovan put his hand on Soon's shoulder. "Then we need to do everything in our power to make it happen."

"Do you think we can, Major? The Monster was genius, but our luck seems to be out. We're stranded, and our position is way too open. I came in here, and now I'm hoping Daphne knows how much I miss her, and how much I want to give this outfit to her, even if I have no idea what it says on it. Even if the odds of that happening are getting lower by the minute."

Donovan dug his fingers into Soon's arm, turning the pilot toward him. A wave of anger bubbled up, pouring from the wounds he had buried.

"We aren't going to die here, Captain. You hear me? Not you. Not me. Not anyone else. We got you away from the Dread; we escaped Mexico City and San Luis, and we made it all the way here. Nobody said it would be easy, but we're going to survive this thing. We're going to topple the Dread, and we're going to bring your wife home. Do you get that, Captain? She's going to come home to you, right here on Earth."

Soon stood in front of him, shocked into silence for a moment. Then he nodded, clutching the cloth he had picked up tightly in a fist.

"Yes, sir," he said.

"Come on," Donovan said, turning back to where he had left Ehri and Murphy.

He looked just in time to see Ehri running toward him, her mouth opening in a scream, her arms waving at them to get down.

Then the gunfire started, bullets hitting her body and throwing her to the ground. He felt his heart jump again as Murphy fell to the ground behind her, his body riddled with holes, his face vanishing under the barrage.

42

DONOVAN HIT THE GROUND BESIDE Soon, lying prone as the bullets continued to pass over them for a few more seconds.

Then it stopped as quickly as it had started. The world fell silent again, the smell of blood and metal leaving a thick taste in the air. Donovan looked up, trying to find the attackers and trying to find Ehri. How could he have just lost her like that? She had enhanced senses, and she hadn't heard them coming. He still didn't see anyone in the hallway. Where the hell were they?

"Get up," a voice said. It came from all around them. From the building's comm system.

Donovan remained on the floor. He looked over at Soon. He was unharmed.

"Look in front of you," the voice said.

Donovan did. The red point of a laser was hitting the floor there. He followed it to the source, an opening in the ceiling ductwork that he had failed to notice earlier. The building had been occupied the entire time. They just hadn't known it, and now Murphy and Ehri were dead.

"We could have killed you already if we wanted to, Major," the voice said. "Lucky for you, we have a soft spot for the military. That was a pretty killer pep-talk you were giving, by the way. I couldn't have done it better myself. Oh, and you, Captain. Oh, my. So emotional. So sweet. I cried a little bit." A moment of silence was followed by a sharp command. "Get up."

Donovan pulled himself to his feet, staring up at the laser. Soon stood beside him. "Who are you?" he asked.

"My name is Kraeger. Welcome to my honeypot."

"What do you want with us?" Donovan looked over to where Ehri was laying on the ground. She wasn't moving.

"Honeypot, Major. Do you know what that is?"

"A trap," Donovan said.

"Exactly. One that you and your friends walked right into."

"You didn't have to kill them," Soon said.

"That's a matter of opinion," Kraeger replied. "I needed you to know I mean business. Like I said, the only reason I didn't kill you is because I have a soft spot for the resistance. Step forward, to the center of the corridor. Oh, and lose the guns."

Soon looked at Donovan, who nodded. They both dropped their guns and moved to the center of the space.

The laser remained in front of them. Donovan heard footsteps in the building, and a minute later a muscular older man in a white t-shirt and stained jeans appeared, flanked by a dozen other men and women. They were all heavily armed with weapons that looked much more modern than anything Donovan had seen before. Somehow, these jackals were better armed than the resistance.

"Major," the man said, stepping ahead of the others and putting out his hand. "Kraeger."

Donovan didn't take the hand. Kraeger smiled at that.

"I could kill you for being rude."

"You won't," Donovan said. "You want something from me."

"I want a few things from you. Seeing that I've got you by the balls, I think you're going to give them to me, too."

"What makes you say that?"

"Grab him," Kraeger said.

187

Three of the men broke off from the others, approaching Soon. One took each of his arms, holding him tight. The other produced a knife, moving to Soon's left hand.

"How many fingers will it take, Major?" Kraeger asked. "Two? Three?" He nodded, and the man grabbed Soon's hand.

"Wait," Donovan said. "What do you want from me?"

Kraeger put up his hand. His lackey let go of Soon's.

"I knew you would be reasonable. I don't want to hurt you or the Captain here. What I do want is to know how you managed to capture a Dread transport? That is beyond impressive, Major."

"I took it," Donovan said.

"From the Dread?" one of Kraeger's people said. "Not likely."

"From the Dread," Donovan said. "Look, I don't know you, and you don't know me, but we don't have to be enemies. The Dread can be fought. They can be hurt. They can even be killed."

"With their own weapons. Yes, Major, we intercepted that message."

"What do you mean, intercepted?" Donovan asked.

"We've been tapping into resistance channels for years, Major. Not always from here, we've only been here two or three, but out there. Following the tides, waiting for some kind of hope."

"Then you know there is hope. We've been in contact with the space forces. We got one of the weapons to them, to learn how to defeat their armor. We're working together to stop the Dread. You could have helped us, instead of shooting first."

Kraeger laughed. "Help you? You're lucky I haven't killed you already. Do you know what your little victory did, Major? You haven't been listening to the chatter, so let me tell you. A month ago, there were twenty-two free settlements positioned around North America. These are civilians, regular men, women, and children, not murderous assholes like me and mine. Do you know how many are left?"

Donovan knew what Murphy had told him about Washington. He felt a cold chill settle over him. "No."

"Six," Kraeger said. "Feel proud of yourself? Feel like you're winning?"

"At least I'm trying instead of luring innocent people in and killing them for what they have."

"Careful, Major," Kraeger said. "It is possible for my good will to run out. You don't know enough about what we do here to make statements like that."

"The Dread were coming before I did anything. You know it was only a matter of time."

"Maybe." Kraeger shrugged. "It doesn't matter now, does it. The resistance is falling apart, Major. You've seen it yourself. It's too little, too late, which means it's more important than ever for those of us who want to survive to do whatever it takes. Whatever. It. Takes. Do you hear me?"

Donovan glanced over at Soon. "Yes, sir," he said.

"Sir?" Kraeger replied, laughing. "I like that. We've been watching you since your rig got stuck outside. I know you have people and equipment inside that transport. I want it."

"The equipment?"

"And the people."

"What for?"

"They managed to create that monster out there. It looks like they got the Dread power source hooked up to the tractor's battery. We need people with skills like that. The ones who don't have any? We'll find a use for them, too."

"I can't turn them over to you."

"Yes, Major. You can. And why not? We don't have to be enemies. I'd be happy to bring you and the Captain on. Like I said, I need people with skills."

"How do you know you can trust us?"

"Because you have morals. You won't say yes unless you mean it. You'd rather die."

"I'd say yes to keep you from torturing my friend."

"Fair enough. I'll tell you what. I'm going to take torture off the table. Let him go."

The men dropped Soon's arms and backed off.

"There. You see? We can be civilized. The Dread are coming for us,

Major. They want to wipe humankind off the Earth. I'm not like the other assholes out there. I know what's going down. The difference is, I want to save what I can, and I have a plan to do it."

"Which is?"

"I've been here for almost three years. The Dread have been in this building four times already, searching. They haven't found us yet. Do you know why not?"

"You hide?"

"Yes, we hide. But the answer isn't that we hide. It's how we hide. It's where we hide."

"And where is that?"

"I want to show you, Major. I do. I can't unless you join up."

"You killed my people."

Kraeger sighed in frustration. "Yes, I killed two of your people. We kill people all the time. So do the Dread. That's the way the world works now. You give something to get something. In this case, your people gave up two of their own in exchange for a chance at something better. I'm not saying it will be an easy life for them, but at least they'll be alive and contributing, and who knows? If the space forces do come back, maybe we'll all survive."

"Have all the people who came here gotten this offer?" Donovan asked.

"Not even half," Kraeger said. "We take people who can help us. We kill the ones who can't. We can't risk word of our community getting out. We can't take the chance that the Dread will discover us."

"What are the Dread going to think when they find our rig right outside your front door?" Donovan said.

"They'll search the building again. They'll find nothing, again. No bodies, no blood. We've been doing this long enough to get it right."

"And if I say no, you kill me?"

"And everyone with you."

"You can't get into the transport."

"Then the Dread will kill them when they show up. How did you make it this far without them stopping you, anyway, Major?"

"I got into an Honor Fight with one of them. I won three days of peace."

"Well hell, I'm even more impressed. You should join up, Major. I know it wasn't the plan when you showed up here, but I think you'll be glad you did. A guy like you can get ahead in a hurry."

"I'm with the resistance," Donovan said. "I want to stay with the resistance. What if I give you the others and walk away?"

Kraeger laughed. "See? That's what I mean. We get to talking, and things change. But what if I had talked first, instead of killing your friends? You wouldn't be taking me seriously right now. You wouldn't be so willing to negotiate. I can't let you walk, Major. You know we're here, and I don't take risks."

"No exceptions? I promise I won't talk."

"Sorry, Major. No exceptions."

Donovan glanced over at Soon, and then back to Kraeger. He wasn't ready to give up his mission to reach Austin, but what choice did he have? The man had him by the throat and was offering him and the scavengers a chance to live. It was more than most got.

He glanced over Kraeger's shoulder again, to where Ehri had fallen. He had murdered her in cold blood to make a statement. Could he live with a man like that? Could he turn the scavengers over to a man like that? It didn't matter what his reasons were. The fact that he was even capable of the act spoke volumes.

He bit his lip, casting his eyes to the ground and putting his hand to his head like he was considering. He fought to keep himself calm and not give anything away.

Ehri was gone.

43

"ANYTHING NEW TO REPORT?" THEODORE asked, rolling smoothly onto the bridge.

Colonel Choi stood as he entered. "General on the bridge," she said.

The rest of the crew stood to face him.

"At ease," Theodore said.

The crew returned to their positions, Gabriel included. He had spent the last forty-eight hours splitting time between resting in the cockpit of his starfighter, running through the corridors of the Magellan with Wallace and Miranda in an effort to get some exercise, and manning the pilot station on the bridge. He wasn't required to be there, and Maggie could handle the flying duties while they continued on their course along the edge of the star system, but he didn't want to miss anything.

"Colonel, what's the status of the Dread fortress?" Theodore asked.

"They're remaining in position behind us, General," Choi replied. "I don't think they're near full thrust."

"Me neither. It's been a couple of days, which means if Guy was right about them being slipsick, all but the weakest will be recovering, and the rest will be dead." Theodore looked over at where Sarah Larone was sitting by herself. "Mrs. Larone, why are you on the bridge?"

She stood and faced him. "Sir, Guy and Reza asked me to be here to liaise with you."

Theodore's brow creased. "How do you mean?"

She smiled. "They're onto something sir, the two of them. They have a new theory regarding slipspace, based on the ideas we've come up with on the Dread technology. They asked me to be here when you arrived, to keep you updated on their progress."

"I see. In that case, Mrs. Larone, update me."

"Yes, sir. Can we go to the conference room? I have a sim I can show you."

"Of course. "Major St. Martin, can you please attend? You too, Colonel. Sergeant Abdullah, you have the bridge. Don't let Maggie do anything I wouldn't do."

"Yes, sir," Abdullah said, standing to take the command chair.

Gabriel retreated to the rear of the bridge to stand beside Theodore as he swung himself easily into his chair. He was still amazed at how much stronger and healthier his father looked, though he did notice a wince as Theodore settled himself in his seat. How much pain was the General masking?

They crossed the corridor into the conference room, the four of them sitting in a semi-circle around the end. Sarah withdrew her tablet and placed it on the table. It projected the Dread rifle in front of them.

"As you know, we had to bring the rifle back down to the lab after Reza began disassembling it. Once we started opening it up, we realized what a poor job our scanners did in picking up some of the components."

"Because they're organic in nature," Theodore said.

Sarah seemed surprised. "You spoke to Guy already?"

"Yesterday. It seems like you have more for me today."

"Yes, sir. As you said, we discovered that some of the internals are made of organic compounds. Some further studies I've done have proven that these compounds are basic in nature, but by our standards, they can be considered living organisms."

"You're saying the gun is alive?" Gabriel asked.

"Yes, Major. In a sense. The organisms are fueled by the same electrical supply that powers the weapon. They take the energy and excrete trace elements of waste that we believe get burned off when the weapon is fired. That's not too important in itself. We believe the Dread have found a way to use organic compounds to replace common minerals used by humans. Copper, for example. It is likely they didn't have these minerals on their homeworld, and so their technology emerged differently than ours."

"But it isn't related to how the weapon functions overall?" Choi asked.

"We don't believe so."

"How does the weapon work, Mrs. Larone?" Theodore asked.

She waved her hand over the projection, pulling it apart the way Reza had done earlier. Except now there were at least three dozen more parts.

"There are two parts to this equation, General," Sarah said. "The first is the weapon itself, able to pierce the Dread armor. The second is the armor, able to deflect pretty much anything without taking noticeable damage."

"Sounds about right."

Sarah manipulated the weapon, turning it so that the center was right in front of them. She pushed the rest of it aside, leaving what appeared to be a simple, rippled ring in the view.

"We're calling this a phase modulator. This is the visible part of it, but once we took the weapon part we were able to examine it under magnification." She reached for a piece of the image and blew it up, expanding it until a web of circuitry became visible. "Everything here is nano-scale. There are almost two billion of what we're calling 'phase points' embedded into the ring. Each phase point is connected to a small node that we think is a controller that manages the point."

"I'm an old gator, Mrs. Larone," Theodore said. "Keep the next part simple for me."

"Essentially, when the weapon is triggered and the phase modulator is engaged, it puts whatever passes through it into what Guy is calling a quantum vortex." She paused, the excitement of her next statement clear on her face. "His new theory is that it phases the plasma through another dimension of spacetime. One that humankind hasn't discovered yet."

"A third dimension?" Choi said.

"Yes," she replied, almost giggling. "One with properties we don't completely understand. What we do know is that it allows the plasma to pass through the enemies' shielding. We believe that the enemy shields may also be utilizing this dark energy as part of their function. Guy and Reza are exploring that concept right now."

"How is that possible?" Gabriel said. "I mean, slipspace is composed of ripples in space and time. This other dimension is composed of what?"

"Matter and energy. Like realspace, but different. Reza thinks this new dimension may be the source of dark matter. In fact, he's taken to calling it darkspace. His idea is that it leaks through into our space because darkspace is so dense that it can't contain it."

"The majority of the universe is made up of dark matter," Choi said.

"Yes, Colonel. If he's right, we may have found a clue to the origin of our universe itself."

"For all we know, the Dread already understand the origin of the universe," Gabriel said.

"It is possible," Sarah agreed.

"You got all that from looking at the gun under a microscope?" Theodore asked.

"No, sir. To be honest, it's all theoretical, based on one observable calculation. Reza isolated one of the phase points and was able to trigger it. It broke our sensors, but not before he was able to take measurements."

"What do you mean, broke?"

"They were too close to it, I guess. Without being inside the weapon's shielding, it caused a small electromagnetic pulse that killed the equipment."

Theodore smiled. "You're saying you could have shorted out the entire ship and killed every last one of us?"

Sarah's face turned red. "Uh. I suppose I am, sir."

"Ha! Wouldn't that have been a real kick in the pants?"

"I don't understand," Gabriel said. "If this isn't related to slipspace, why are the Dread ships vulnerable in slipspace dead zones?"

"It is related to slipspace," Sarah said. "Directly related. Think of it like a ligament holding muscle to bone. Darkspace is a thin layer that sits between realspace and slipspace. In fact, it's quite possible that we pass through it every time we slip, it's just that it's so narrow that our equipment can't detect it. In fact, we think the slipspace dead zones aren't caused by a lack of waves, but a detachment between darkspace and slipspace within them."

Gabriel waved his hands in the air. "You're saying it's the stuff that holds all of this together?"

"It may be, Major. We also now think the reason that slipspace is black instead of white is because the density of darkspace is keeping the light in realspace from penetrating through."

Theodore whistled. "Mrs. Larone, I have to say that you and your husband and Reza have done fantastic work here. Simply fantastic. I'm happy to hear we may be breaking new ground on our understanding of the universe, and I hate to spoil the fun, but what does it mean for us today? We've still got a Dread fortress on our tail, and they ain't going to stay back there forever."

44

"AH, GENERAL," GUY SAID, LOOKING up as Theodore entered the makeshift lab with Gabriel, Sarah, and Colonel Choi. He was hunched over his tablet, his hair messy and his eyes red from lack of sleep. "I assume you spoke to Sarah." He stumbled to his feet.

"That's why we're here, Mr. Larone," Theodore said. "She gave me the rundown on this so-called darkspace. Where is Mr. Mokri?"

"He went to retrieve some of the phase paint from inventory," Guy said. "We were about to test my theory."

"Which one?" Theodore asked. "You seem to have come up with a whole barrel of them."

"It's amazing what you can do with the right motivation, and with a little push from alien technology. I haven't been this excited about anything since I met Sarah." He looked at her. "You're still more exciting, darling."

She blushed and smiled in response, acting demure. Gabriel didn't know what the current situation was between the three scientists, and he didn't care. At least they were working together on the problem.

Reza approached behind them, holding a container of the paint.

"Oh. Uh. General." He put the paint on the floor and saluted. "Sir.

M.R. Forbes

You're just in time to see if we're onto something."

"I hope for all our sakes you are, Mr. Mokri," Theodore replied.

"Yes, sir." He picked up the paint and carried it across the lab.

They had taken root in a large space deep inside the Magellan. They had moved a ton of equipment from its original place on the ship into a corner of it, along with a simple workbench and stools, tablets and projectors. It was an organized chaos of tools and devices that Gabriel didn't recognize or understand the purpose for.

Reza walked to the far end of the space, a hundred meters distant from them. He lifted the paint container and began spraying it against the inner bulkhead. It dried nearly instantly, leaving a dark, uneven film across the area.

He came back to them. A battery was resting in a cart nearby, attached to his tablet and connected to the Dread rifle, which was protruding a thick wire. He grabbed it and began pushing it toward the painted wall.

"Mr. Mokri," Theodore said. "Would you mind telling me what you're doing? We don't have much of that paint as it is, and last I heard we needed it to repair the nacelle."

"We would have to be able to get someone outside to repair the nacelle, sir," Reza said. "Which we can't do as long as they're vulnerable to attack."

"Gabriel can keep the Dread away from the repair team."

"Maybe. Maybe not. You may not have to take that risk if our theory holds up."

"My theory," Guy said.

"Whatever," Reza replied. He kept walking back to the paint, kneeling beside it and rigging the wire against the surface of it. "The paint is conductive," he shouted back, his voice echoing in the chamber. "In simple terms, the quantum phase generators pass energy into it in a defined frequency, which causes the nanoparticles within the material to accelerate and spin. The spin creates a bond between the material here and sibling particles in slipspace, which drags the Magellan out of this spacetime and into that one. These particles travel through slipspace in various densities, always moving and spinning. It is these densities that

198

make up the waves. When we create a strong enough bond, we join the wave, and move from our space into that one."

"I'm a soldier, not a scientist. I'll take your word for it, son," Theodore said.

"Uh. Right. Anyway, the theory-"

"My theory," Guy said again, interrupting. "Is that we can use the phase modulator on the Dread rifle to alter the spin of the particles, so that instead of pushing us toward slipspace, we pull slipspace to us."

"And how is that going to help?"

"My dearest Sarah explained the concept of Laronespace to you?"

"Darkspace," Reza said.

Guy looked back at him.

"Darkspace," Theodore said, confirming Reza's naming. "Yes, she did. Go on."

"To pull slipspace to us, we have to lift Laronespace with it. How do I explain simply?" He paused, considering. "You were born on Earth before the invasion, so you'll understand this simile. It is like swimming instead of sinking. We want to skim the surface, to bring the Magellan into phase with Laronespace instead of slipspace. But, as you know, it's a lot easier to sink than swim."

"Not if you just relax and let yourself float," Theodore said.

Guy paused. "Not exactly like swimming, then."

"You said darkspace is dense," Gabriel said. "Wouldn't that make it easier to sit on top of it, not harder?"

Guy's face tightened. "I'm trying to put things in layman's terms so that you all understand. Density is a relative analogous synonym, in this case. I can show you the calculation that describes the properties we have theorized, but that will be even less meaningful to you."

Gabriel opened his mouth to reply. Theodore interrupted him. "I get the point, Mr. Larone. What exactly are you preparing to do?"

"We've been skirting the edge of the dead zone for the last two days. We're going to cross a short break in it in about a minute. Ten seconds at most, but that's all the time we need."

"Mmm. What exactly are you going to do?" Theodore asked again.

"You might want to roll back, General," Sarah said, putting her hand on his shoulder. "We aren't completely sure about the results."

"Are you telling me you're putting my ship at risk again?" Theodore barked.

"No risk, no reward, General," Guy said. "My calculations are good. Sarah checked them. So did Reza. Besides, I don't think it will damage the ship if it doesn't work."

"Let's hope not."

Guy watched his tablet as the seconds passed. Gabriel, Theodore, and Colonel Choi stood behind them, waiting to see what they were going to do. Gabriel glanced down at his father at the same time Theodore looked up at him. His face hopeful and doubting. This was the culmination of the effort Major Peters and his team had made to get the weapon to them in the first place. It was what Soon had sacrificed himself for. What so many had sacrificed themselves for.

Gabriel felt his heartbeat increasing, his body tensing as the seconds ticked away. He put his hand on his father's shoulder, squeezing it lightly. His other hand landed on his mother's crucifix. Would this work? Would they finally have a way to fight back against the Dread?

A small chime sounded from Guy's tablet. He bent over, retrieving a standard issue assault rifle from beneath the workbench. He held it out to Gabriel. "Major, if you would shoot the wall." Then he turned to Reza and shouted, "Turn it on."

Reza responded by tapping something on his own tablet. There was no change in sound, no difference in the before or after, but the scientist gave them the thumbs-up and then backed away from the area.

Gabriel approached Guy, taking the rifle from him. He pointed it at the bulkhead. He had no idea what was supposed to happen.

He pulled the trigger.

The noise of it echoed across the room. At the far end of the wall, an inky blackness appeared around wherever the bullets struck, flashing for the briefest of instants before vanishing again.

Reza stood at the end of the space near the wall, his fists up in triumph as he whooped and cheered. "Yes. Yes. It works. I don't believe it. It works."

45

HE TURNED TO FACE THEM, a huge smile on his face. A moment later, smoke began pouring from the battery.

His smile vanished, and he ran to the cart, grabbing the Dread rifle and running back toward them. "Watch out," he shouted. He threw himself to the ground as a small flame erupted from the battery and then went out, leaving the entire chamber in silence.

Reza pulled himself to his knees, looking back at the smoldering, half-melted battery, and then at them. "I think we were a little off on the power requirements," hc said. "We can work on that."

"Did you see it, General?" Guy said, smiling.

Gabriel thought it might be the first time he had ever seen the man smile.

"I saw something," Theodore said. "Now tell me what it was."

"Darkspace," Guy said, forgetting to use his name for it in his excitement. "We modulated the phase of the paint at the point of impact to bring it into this spacetime, using it as a shield against the Major's projectiles. Because the impact occurs, it still exerts a force on the surface, but the interceding layer of darkspace absorbs most of the energy, limiting its penetrating effects."

"In other words?"

"In other words, we just replicated the Dread's shields."

Theodore smiled. "That's a fine step forward, Mr. Larone. I assume that since you now know how the shields work, you can find a way to defeat them?"

Guy's smile vanished. It was as if Theodore had punched him in the gut.

"What is it?" Theodore asked.

"General, the Dread plasma rifle has two billion phase modulators in an area the size of your first. That's billion, with a 'b.' We don't have anything that can come close to replicating that kind of nano scale construction, and even if we did, it might take months to design a template."

"The other problem is power," Reza said, joining them. He handed the Dread rifle to Gabriel. "That was the largest battery we had in inventory, and it was enough to power the system across a two-meter square section of the wall for about five seconds. Based on that, the power supply in the Dread weapon contains fifty to sixty times more energy. Our battery might be able to fire ten to twenty rounds, and that was the only one we had."

Theodore stared at them. Gabriel could tell his mind was working, taking in the cold facts and trying to adjust strategy around them.

"You said if it worked we might be able to get the nacelle repaired without risking our people."

"Yes, sir. We could theoretically create a shield that would cover the team as they worked on the repairs. If we hook into the Magellan's power supply, it should be enough to protect them from attack."

"Except the Dread can shoot right through their own shields," Gabriel said. "Remember? How would that help?"

"On its own, it wouldn't," Guy said.

"We have another theory," Reza said. "But it's a little harder to test out."

"Which is?" Theodore asked.

"Phase modulation," Guy said. "We think we can alter the phase such that it cancels out the ability of the Dread's weapons to bypass it. Or at a minimum reduces the impact."

"You mean to create a shield against their weapons?" Theodore said.

"Yes, sir. If we had two of the Dread rifles, we could use one to power the shields, and another to test the theory, but-"

"But you don't have two weapons," Theodore said. "And I don't think we'll be getting another anytime soon. There's no way to prove your theory without them?"

"The math seems to be holding up," Reza said. "But without a real test, there's no way to be completely confident."

"Sir," Colonel Choi said. "We need to repair the nacelle if we're going to get out of the system and back home. If we put our fighters out there at the same time, we can minimize the risk."

"Understood, Colonel," Theodore said. He shifted his attention to the wall at the end of the space, staring at it in silence.

To Gabriel, it seemed like the decision was cut and dry. Like the Colonel had said, they had to fix the nacelle, and this was a chance for them to do it. The Dread would undoubtedly target the nacelle, knowing that destroying it would keep the Magellan stranded here forever. They wouldn't even need to do any further damage at that point. They could just leave them here to drift and starve to death.

Wouldn't it be a shock when their attack proved ineffective?

"No," Theodore said a moment later. "I'm not going to do that."

"Sir?" Gabriel said, surprised by the response. "What do you mean?"

"Am I speaking another language, because that sure sounded like English to me? I said I'm not going to do it. Maybe it will work, maybe it won't. It don't matter because either way, it's short-sighted, plain and simple."

"Short-sighted?" Sarah asked.

"Yes, Mrs. Larone. Short-sighted. As in, it ain't going to solve our bigger problem."

"Which is what?" Gabriel asked.

"Power, son. Energy. According to our resident geniuses, we need a pool of it the size of a bayou to feed the tech the Dread are using. What we've got on board is more like a single drop on the head of a pin."

"We can work on the power problem, General," Reza said. "I'm sure we can reduce the overall requirements."

"Can you?" Theodore asked. "The Dread haven't been able to, and I bet they've had a long time to do it."

"We have different materials to work with. There may be limitations to their organic compounds that we can avoid with minerals."

"How soon?"

None of the scientists replied.

"My point exactly."

"Do you have another idea, General?" Choi asked.

"As a matter of fact, I think I do."

46

THE REPORT OF A SINGLE round echoed in the hallway. A soft grunt, and then a rifle fell from the open space in the ductwork, clattering on the floor.

"What the?" Kraeger started to say.

Donovan threw himself forward at the man, grabbing him around the waist and pushing him to the ground. There was no time for him to worry about what was going to happen next, or if Soon had caught on quickly enough to survive. They had one chance to try to get out of this, and he had to take it.

A second report sounded. Then a third and a fourth. Donovan felt blood land on him as he fell to the ground on top of a surprised Kraeger, whose face curled into a snarl as he punched Donovan in the ribs. He couldn't see the Dread cloth beneath the other clothes. He didn't know the punches barely had an effect.

"You son of a bitch," Kraeger cursed, still hitting him. Donovan punched back, hitting him in the jaw and then the eye. The older man shouted, using all of his force to turn himself over and push Donovan off.

Donovan rolled away to his feet. One of Kraeger's men was there, raising his rifle to shoot him point blank. Then the butt of a second rifle cracked against the man's head, dropping him and leaving Soon standing behind him.

"Watch out," Donovan said. Another jackal was coming at Soon with a knife. He went down as a fifth shot sounded, hitting him square on the side of the head.

Donovan started to turn back to Kraeger, suddenly pulled off balance as the man tackled him from behind. They sprawled on the floor, but Donovan managed to get his balance and roll his assailant off again. They both got to their feet facing one another.

A gun appeared against Kraeger's head.

"Don't move," Ehri said, holding the pistol against his temple.

Donovan looked at her. Her arm had been bleeding, leaving a stain around the wound. There was another stain on her leg.

"Tell your people to back off," Donovan said, noticing the four jackals still standing were regrouping.

Kraeger looked defiant. Ehri pushed the gun harder against his head.

"Do it," she said.

"Okay. Okay. Back off," he said. He glared at Donovan. "I'm sure we can work something out."

"Are you okay?" Donovan asked Ehri.

"Yes. The gori'shah reduced the impact sufficiently. The wounds are healing. I didn't think it was wise to give myself away."

"Good call."

"Gori'shah?" Kraeger said. "You sound like one of them. You should have been dead."

"You should have checked the bodies instead of assuming," Donovan said. "She sounds like one of them because she is one of them. The clones are turning on their masters. We have their weapons. We're killing their pur'dahm, and stealing their transports. Don't you get it? Whatever you think you're trying to do, you're wrong. The tide is turning. We have a chance to fight back. To really fight back. I don't like what is happening to the civilian settlements, and I don't feel like a hero. But I do think we can win."

Kraeger laughed at that. "You're crazier than I am if you think you can win. One Dread warrior. One transport. Big deal. They have hundreds of both."

"Everything starts with one," Ehri said. "One escaped starship. One unsecured rifle. One clone who wants to choose for themselves."

"Whatever. It looks like you've got me by the balls now, Major. You're right. I screwed up. Now I've got to face the consequences. If I were you, I would kill me. I would kill every last one of us. We've done things, Major. Terrible things. Torture. Murder. I even ate human flesh once. I don't regret it, either. I survived the way I had to. We all survive the way we have to."

Donovan looked at Kraeger. As much as he wanted to despise him, he found that he couldn't. He could have just as easily ended up like him if his situation had been different. All of humanity was doing what it could to survive. It didn't mean fighting with one another was the right thing, but what if there was no other choice? What if it meant living or dying? At least Kraeger was trying to put something together, to build some kind of community, even if he didn't understand how it worked yet. The man wasn't killing for sport.

At least, Donovan didn't think he was.

"Where did you get these weapons?" he asked, taking the rifle Soon was carrying and holding it up to Kraeger. "These are newer than anything I've seen."

"This is the honeypot, Major," Kraeger replied. "Not home base."

"Where's home base?"

"Kraeger," one of his followers said. "Don't."

Kraeger looked at him. "It's over, Julio. Can't you see that? We lost. Besides, the Major here isn't going to hurt anybody. Are you?"

"Not unless they try to hurt us," Donovan replied.

"Yeah, but-"

"Am I in charge?" Kraeger shouted.

Julio backed down without another word.

"I'll take you there. Maybe once you've seen it, you'll change your mind about joining us."

"Are you planning to become part of the rebellion?" Donovan asked.

"Not if I can help it."
Donovan smiled. "What if you can't?"

47

DONOVAN TRAILED BEHIND KRAEGER, WHILE Soon and Ehri covered the rest of his remaining followers, keeping them at gunpoint while they traversed the building. Kraeger hadn't stopped talking the entire time, keeping up a litany of chatter about how he wound up first in Mexico, and then at the rest stop between San Luis and Monterrey.

"I almost died five, six times on the way down," he was saying as they reached the small security room in the back corner of the structure. "Not Dread, mind you. Jackals. It isn't just the innocents they go after, you know. Anybody who looks weak is fair game, and I was pretty weak at the time. Not by choice. Just a series of bad decisions that didn't pan out in my favor." He laughed. "All because of a girl, believe it or not."

Donovan didn't answer. He kept hoping that not engaging would get the man to quiet down. It didn't seem to be working.

"So, I came into this place, and there was just blood and guts and death everywhere. At first, I thought it was more jackals, and I was ready to get the hell out, but then I came across the dead clone. The Dread had cleaned this place out maybe a day or two before I got here. Just wiped everyone out. They had used small arms, though, not heavy slugs like their mechs fire. They wanted this place intact. They wanted to use it to bring people in. Their honeypot."

They filed into the space. There was power being fed to the equipment, and screens displayed the inside of the building from almost every angle. There were even cameras on the outside of the space, and Donovan could see the Monster clearly through one of them.

"Standard security," Kraeger said. "Low cost, easy to maintain. Nothing fancy like they had up in the States. It was out of order when I got here. Like I was saying, the Dread were using this place to bait humans. It got me thinking about the idea as I explored. What if I could do the same? What if I could start rebuilding my resources, start a new community, do my part to save humankind? It was all wishful thinking at the time. I knew if enough people showed up here the Dread would come back and wipe them out again. I'm sure you've heard of it happening before?"

"Too often," Donovan said.

"Yeah. So I was just daydreaming about it. I didn't think it would ever work. Then I came in here, and I learned the most important lesson of my life."

Kraeger paused and looked at Donovan, waiting for him to ask.

"Which was?"

He smiled and reached under the security desk, feeling the bottom. He did something, and a piece of the floor slid aside, revealing a ladder the descended into darkness.

"Always be on the lookout for narcotics trafficking tunnels," he said.

"Narcotics?" Donovan said. "As in, illegal drugs?"

"Yup. I came in here and looked around a little bit. I found a frayed wire leading into the floor, and that made me curious. So I ended up on my hands and knees below the desk until a cat or something made noise and I tried to jump up." He laughed. "I hit my head on the switch to activate the hidden door. It was a total accident, can you believe that? Anyway, I followed the rabbit hole. The tunnel to the drop point is about a kilometer long. That was where I found a stash of drugs and guns. There's another tunnel that goes five kilometers out that way, toward the mountains. That's where the bunker is."

He moved to the ladder, turning around to climb down.

"From what I've been able to learn, it used to belong to a guy named 'El Diablo.' The Devil. He was a pretty high and mighty drug kingpin until the day the Dread attacked. The bunker was his hiding place away from all the rivals and government agencies that wanted to take him down. It was like his own private estate, tucked away from prying eyes and offering a level of comfort and security that should have carried him through a pretty peaceful life hiding from the aliens."

"Should have?"

"When I found the place, the generator was running, and the power was on, but nobody was home. It seemed that El Diablo and his entourage never made it to the bunker to hide. They probably got blasted on the way here."

Kraeger started climbing down the ladder. Donovan followed after, careful to keep him in view. They descended twenty meters until the walls around them opened up into a fairly large tunnel.

"I always guessed that he owned the building through some shell corporation or something and that the whole thing was a front for his real operations. It's easy to access from the highway, but also pretty nondescript and utilitarian. Who would ever have thought it was a facade?"

"How many people are down here?" Donovan asked, staring past Kraeger and into the long corridor. He couldn't believe a place like this had been so close to the resistance base the entire time, and he had never known about it. Then again, wasn't that the point?

"Four hundred," Kraeger replied.

"How do you keep that many people fed down here? There's nothing to forage nearby." He remembered that Kraeger had mentioned eating human flesh, and he began to feel sick.

"That was a part of a darker past," Kraeger said, noticing his discomfort. "The bunker is self-sufficient, Major. Indoor farms provide more than enough veggies to keep everyone healthy without resorting to cannibalism. It's funny when you think about it. El Diablo must have spent billions to get it assembled, and then he got offed before he ever got to use it. But now we have a growing community here. A thriving community.

It's like a fairy-tale."

"Except for the part where you kill people," Donovan said.

"I won't lie and tell you I never enjoy killing. But the difference between me and some random asshole is that I have a reason for it. You come into my house looking for food or shelter; I'm happy to oblige if you can be of service to me. If you have skills. If you've been out there too long, if you're rabid, or if you're too damn weak and useless, then I don't have a use for you and the rest of the world doesn't either. You're Dread fodder regardless, so is it a big deal if I keep you from grabbing that last candy bar that might keep someone strong alive for another day? If that little bit of sustenance can get them to me?"

Kraeger stopped walking, turning and facing Donovan. He raised his gun in response, uncertain about the man's intentions.

"Answer that for me, Major. Should I let weak people live and risk that the strong people will die? Do you think there's a place for that kind of charity in the world today?"

Donovan would have known the answer to that a month ago. The world they lived in had always been dangerous, but there had been room for everyone in the security of the silo. But now the resistance base was gone. Matteo was gone. His mother and Diaz were gone. Thousands of people were dying every day at the hands of the Dread. Maybe there was some truth to Kraeger's words, even if it was a truth he didn't want to see.

"I can tell you're not as sure as you were an hour ago," Kraeger said. "I call that progress. I can show you more, Major, but I know you have somewhere else you want to be. So what do you want to do with me? With us? I can't stop you from taking your people and leaving, or from killing me and claiming this place for yourself. So the question is: now what?"

48

"HOW LONG?" DONOVAN ASKED.

KRAEGER turned his wrist, checking a heavy, antique gold watch he had recovered from his quarters in the bunker the residents affectionately referred to as Hell.

"The situation's a little different this time, Major," Kraeger said. "Usually, they come to check their trap, find nothing, and head out. You left their transport sitting out there on the back of a big-rig. Not to mention, they appear to be more than a little worried about you."

They were inside what Kraeger had called the Ready Room, a secondary, heavily fortified space inside Hell that contained remote links to the cameras positioned throughout the external complex. Through them, Donovan could see the new Dread troop transport that had arrived. Clone soldiers were crawling all over the interior of the former shopping area, examining every nook and cranny for evidence that Donovan, Ehri, and the rest of the scavengers were hiding inside.

According to Kraeger, that was the typical Dread deployment. In this case, their forces had been bolstered by a pair of mechs and the presence of a squad of fully armored pur'dahm. Ehri had identified them as more Hunters.

"But we're safe down here, right?" Donovan said.

"So far, so good," Kraeger replied. "But we left your people out by the tunnel armed to the teeth for a reason."

Donovan checked the camera feed that showed the scene by the heavy steel door that could seal the bunker off from the tunnel. Soon was leading a group composed of both scavengers and jackals there, the men and women who had agreed to be part of their overall defenses. They had ten of the enemy plasma rifles in all, enough to put up a pretty good fight if the Dread found the tunnel and entered it.

It had taken Donovan nearly the entire remainder of the hour he had had given them to free the Monster to come to the decision to work with Kraeger. Then it took almost another hour to forge an agreement with him to allow any scavengers who wanted to stay to stay, and to swear to let them become part of the community regardless of their skills. Donovan hadn't known exactly what he was bargaining for until he returned to the scavengers, explained Murphy's death, and led them down into the tunnels and to the bunker.

Hell wasn't a bad place overall, but it did come with a well-defined hierarchy of status based on usefulness. Women were valued for one of two things. Either you had a trade the community could use, or you had a body the community could use. It was a hard idea to accept, but the cold truth was that humankind needed more humans, and there was only one way to get them. At the same time, the pregnant women Donovan had seen were treated like royalty, given every comfort they could want as well as the best pick of the available food.

The process was similar for the men, though they were typically culled based on age, physical health, and personality along with skill set. And when Kraeger said culled, he meant culled. The majority of the travelers they killed were men who didn't fit into the community; the decision made after an ambush and a quick interview. While Donovan had made Kraeger promise to spare the scavengers, he had a feeling that treaty was only going to be good for as long as Donovan was in the bunker. Kraeger claimed to be an honorable man, but he was also a pragmatist, and those two things didn't always mesh.

"They're in the control room," Donovan said, watching one of the pur'dahm Hunters move in. The armored bek'hai stared at the equipment, tapping on the panel to see if it was functional before turning and running his eyes across the room. He walked out a moment later.

"A good sign," Kraeger said.

"Where do you think they're going to think we are when they can't find us?" Donovan asked.

"Scattered into the brush, most like," Kraeger said. "That's what usually happens. They'll try to track you down, find a few stragglers out there, and then kill them and call it a day."

"You've seen it happen?"

"Plenty of times. I spent twenty years out there before I came here."

"Before or after the woman was involved?"

He laughed. "Both. I had a couple of years in the middle that were damn good. A few on either end that made me question my sanity." His face suddenly turned dark, and he cast his eyes to the floor. "You have to learn to accept who you become, or you can't ever come back."

"I've only ever been one thing, and I plan to keep it that way. A soldier."

"I wish you the best of luck with that, Major."

They sat silently for a minute, watching the Dread. It was obvious when they finished the sweep because they retreated as one back to the transports. The Hunters loaded themselves into the one Donovan had taken, and it lifted off with the others, heading out toward the brush. The two mechs abandoned the facility as well, moving west.

"Looks like they gave up."

"They never see us coming or going because we hardly ever go outside. They have no reason to think there's anything hidden in here. Wasn't that the reason El Diablo built the bunker here to begin with?" Kraeger was silent for a moment before he looked at Donovan. "You know, Major, I've been thinking about what you said earlier. About bringing the fight to the enemy. Were you serious about that?"

"We're on our way to join the resistance in Austin," Donovan said. "General Rodriguez told me there's a force massing there, one that's still hidden from the Dread."

"You mean you hope it's still hidden from the Dread."

"There's no way to know for sure until we get there. Unless you've heard otherwise?"

Kraeger had shown him the equipment they used to sniff packets out of the hard-wired network the resistance was utilizing to communicate with one another. He had been eavesdropping on the rebels for some time, keeping up with their messages back and forth.

"Not so far, but things can change in a hurry, and they don't always get a message out. With all the activity out here, the odds are that the enemy is hitting Austin hard, or at least has the potential to. So I was thinking about what you and the clone said. There always has to be a first, right?"

"Right. You have something in mind?"

"I think we should hit them back."

"We? You said you didn't want to be part of the resistance."

"I don't, especially. But I also told you I have a soft spot for the military. The thing is, there's a Dread base not too far from here. It's not a fortress or anything. It's a smaller outpost. I think the mechs are headed back there. Anyway, with the contingent out searching for you, I have a feeling the defenses are going to be relatively light. A quick, coordinated strike could net you a solid victory against the enemy, a victory that we can broadcast out to the rest of the world. It's just the kind of thing you need if you want humans to stop being so helpless, stop killing each other, and maybe get them to seek out the rebellion."

"You almost sound like you're feeling a little more hopeful already," Donovan said.

Kraeger smiled. "I see that they're worried about you. I like that. Besides, you seem hell-bent on going forward no matter what I do. You may not be a hero, but you're a stubborn son of a bitch, and I admire that just as much. Even if you are just a kid."

"Thanks, I think."

"Yeah, so this base I'm talking about is about ten klicks west of here. They'll probably have left a couple dozen clones behind, and those mechs, but that's about it. I found some explosives in the armory here when I moved in. It won't do shit to the outside of their structures, but maybe we can wreak some havoc on the inside."

Donovan considered it. The whole reason to head to Austin was to join the resistance there and to tell them how they could get ready to fight back. There was a certain appeal to being able to show them, and to lead by example.

"If we attack their base they're going to come back at us even harder than before," he said. "They might not give up on this place so easily."

"Yeah. That's the rub, Major. If you do this, you and whoever decides to come with you can't come back here. You hit the base, and you vanish into the night. Head to Austin, go back to Mexico City, whatever you want, just not this place."

They shared another moment of silence. Donovan wanted to pretend he had a choice when he already knew he didn't.

"I guess you're going to get rid of me a lot sooner than you were expecting," he said.

Kraeger laughed. "I guess you're going to be stuck with me a little longer than you were expecting, Major. I'm getting old, and while I'm proud of what I've done here, I know that nothing stays the same. I can try to hold onto it, or I can accept it. You're exactly the sign I didn't know I was looking for.

"In other words, I'm coming with you."

49

"HOW'S THE PATIENT?" DONOVAN ASKED, entering the bunker's medical facilities.

He paused to take them in as he did, impressed with the space. The equipment was the latest humankind had produced before the invasion, and the room was spotless and sterile. El Diablo had spared no expense on the place, prepared for the worst in the event of an emergency. For criminals, emergencies probably weren't that out of the ordinary.

"Her recovery is not human," Doc Iwu said, turning to face Donovan as he entered. She looked more relaxed and at peace now that she was back in a room filled with stainless steel and gauze.

Ehri was sitting on the edge of the exam table, her gori'shah in a pile behind her. She was dressed in her underwear and a tank top, with one bandage wrapped around her shoulder and another around her leg. She smiled when she saw Donovan.

"Another genetic enhancement?" Donovan asked.

"Partially," she replied. "The gori'shah also assists in healing underlying wounds. If the bullet had not gone through, the symbiotes would have worked to remove it. They also leave their saliva on the damage itself, which promotes healing. I tried to convince Nailah to leave it alone and let them do their work, but she wouldn't have it."

"I'm not about to trust something I can't see," Iwu replied. "Especially not microscopic worms."

"They aren't worms," Ehri said. "They're larvae."

"For what?" Donovan asked. "You've never answered that."

"I don't know what they become," she replied. "The gori'shah are replaced on a regular basis, cycled through by the ones we call the lek'hai. The Keepers. It is said that the gori'shah are the backbone of our technology, much of which is, or was at some point, organic."

"So it's like raising cattle for meat?"

"Not exactly, but an adequate simile. I trust that since you are here the bek'hai have gone?"

"Yeah. They didn't find anything, and they headed off to the east to search the wilderness. Kraeger is convinced they'll find a few random humans out there and slaughter them before giving up."

"I don't think they're going to give up that easily. Not on finding us."

"Me neither, but Kraeger put me onto something. He said the Dread have a base not too far from here. An outpost. He thinks the mechs came from there. He suggested that we attack it."

"What?" Iwu said. "Donovan, I don't think that's a good idea."

"Why not?"

"You're going to bring the entire Dread army down on you if you go after them like that. You've been lucky so far, but that's asking for a little too much trouble."

"I've been thinking about that. I don't disagree with you, but the truth is that we need to do something. We don't know Austin will still be viable by the time we reach it, and based on what we know there's a good chance it won't be. If that turns out to be the case, we'll have wasted an opportunity to make a statement that we can fight back, really fight back, against the Dread. To rally the resistance everywhere by hitting them directly and doing some real damage. We've got a tiny bit of momentum here, and I'm worried about losing it by playing it too safe."

"Play it too reckless, and you'll lose everything for everyone."

"You mean this place?"

She nodded. "There are sixty pregnant women here. Forty-six children. I don't want them to die the way they did back at the silo."

"Neither do I. When we go, we won't be coming back." He looked at Ehri. "What do you think?"

"This isn't my decision to make, Major. It is yours."

"I'm asking for your opinion."

"I pledged my loyalty to you. I'll follow wherever you go, and fight as hard as any other human. Kraeger is an interesting man, an odd mix of selfishness and patriotism. He's based his community on keeping only the strong, and yet he weakens its ability to survive and adapt by anchoring it with the young. I think his motives are also mixed. He knows the bek'hai want you, or me through you, and so he wants you gone from here. At the same time, he wants you to succeed."

"He's decided he wants to come with us."

"Interesting. He understands what he has created here. For as much as he has said we can't defeat the bek'hai, deeper down I think he knows the only chance this community has is for us to fight, and to win."

"And you think we should fight?"

"Yes."

"Me, too. After everything that's happened, I wasn't sure if I should trust my instincts."

"They've carried us this far, Major."

"And gotten a lot of people I cared about killed."

"No. They have always been dying. Now they are dying for something."

Donovan couldn't argue with that. It was the one thought that helped ease the guilt. It slipped away from him sometimes, but Ehri was always there to bring him back in line. He caught her eyes with his own, holding them for a minute. He couldn't imagine where he would be if Kraeger had been successful in his efforts to kill her. He wasn't sure he could take one more loss like that.

"When are you leaving?" Iwu asked. "The wounds are in good shape, but it would be better for her to rest a day or two."

"Within the hour," Donovan said, breaking eye contact with Ehri. "I assume you're staying here?"

"There aren't many doctors left in this world," she replied. "The mortality rate for the women here is over fifty percent. They have the right tools, but they didn't have anyone with a medical background to teach them. I think I can bring that down to near zero, and train some of the people we saved. I can give them a skill that will make them valuable, not only here and now, but after you get the Dread off the planet once and for all. Besides, I'm an old woman, Donovan. We both know I've been slowing you down. I do appreciate you looking out for me."

"I'm glad you made it out," Donovan said. "The world does need people like you. Not just your medical skills, but your compassion and spirit."

Doc Iwu surprised him, approaching and wrapping her arms around him. He returned the embrace once he got over his shock. He had never known her to be affectionate. Her care was business-like and rational, not emotional. At least not until now.

"Take care of yourself, Major," she said. "I know you'll make the General proud."

"Yes, ma'am," Donovan said. He looked at Ehri again. "We'll be meeting near the entrance in forty minutes."

"I'll be there."

Donovan turned to leave. He paused there, a sudden thought creeping into his head. Kraeger had given him the idea that they should go in and do as much damage as they could, but maybe that wasn't the only option.

"Ehri, how much can you teach Soon and me about piloting a bek'hai mech in thirty minutes or less?"

50

TEA'VA PEERED AROUND THE CORNER, taking extra care that the corridor was clear before darting across it to the other side. He pressed the panel to his right, and a small hatch opened beside him. He crossed into it, leaning back against the wall as the hatch slid closed and left him in near total darkness.

Two shifts. That was how long it had taken for him to navigate from the bowels of the Ishur up three decks. It was impossibly slow, every step made challenging by the arrival of another batch of clones, and by Gr'el's sudden domination of the ship. His Si'dahm had managed to tear him from power with almost zero resistance, and in a way that made the failure look like Tea'va's alone. Did the Domo'dahm know what Gr'el had done? Did he approve?

It didn't matter. Gr'el's worst mistake was that he had failed in his initial assassination attempt, and he had failed to capture Tea'va since. Tea'va was certain it was because the pur'dahm had underestimated him and his deep knowledge of the fortress. The ships were so large that few beyond the clones made to care for them knew every service tunnel and access point, every ingress and egress.

But he knew. He knew because he had never trusted. Because he had never believed that any would seek to aid him in his mission of conquest. Why would they, when they all sought the same station? If he were going to rise to power, he needed to not only be stronger, not only be smarter, but also be more tolerant to change and more able to adjust. Knowledge was power.

It had allowed him to hide from Gr'el's patrols as they began to hunt him. It had allowed him to drop down on them unaware, to destroy an entire squad of clones and vanish back into the dark. It had permitted him to put fear into the pur'dahm traitor, to show him that he would not be an easy kill and that if he wanted to maintain control of the Ishur he would need to earn it.

Of course, the odds were still against him. Every drumhr who may have been loyal to him had been retired and almost every clone that had lived before they arrived in Pol'tik had been destroyed.

Almost every clone.

He had seen Zoelle earlier, walking the corridors from her lab with her two assistants, who were also Children of the Un'hai. She had passed one of Gr'el's patrols unharmed, an act that proved to him beyond all doubt that she had betrayed him, earning his trust and then turning on him at her convenience. She had helped Gr'el make his new clones in secret, knowing what the Si'dahm planned. He didn't know how they had managed to make this alliance ahead of time before he had even been assigned to the Ishur in the first place.

He was about to find out.

The back routes of the fortress were narrow and normally occupied by drek'er, Cleaners, small-statured clones who were in charge of maintaining the inner workings of the ship. They would skitter about from one location to another in a constant cycle, testing power outputs, optimizing flow, and ensuring that the millions of components remained in working order. The fortresses didn't require much maintenance, but constant monitoring was what kept them that way.

The Cleaners were in another part of the ship, and so their passages were barren. Tea'va was able to move through them unhindered, without worry of being captured. While he was sure Gr'el knew the corridors existed, he also doubted the pur'dahm had any idea where they were or how to reach them. His rival also probably couldn't conceive of traveling like this. It was an affront to their ideas of honor. One that had allowed humankind to survive far too long.

It was a weakness he was not afraid to exploit.

The passage took him behind the private cells assigned to each member of the crew. This deck was for the scientists, Zoelle and her lor'hai. He had seen her return here earlier. He knew she would be inside, likely asleep.

From that passage, there was a small crawlspace that went up and over the top of the cells, an area purposely left open for ventilation. Tea'va pulled himself up into the narrow space, for a moment frightened that he would get stuck there as the floor and ceiling pressed against him. He pulled himself along on his elbows; his head cocked to the side to fit it through the passage, stopping as he reached the center of one of the cells. A thin screen separated him from it, one that he could peer down through at the occupant. An un'hai, but not Zoelle. While they were identical in appearance, he was certain he would know her when he saw her. This one was asleep in her bed, mouth open and head lolled to the side.

He continued, dragging his body through the tight confines to the next cell. He looked down into it. The un'hai inside was sitting up in bed, staring at the wall.

"I knew you would come," Zoelle said without shifting her gaze.

How did she know he was there?

He held back the sudden rage he felt at her betrayal. She was calm and collected. He had to be the same.

"Why?" he said. It was the only word he could manage without his voice shaking.

"I told you why," she replied. "Power."

He clenched his fists; his knuckles white around the grip of his weapon. "I offered you power."

"You offered me something you don't yet have. Gr'el offered me something he already controls. It is not personal, Tea'va."

She didn't use his title. He bristled at that while he angled his plasma pistol, getting it into position to end her life.

"I trusted you."

"That was the idea. You are so aloof from the others, and you are so suspicious. It makes you easier to manipulate, not harder."

"What did he promise you? To be his heil'bek? To overthrow the Domo'dahm with him, as I did?"

There was so little space; it was hard to get a bead on her from where he was. He could spray the room with plasma. It would have to be enough.

"Yes. And he has already delivered the first of those. He has named me his heil'bek and afforded me Si'dahm status on the Ishur. A clone as a Si'dahm, Tea'va. It is the first time." She looked up at the screen now, though she couldn't see him through it. "You disregarded me. You removed me from the bridge before the battle. That was one of your mistakes."

"If you are Si'dahm, why are you still down here?"

"Because I knew you would come. Of the things you are and are not, Tea'va, I will agree that you are resourceful; however, I would not judge you intelligent."

Tea'va felt his heart pulse. He knew what she was saying, and she was right. He shouldn't have lingered when he saw that she was waiting. What was he thinking?

He didn't waste time shooting. There was no point to it now. He should never have been there at all. Why had he come?

He began to push himself back, fighting against the friction of the small space to return to the corridor. He could hear the sounds now. The soldiers were coming for him.

Fool. He was a fool. All of that time and energy wasted, and for what? A word with a traitor? He had gained little from her. Only that he now knew Gr'el also intended to kill the Domo'dahm. Was that something he would survive long enough to use?

He slid along the top of the passage, feeling a bit of relief as his legs came clear of the floor and dangled down. One last push and he was free, back upright and clear.

He looked to his left. A squad of soldiers was approaching.

He looked to his right. Another squad.

He held up his weapon. He was going to die in here if he didn't do something.

He looked both ways once more. Then he dropped the weapon and put his hands out.

"I submit," he shouted, the taste of it like acid on this tongue. "I submit."

51

THEY DIDN'T KILL HIM RIGHT away. It would have been against their laws to do so. A pur'dahm who surrendered had the right to retire themselves after a suitable time for preparation that usually consisted of composing a history of their life and accomplishments.

As the soldiers led him from the back routes to the main corridor, Tea'va thought about how little he had accomplished and how many of his deeds had ended in failure. For all of his goals and plans, was Zoelle right about him? Was he simply not very intelligent?

It was an idea that was difficult for him to accept. An idea that he refused to give in to. Bad luck, that's all that it was. A history of close calls and late decisions. He had been so close to shooting down the Heil'shur. He had almost been a hero before this journey. Before the opportunity had arisen for it to all fall apart.

Zoelle met the soldiers in the corridor; her head held high as she reached them. They bowed before her, causing her to smile.

"I see you surrendered," she said. "It won't save your life."

He looked at her without speaking. He was done with her. With all of them. He was the future of the bek'hai. His story was not fully written yet.

"Do you have anything you want to say?" she asked.

He didn't respond.

"Very well. You will be returned to your room and allowed one day to prepare, in accordance with our laws. Don't think to delay your retirement somehow. Gr'el will not allow it."

She turned on her heel, heading away from him. He watched her go. He hadn't bothered to kill her before. When he did, he would make sure she looked him in the eye.

The lead soldier pointed him in the opposite direction. He walked ahead of them, unencumbered. He was still a pur'dahm. He still commanded respect.

He led his captors through the hallway toward a transport beam. The squad leader took his arm when they reached it, a precaution against him trying to escape. He clenched his teeth at the touch. It was demeaning to be handled by a lor'hai. It had been demeaning to surrender to one.

He stepped into the beam, transporting himself up to the officer's quarters. One of the bridge crew was there, and he looked away as Tea'va passed. Another traitor to his Dahm. Tea'va wanted to destroy him. He glared at the drumhr as he passed, but still didn't speak. He decided he would not speak again. Not to traitors. Not to lor'hai. He was done with words. He needed a way out.

He expected that Gr'el would be in his quarters when he arrived. He assumed the pur'dahm would come to gloat and to mock. He had done so little to succeed in outmaneuvering the most advanced drumhr bek'hai science had produced. All it had taken was a single un'hai to disarm the one who claimed not to be taken with them.

Gr'el wasn't there. Neither was the Mother he had killed. His room was empty and clean, as though he still owned it. As though he was still commanding the Ishur.

It was a greater statement than anything the pur'dahm could have said in person, and it drove Tea'va to slam his fists against the walls in anger.

He caught himself a moment later. He had been foolish, and displaying his anger would only make him more so. He needed to be calm and think clearly. He was still growing weaker from his time outside of the regeneration chamber. He could spend some time in it, heal his body and his mind and still be able to... To what? He had surrendered. It was on his honor to retire himself. What use would healing be for that?

He crossed the room to his terminal. Surely he had done something in his life worth recording? Surely not all of it could be a failure? He had risen to the Second Cell after all. He had convinced the Domo'dahm to give him command of the Ishur.

Or had he? Did the Domo'dahm really want him as a successor? He was more human than any of the other drumhr.

Was he too human?

He glanced out of the viewport at the end of his quarters, staring into space. He had never considered that possibility before. His functional sex organs and his ability to breathe Earth's atmosphere freely were supposed to be the herald of bek'hai resurgence, but what if everything else about him was loathsome? His skin. His lips. The smoothness of his skull. What if his refusal to breed had made him expendable? Had given the Domo'dahm cause to want to displace him or at least to allow it?

His anger flared again. He was a bigger fool than he had even realized. The Domo'dahm hadn't given him command of the Ishur as an opportunity to earn his place. He had set him up to fail. He had set him up to die.

There had to be a way out. He would think of something. He approached the viewport, still looking out into space. He could see the light from the human starship's main thrusters ahead of them. All he wanted was one more chance at the Heil'shur. One more battle to decide who was the superior pilot.

He felt something wet on his eye, and he reached up and lifted it with his finger. He stared at it for a moment. A tear? Was he crying? Bek'hai didn't cry. Drumhr couldn't cry. None, except for him.

He blinked a few times, and then wiped the tears away with the sleeve of his gori'shah. He was pathetic. Simply pathetic.

He looked out the viewport again. He let his eyes trail along the space ahead of him, expecting them to come to rest on the glow of the thrusters once more.

He froze when he didn't see them, squinting his eyes and leaning closer to the clear lek'shah until his head was pressed against it. He found the human ship a moment later.

It was coming about, and heading straight for them.

52

"Alpha Squadron, report," Gabriel said as he slid down into the seat of his starfighter.

"First Lieutenant Bale, ready."

"Second Lieutenant Celia, ready."

"Second Lieutenant Gerhardt, ready."

"Captain Sturges, ready."

Gabriel smiled when he heard the older officer's voice. They had scrambled to get one more of the fighters online and then scrambled again to find a pilot to fly it. Sturges was past his prime, and hadn't flown a fighter in years, but they needed every extra hand they could get.

The General had a plan, and it was a doozy.

It was also already underway. Theodore had taken them all by surprise, barking orders from his wheelchair down in the science lab. He knew exactly what he wanted to do, as crazy as it was, and there was no time to waste in doing it. They had a small window of opportunity to get this right.

"Alpha Squadron, prepare to launch." Theodore's voice cut across the comm channel. Gabriel had never heard his father so determined.

The main hangar door began sliding open.

"Roger," Gabriel said. "Alpha Squadron is loaded and ready."

"Good hunting, Major," Miranda said through his channel.

"Remember," Gabriel said, taking the fighter's controls in his hands. "We're going to be moving out of the dead zone. Once we do, they'll be invulnerable."

"Yes, sir," the other pilots replied.

"Alpha Squadron, you are go," Miranda said.

"Roger," Gabriel said. "Let's do this." He reached up and squeezed the crucifix below his flight suit. "Give me strength."

The fighters added thrust as one, bursting from the hangar in the Magellan's side and making a quick right turn. They spread apart, taking up a large diamond formation above the starship as the General cut the main engines and fired the vectoring thrusters, rolling her over at the same time. The turn wasn't quite as tight as it had been the last time, but the result was identical.

It left the Magellan pointing straight at the Dread fortress.

Gabriel watched as a stream of superheated plasma poured out from the rear of the starship, the mains firing at full thrust. It pushed the craft forward once more.

"Let's stay ahead of her," Gabriel said, pushing his thrusters.

The fighters shot forward, swooping down in front of the Magellan and continuing to add velocity.

Five seconds passed. Then ten. They rocketed toward the fortress without a response, the fighters closing the gap much faster than the Magellan.

Gabriel's fighter beeped, the targeting computer picking up new obstacles. A dozen bolts of plasma suddenly lanced the sky, streaking past a little too close.

"Here we go," Gabriel said. "Stay alert."

The Dread fighters came into view a moment later, a dozen in all. It was a much smaller number than Gabriel had been expecting.

He didn't want to be ungrateful, but why?

There was no more time to think about it. The first of the Bats began shooting at them.

"Take evasive. Celia, Gerhardt, Bale, you're on the fighters. Keep them off the Magellan." His father was going to have a hard enough time evading the fortress' plasma without having to worry about them, too. "Sturges, you're with me."

"Roger," Captain Sturges replied.

Gabriel opened fire as the Dread Bats approached, sending his fighter into a sine-wave flight pattern and adding a bit of spin. Plasma streaked around him, the flashes bright enough to be blinding if he wasn't careful. He blew past one of the fighters, throwing his craft into a tight flip and triggering his guns. His rounds caught the Dread Bat in the tail, the dead zone stealing its shields and allowing the energy to penetrate. It exploded a moment later in a short fireball that Gabriel didn't see. He had already flipped his fighter back toward the fortress.

"We're coming up too slow," Sturges said.

Gabriel checked his screen. He was sure his father saw the same thing. "We're almost there. Stay alert."

The fortress drew closer, looming over them within seconds. It was even larger in space than it had been on the ground, a large part of it having been settled within the earth. Gabriel gasped at the sheer immensity as his fighter came within a few kilometers of the side and he adjusted his thrust to keep from crashing into it.

"How do we fight this?" Sturges said.

"We are fighting this," Gabriel replied.

"Bale, I need assistance," Celia said through the comm. "I've got two Bats on my tail."

"I'm coming," Bale said. "Hard port, drop ninety degrees."

"Roger."

Gabriel's computer beeped again. He looked ahead as another squadron of bats appeared ahead of them, launching from the fortress. They cut immediately, vectoring right toward them.

"Major," Sturges said.

"These are ours," Gabriel replied. "Keep them busy." He checked his screen. "We've got thirty seconds."

"I can't get them off me," Gerhardt said. "Celia. Bale. They've got me in a cross-"

His signal vanished.

Gabriel cursed under his breath, hitting the trigger on his cannons as they swept past the incoming Dread bats, keeping his starfighter rotating and vectoring as he did. A plasma blast scorched the side of his cockpit, leaving a dark stain to his left. It had missed by centimeters at best. He had to focus. Forget about the others. His mission was to clear the way here.

He dropped his thrust, rolling the fighter over again. Sturges had turned around ahead of him and was shooting away, putting distance between them while the Bats gave chase. Gabriel slammed on the thrusters, watching his power levels drop as he moved up on the enemy. One of them slotted in behind him at the same time, and he zigged and zagged to stay out of its crosshairs.

Plasma bolts took aim at Sturges' craft, dozens of them bypassing the fighter as the old Captain showed himself to be closer to his prime than anyone had thought. He maneuvered like a pro, moving across every plane to keep the Dread fighters close.

"We're running out of time," Sturges said. "I'm going to bring them to you. You hit these; I'll get the one on your tail."

Gabriel checked his screen. "Negative. You can't make that pattern without leaving yourself wide open."

"Already doing it, son," Sturges said. "Be ready."

Gabriel felt his heart lurch. Damn it.

Sturges' fighter rolled and flipped, a burst of the rear thrusters sending him on a collision course with Gabriel. Gabriel stopped watching the screen, scanning the field ahead of him for the enemy fighters. It wasn't his decision to make. Not now. It was his job to ensure it wasn't for nothing.

The two human fighters closed within seconds of one another.

"Now," Sturges said.

Gabriel bounced his fighter up as the older pilot's fire trailed below, slamming hard into the oncoming Dread Bat. Gabriel tracked the three Bats on Sturges' tail, trying hard to ignore their fire as the straight line allowed them an easier target. He held the trigger down while he rocked his starfighter, sending a stream of ion blasts on a collision course with them.

Sturges' starfighter exploded.

His rounds hit the Bats. One of them exploded while the other two lost power. The path was as clear as he could make it.

Gabriel checked his screen.

Time was up.

Where was his father?

53

THEODORE SHIFTED IN THE COMMAND chair of the Magellan's bridge. "Colonel, get me a status from Guy and Reza."

"Yes, sir," Choi replied.

He returned his attention to the view ahead. The Dread fortress was growing larger and larger, its defensive plasma fire growing more intense.

"Come on, Maggie," he whispered. "We made it off Earth; we can make it through this. For her sake."

The starship shook slightly as it took another hit.

"Deck L," Abdullah said. "It pierced the armor. Emergency bulkheads are sealing."

Theodore cursed to himself and renewed his focus on the controls. He fired starboard vectoring thrusters six and nine, then port four and eight, then hull number seven, his fingers working an intricate pattern across the controls. Flying a starship like the Magellan was supposed to be easy. The vectoring thrusters had always been intended for docking, not for war, and using them this way was akin to playing a musical instrument. Some people couldn't play a note. Some were adequate amateurs. Some were cool and professional.

He was a virtuoso.

Gabriel would be too, he knew, with more experience. He had done well the first time, managing to handle the ship with one hand tied behind his back because he didn't know the intricacies of managing the separate thrusters, or how they would affect the ship's overall vectors and profile. Gabriel could be better than him if they survived long enough.

Hell, he was sure Gabriel was already better than him. He felt a sense of pride in that. The pride helped him focus.

His boy was out there, and he wasn't about to let him down.

He triggered more of the thrusters in an uneven sequence, kicked the Magellan's stern out to the left, then up, bringing it around and down. Plasma bolts streamed around her, most passing in the spaces left behind by the evasive maneuvers, some striking the heavy armor plating.

"Colonel," he snapped, still waiting for an answer.

He hadn't given the scientists much time to prepare, but he also had a feeling they would work better under pressure. They had already accomplished so much in so little time after he had set them straight. He didn't fault people for occasional weakness. He had been forced to deal with his own, and nobody was perfect. Infidelity? That was one flaw he couldn't stomach. It had made even looking at the Larones and Reza difficult.

"They're hooking everything up now, sir. Guy wants you to know that none of this has been tested, and the odds of success are relatively low."

"Not what I want to hear, Colonel," Theodore said. "Tell him he has to make it work, or we're all gonna die."

"Yes, sir."

There was a chance they would all die anyway. Their part of the plan was only the first part. But what a victory it would be in itself to make it that far.

"We just lost Gerhardt," he heard Bale say over Alpha Squadron's comm. "We can't keep this up for long."

"You don't need to keep it up for long," Gabriel replied. "General, the path is clear. Passing coordinates."

"You got that, Maggie?" Theodore asked.

"Data received," Maggie said.

Theodore looked down at his screen. The Dread fortress was covering most of it, but now a red target had appeared against it.

The Magellan shook again. A warning tone sounded.

"Life support systems were hit," Abdullah said. "Main control is down."

"Initiating emergency support systems," Maggie said.

Theodore forced himself to stay calm. Even a virtuoso couldn't get through the fire they were taking without a scratch. He knew his plan was a risk, a Hail Mary chance to get them out of the situation they were in. He had to trust in himself, and in God.

The way he saw it, the Man Upstairs owed him for taking Juliet away, and this was his moment to cash in.

"Time?" he shouted.

"Ten seconds, General," Spaceman Locke replied.

He smiled to hear her voice. Gabriel had been spending more time with her lately. That was good. They had been friends for a long time, but Jessica's death had hit his son hard and kept him away from romance all of these years. He trusted Gabe not to get involved in anything that would diminish his capacity as a soldier. He also knew from experience that the love of a good woman could be the difference between being mediocre and being exceptional.

"Mr. Larone," he said, opening a channel and communicating with the scientist directly. "You have ten seconds."

"Ten seconds?" Guy replied. "General-"

"Do it," Theodore shouted.

The fire was getting more intense. The Magellan shook again. The closer they came to the fortress, the larger their profile, and the less time they had to avoid the attack.

"Five seconds," Spaceman Locke said. "Four seconds. Three seconds."

"Got it," Guy shouted over the comm. "We're active. I hope this works."

"Two seconds."

The main plasma cannon on the Dread fortress lit up, a bright blue light way too close for comfort. Secondary plasma peppered the hull, and a second warning began sounding.

"We're not going to make it," Choi whispered.

"Yes we are, damn it," Theodore growled.

The Dread cannon erupted, a bright beam of energy only a thousand kilometers away. It arced toward the Magellan in a path that made it unavoidable, the light of it becoming blinding as it reached them.

There was no sound. There was no impact. There was no explosion. The plasma struck the front of the Magellan, vanishing into a black void that appeared along the surface of the bow. The force of it slowed their velocity, pushing against them, but the energy, the destructive power, disappeared beneath the darkspace shield.

It was over within a second, the main cannon's fury absorbed. Secondary fire was caught along the other painted edges of the Magellan, the hull, and the nacelles.

Nobody cheered. Nobody even breathed. The tech worked, but they weren't safe yet.

"Power levels critical," Maggie said

Power. It was all about power. The Dread fortress was huge in front of them. For all the size of the Magellan, it was nothing in comparison.

"The left nacelle is gone," Abdullah said.

Theodore nodded. He knew they weren't getting home that way.

"Gabriel, what's our status?" Theodore said.

"Still clear, General," Gabriel replied. "Follow the target. I'm holding them off."

He fired the vectoring thrusters, managing the distance between the Dread fortress and the Magellan. The enemy plasma stopped coming as they moved in too close to be targeted.

It was working. As impossible as it was. As impossible as it seemed. His plan was working.

The Magellan continued to drop as the fortress moved closer, from hundreds of kilometers to less than a dozen within seconds.

"Let's hope we have enough power for one last push," he said. "Gabriel, clear out."

"Yes, sir," Gabriel said.

The hangar appeared in front of them a moment later, as Theodore aligned the Magellan with the target. They were close now, so close they had no other options. As if they did before.

A single starfighter streaked out of the hangar, whipping past the viewport. Theodore cringed when he saw the number of plasma burns across the fuselage, and against the cockpit. It made him as sure as anything that his son was blessed.

"Power levels at ten percent, General," Maggie said.

"Brace for impact," Theodore said.

The fortress' hangar was big. So was the Magellan, and it was coming in hard. He had no idea what would happen when their shields struck the enemy's shields.

They were about to find out.

He fired reverse thrusters, pushing them to full. It would help, but it wouldn't be enough. The fortress vanished into nothing but a solid line of black with a giant open mouth. He could see the inside of the hangar now, the Dread tech keeping the atmosphere contained and gravity in place. He could see the soldiers that Gabriel had killed, the unpiloted ships he had destroyed.

The Magellan passed into the hangar, the gravity instantly pulling it to the floor. It hit with a deafening, grinding whoomp, pulling them hard in their seats, the din continuing as momentum dragged the starship across. The rear of the hangar approached in a hurry, and Theodore couldn't help but close his eyes as the impact grew imminent.

He felt and heard the crash as the shielded bow of the Magellan struck the shielded interior of the fortress. The noise was louder than anything he had ever experienced, the forces involved threatening to break every bone in his body. If the seeming magic of the dark shields hadn't reduced the overall impact, he was sure it would have.

He opened his eyes. The black material ahead of him rippled outward, the shockwave of force spreading across the fortress, being distributed throughout the alien ship like an earthquake. The rumbling continued for another ten seconds as if they were sitting in the center of a volcano.

And then everything was silent.

54

THEY LEFT AN HOUR LATER without much fanfare, and with a surprising ambivalence from the residents of Hell at the idea of losing their leader.

"I took them in and made them tough," Kraeger said. "They're too strong to give a shit about me, and Fox will do a better job than I ever did."

They numbered nearly three-dozen, having accepted over forty volunteers from the ranks of both the community and the scavengers and cutting some back out after a rudimentary examination of their overall health. Just because someone wanted to fight didn't mean they would be an asset over a liability, and Donovan discovered that Kraeger did have a sharp mind for making that determination. They were fewer in quantity because of it, but greater in operational efficiency and strength.

They were also greater in overall firepower. Beyond the bek'hai plasma rifles, the community had access to a massive supply of guns, ammunition, and explosives. It was all military grade, the type of equipment the resistance had run out of or lost control of a long time ago. It was nothing that could damage the enemy's armor, but it would be effective against clones.

They were careful up until the point they left the base, filing out into the night, making a quick, concerted dash across the open highway to the tractor cab of the now defunct Monster. A lookout was keeping a close eye on the cameras back in the bunker, ready to transmit a signal to Kraeger in the event of an emergency.

They scaled the industrial machine, taking position along its sides and top, dropping prone and keeping their rifles aimed out into the night. If the Dread were close enough they would be sure to take notice as soon as the rebels powered on the machine and heated it up, but there was no sign of them anywhere nearby. The brush was thick but relatively flat, giving them a long line of sight in every direction.

There was nothing. At least not yet.

"Start it up," Donovan said.

Ehri pressed the button to begin sending power from the battery to the huge, studded wheels. She tapped another button to release the brakes and allow the tractor to move again. It went forward, accelerating smoothly as she increased the throttle and began turning it to the west.

"Here we go," Donovan said.

His heart was racing, but his nerves were calm. He was excited about this, more excited than he had expected. The Dread had taken so much from him and from humankind. He was eager to take something back.

The tractor angled toward the building, picking up speed as it left the roadway and jostled onto the dirt and vegetation. It rolled over it all with ease, gaining momentum and sliding deeper into the wilderness. Within minutes the road was hazy behind them, and a small incline began to appear on the horizon.

"It's right over that hill," Kraeger said. "Eight minutes out."

The tractor was surprisingly fast with the transport unhitched from it and Ehri pushing it to full throttle. It wasn't long before Donovan could feel the heat of the vehicle's exertion begin filtering into the cabin, leaving him sweating.

"There's no way they aren't going to spot us like this," Soon said.

"It's okay if they see us," Donovan said. "They just need to see us too late."

It was Kraeger who had presented the haphazard plan. It was Donovan who agreed with the logic of it. They would lose a lot of time going to the Dread facility on foot, time that would allow the larger force to return. By charging in the tractor, they might be able to catch the Dread off-guard in more ways than one.

They reached the hill in no time, coming upon the incline and rumbling up it with only a minor slowdown. Donovan leaned out the door of the cab, looking behind them. There was a light in the distant sky. A Dread fighter, or the transport heading back to base?

He grabbed Kraeger's shoulder and pointed to it.

"It's going to be close," Kraeger said.

"We have to reach the mechs before the reinforcements get here," Donovan said.

"I'm going as fast as I can, Major," Ehri replied.

The tractor trundled up the hill, slowing to almost half the speed as it neared the crest.

"That's it," Ehri said.

"Kraeger, you know what to do," Donovan said.

"See you in Hell, Major," Kraeger said. "The real one." Then he moved to the side of the vehicle and jumped off.

The rest of their small army jumped with him, abandoning the tractor to make the remainder of the trip on foot. They rolled beside and then behind the vehicle as it reached the apex of the incline, giving them a view of the Dread base a moment before they started dropping toward it.

It was a more open facility than the much larger city, with four roundish main buildings and a few smaller outbuildings all connected by narrow corridors. It gave the outpost an almost insectoid appearance, one that loosely resembled an asymmetrical wheel and spokes.

Donovan quickly spotted the two mechs he had seen earlier. They were moving to the front of the outpost, directly ahead of them.

"They saw us," Soon said, reaching up and pulling the safety restraints over his chest.

Donovan found his seat and did the same. "Let's hope their aim is off."

The tractor shook as it began to roll down the other side of the hill. Ehri kept the throttle all the way forward and began rocking the machine from side to side while it charged ahead. The mechs raised their weapons in unison, sending a spew of heavy slugs at them.

The projectiles slammed into the heavy metal shell of the vehicle, creating a din of clanks and thunks as they tore into to machine. Sparks skittered off the plating in front of the cabin as rounds nearly found them and the entire night sky grew bright white at the onslaught.

Plasma fire began streaking past them, the shots coming close to the mechs but intentionally not hitting them. Kraeger and his team were attempting to distract the pilots, to give them something else to think about and throw their aim.

The tractor continued on its course, racing down the hill toward the mechanized armors. Slugs continued to tear it apart, and Donovan watched chunks of iron explode from the machine, leaving a trail of debris along the sides. Something popped near the back, and a huge plume of smoke appeared in front of them. He expected that any moment one of the projectiles would find its way into the cabin and kill them all. One came close, catching the edge of the cage and tearing a huge hole in the side, taking the door with it.

It didn't matter. They had reached the point of no return. The mechs had also failed to adjust to their tactic. Was it because they didn't think the machine was a threat or was it because they just weren't accustomed to playing defense?

Whatever the reason, the tractor continued its approach, growing ever closer to the mechs until it was right on top of them, nearly as tall as they were and much, much heavier.

The Dread pilots finally realized what was about to happen, and they concentrated their fire on the front of the tractor, trying to slow its momentum.

Of course, they couldn't. Of course, it was too late.

The massive vehicle slammed hard into the mechs, catching one full on and clipping the other. That one spun and tumbled to the ground with a jolt, while the first was pushed backward, sinking into the front of the machine and finding itself pinned. Donovan braced himself as the tractor sandwiched the mech between itself and the wall of one of the outbuildings, slamming into it and coming to a sudden, complete stop.

"Come on," Donovan said

He removed the restraints and got to his feet. They had been hoping they would be able to catch both of the machines with the tractor. They would have to settle for the one. He could see the upper part of it ahead of him. It was struggling to get free, pressing against the weight of the truck.

Soon threw off his restraints, as did Ehri. They had an easy exit from the torn cage, and they made their way out of the hole and into the open air. Donovan found the first mech getting back to its feet, recovering from the glancing blow it had taken.

They were running out of time.

"Ehri, go," Donovan said. She was already moving, rushing toward the mech. He hoped they hadn't hit it too hard. They needed it to get loose.

"This is even crazier now that we're here," Soon said, watching along with him. Ehri jumped from the front of the tractor to the shoulders of the mech, a fifteen-foot leap that she made look easy.

"We're just getting started, Captain," Donovan replied.

The Dread forces were beginning to pour out of the buildings, getting mixed up with heavy fire from Kraeger and his approaching force. Clones were already falling nearby, hit by both plasma and traditional rounds, clearly caught unready for the assault.

Donovan almost fell as the trapped mech managed to get enough force behind it to shake the tractor. He leaned down, putting a hand on the scored metal, looking back to see that it was getting loose. Ehri had scaled the front of it, and he saw her put her hand to a spot on the chest and open a small access panel. She moved her hand across that, and the side of the mech's chest cavity parted, revealing the pilot inside. He could see the surprise on the pilot's face as Ehri shot him.

"What about that guy?" Soon said, pointing at the second mech. It was back on its feet, and facing their way.

"Run," Donovan said, turning and dashing across the top of the tractor. Projectiles dug into the metal behind them as he crossed to the other side. He reached the edge without pausing, jumping without a second thought.

He tucked his shoulder, hitting the ground in a hard roll. Soon was right behind him, trying to copy the move and coming up a little short. He landed hard on his side and didn't get up right away, stunned by the impact.

Donovan rushed back to him. A Dread soldier appeared in the doorway of the building they crashed against, and he got his rifle up in time to bring the clone down. He reached Soon, leaning next to him.

"Captain?"

Soon groaned and pushed himself up. His clothes were torn, but Diaz's gori'shah had survived beneath it, helping absorb some of the fall.

"I'm not dead yet," Soon said.

Donovan helped him up, and they both looked over in surprise as the tractor was shoved back, Ehri working the mech completely free.

"We're going to have company," Donovan said, pointing at the light that had been following them in. It was the transport the Hunters had taken out into the wild. "Bad company. Hurry."

Donovan led Soon toward the doorway. The clone he had shot was slumped there, along with another that had been hit by Kraeger's more distant fire. They stepped over it, moving into the structure. They could hear Ehri's mech join the attack behind them, the whine of the powerful guns and the hard echoes of the slugs pouring into the second armor. Donovan turned his head right before rounding the corner, seeing Ehri's mech ducking around the tractor, using it as cover while she rained fire on the opposition.

"We need to clear the way for Kraeger," Donovan said.

They raced through the structure, catching the clone soldiers by surprise, hitting them with conventional fire before they could make it out the door. Only a few appeared by the time they had reached the first connecting corridor, proving Kraeger's hunch right. The base wasn't heavily defended.

"Honey, I'm hooooommmmeee," he heard Kraeger shout from somewhere behind him. "Get those charges down boys and girls. I'm expecting fireworks."

"Where to?" Soon asked.

Donovan paused. "Command is that way," Donovan said, following the layout Ehri had given them in his head. "There should be a hangar that way. I don't know if they have any equipment we can use in there, but it's worth trying to take what we can. Let's wait here for the others to catch up."

"Yes, sir," Soon said.

Kraeger appeared at the end of the corridor a moment later, flanked by ten men.

"How are we doing?" Donovan asked.

"It's fifteen to six in our favor, Major," Kraeger said. "And I think the odds are going to get better. Your alien girlfriend beat the hell out of that other mech. I'm glad she's on our side."

"Me too," Donovan said, relieved to know Ehri was okay. "We need to split up. Half to the Command Center, the other half to the hangar."

"You heard the man," Kraeger said. "I assume you want the charges in the Command Center?"

"Absolutely."

Soon put his hand on Donovan's shoulder. "If I don't see you again, Major, it was an honor."

"For me, too, Captain," Donovan said.

"Aww. You two are going to make me cry again. I think we should get moving."

Soon saluted, and then started running down the corridor toward the hangar, half of the other rebels following behind him.

"Well, you were right, Major," Kraeger said. "We can fight back. Are you ready to blow the insides of this place to mush?"

55

THE RESISTANCE IN THE HALLWAYS was light, the majority of it coming from a single squad of clone soldiers being led by an armored bek'hai in the corridor right outside the Command Center. Donovan and the others were pinned down there for a few minutes while they traded fire, the battle ending quickly when Kraeger threw a well-placed explosive into the center of them. The blast shredded the clones and left the Dread dazed long enough to get shot.

They filed into the Center. It was similar to the room that Donovan and Diaz had met Ehri in. Sparse and solid and cold. Simple slabs of metal rose up throughout the room, trailing back into the dark, uneven walls and flooring. A raised dais with a single chair resting on it sat in the center, ringed by three more levels of what appeared to be workstations of some kind.

The stations were all deserted, except for the chair in the center. A bek'hai in a flowing gori'shah was sitting there, looking ahead to a feed of the battle continuing outside.

Donovan let his eyes wander to the feed. He saw the tractor first and shuddered at the amount of damage it had sustained. It was a miracle they had survived their initial attack. He found Ehri's mech ducked behind it with the remainder of the rebel soldiers. The transport carrying the Hunters was further afield, on its side against the ground and smoking.

Three more Dread mechs had appeared in the distance and were peppering the tractor with fire, trying to get it out of the way once and for all. Two Dread fighters were circling, staying at a safe distance.

Donovan's heart sank. Either the forces hadn't been as light as Kraeger assumed, or reinforcements were already on the way before the battle started. Whatever the reason, it looked like it was only a matter of time before they were overwhelmed.

"Screw it, Major," Kraeger said. "Let's finish the job and go out as heroes."

"Funny thing for you to say," Donovan replied.

"What can I say? I'm fickle."

The pur'dahm reacted at the sound of their voices, turning his head to look at them. He was uglier than some of the others Donovan had seen, the ridges of bone on his head protruding in odd, asymmetrical angles, his skin thicker and more gray. He looked old.

"Druk'shur," he said calmly. "The resistance ends tonight."

"Maybe," Kraeger said. "You first."

He fired his rifle. The plasma caught the bek'hai between the eyes, sending him tumbling from the dais.

"Set the charges," Kraeger roared. "We aren't dead until we're dead."

The others set about spreading the explosives while Donovan watched the action unfolding outside. Smoke was pouring from the tractor, and Ehri had turned the mech to get it in front of as many of the rebels as she could. He could see some of the slugs were getting through now, digging into the mech's armor, the enemy drawing nearer.

They had tried to do something special. They had tried to claim the first real victory in the war against the Dread. If he was going to die, at least he could find comfort in the fact that he had died doing something, the same way his mother, Matteo, Diaz, and all of the others had. His life was only a waste if he died for nothing.

"Charges are set, Major," Kraeger said. "Let's see if we can get out of here."

Donovan kept his eyes on the feed. Everything seemed to be moving in slow motion out there as the fighters swooped down, unleashing heavy plasma on Ehri's position. The shots hit the tractor, and one of them struck something important. He felt like his heart stopped beating as he witnessed the growing flume of the explosion, the battery detonating, its secure containment structure already turned to slag.

The mech was thrown backward, the rebels incinerated. The building shook from the shockwave, and again when the mech slammed into it once more.

"I don't think we're getting out of here," Donovan said, stunned.

"You don't survive by giving up, Major," Kraeger replied. "No matter how bad it looks. No matter how futile it seems. I know. I've been as low as any man can be."

Donovan nodded. Kraeger was right. He had to keep fighting.

He started toward the doorway.

An armored pur'dahm stepped into it.

Donovan couldn't see the Hunter's face. It was hidden behind a dark mask, still connected to the tanks that allowed the drumhr to breathe more easily outside. He entered wordlessly, rifle shouldered, replaced with an odd, dark blade that was sweating plasma.

"What the?" Kraeger said, raising his weapon to attack.

The Hunter burst forward, crossing the room in three steps, the rebel's defenses too slow. Plasma bolts hit the wall around him as he reached their forces, decapitating the first of them, then the second, and the third.

Donovan and Kraeger backed away, both shooting at the bek'hai. Donovan didn't have a Dread weapon, and his bullets pinged harmlessly against the armor. Kraeger's shots came close, but somehow the Hunter was avoiding them.

"Druk'shur," a voice said from the doorway.

A second Hunter was there, also carrying a blade. He spun it casually in his grip as he entered the room.

"Druk this," Kraeger said, turning to shoot.

Then the first Hunter was on top of him, grabbing the weapon from his hands and throwing it aside. He didn't kill Kraeger right away. Donovan knew why.

"Where is your base?" the second Hunter said in thick English.

"Go to Hell," Kraeger said, smiling.

The first grabbed him by the head and threw him forcefully to the ground.

"There are two ways to die, human. You choose."

Kraeger moved to his hands and knees. He looked a little dazed, but he was trying to get up again.

Donovan stood behind them. They didn't care if he was armed, they knew he couldn't hurt them. They also knew he couldn't escape. He looked around the room, searching for something he could use. A plasma rifle was on the floor a few meters away. Could he reach it in time? He had seen how the Hunters moved. He doubted it.

"How about instead of giving up my people, I give you this?" Kraeger said, raising his middle finger. The Hunter hit him again, the force putting him back on the floor. He didn't get up as quickly.

"You," the second said, turning to Donovan. "You started this with the un'hai traitor. Where is your base?"

Donovan smiled. "Go to Hell," he said, mimicking Kraeger. He gave them the finger for good measure. He was about to die. Why not?

"I did not expect you to reveal your base, Heil'drek," the Hunter said. "You have great honor as a warrior and my respect. For that, I will retire you without pain."

He raised the plasma sword.

The building quaked, rocking so hard it knocked both Donovan and the Hunter from their feet as something large smashed against it.

Donovan didn't get back up. Instead, he scrambled for the plasma rifle, crawling toward it on his hands and knees, not even daring to look back. He had one chance to reach it before the pur'dahm cut him in half.

He almost had it in hand when he sensed the Hunter's presence behind him. He rolled to the side as the blade came down, sinking slightly into the floor and then lifting away. He looked up at the Hunter, knowing he wouldn't be able to avoid a second strike.

A muffled whine interrupted everything, and a split-second later the entire room began to blow apart under the force of slugs coming in from outside. Donovan looked over at the feed just in time to see the front of a mech nearly butted up against it, too clean and fresh to be Ehri.

The Hunter turned to face the new attack at the same time the bullets began ripping into him, hitting him hard enough that his body was sent across the room and into the wall. The other Hunter was down as well, while Kraeger was lying prostrate on the floor, his hands over his head.

The shooting stopped. The wall was in pieces ahead of them, revealing the front of the mech. The feed was destroyed, as was most of the interior of the room.

The front of the mech shifted, the cockpit opening. Soon's head appeared a moment later.

"Sorry I'm late, Major. Ehri made these things sound like they were easy to use."

Donovan stared at the pilot, the shock of the turn of events keeping him speechless.

"I didn't hit you, did I?"

Donovan pointed past the mech. Soon was leaving himself vulnerable, and there was still a battle going on. Or was there? He didn't hear any gunfire.

"It's okay, Major. We won."

56

DONOVAN AND KRAEGER MET SOON and Ehri outside, along with the remaining rebels, six in all. They had lost over two-thirds of their forces.

They had killed a lot more of the enemy than that.

Ehri's mech was a mangled mess, one of the arms missing, the other twisted into an ugly shape. The legs were badly damaged, and there were score marks across every inch of the armor. Somehow, she had kept herself facing the onslaught and prevented the cockpit from being hit. She had jumped out of the machine sweaty but unharmed.

Smoke rose all around them, the field outside littered with dead clones, a downed transport, four destroyed mechs, and even a crashed Dread fighter. It was an unexpected and impressive victory. One that Donovan had never imagined he would live to see.

"We can't linger here long," Ehri said. "The Domo'dahm will be furious at the losses."

"Good," Kraeger said. "It's about time he's the one upset about losing. I'm willing to wait for round two."

"I'm not," Donovan said. "What we did here was a start. Our first victory. Now our job is to make sure it isn't our last."

"It won't be," Soon said. "There's another mech inside the hangar with your name on it, Major."

Donovan considered for a moment before shaking his head. "It'll make us too easy to track. We should go on foot."

"It will shorten the time to Austin considerably, Major," Ehri said. "And will not reduce the fury of the Domo'dahm's retaliation. Besides, the resistance may need the relief these weapons can provide."

"What about the rest of us?" Kraeger asked. "We're supposed to walk?"

"There's a slug looking thing in the hangar, too," Soon said. "Ehri says it's ground transportation."

"A Ped'ek. An armored carrier," Ehri said. "Once used to collect humans for processing. It has been dormant for some time, but it should still be functional."

"Processing?"

"In the early days of the invasion humans were collected for testing, to determine the proper genetics for splicing. This went on for twenty years or so until enough positive samples had been collected. The transports were used to ferry the prisoners to the testing facility."

"Why not put them on a regular transport?" Donovan asked.

"They didn't want to soil the ships by allowing contact with human flesh."

"What?" Soon said. "I don't get it. The Dread are mixing genes with us."

"By necessity, Captain. Not choice. Make no mistake, the Domo'dahm and many of the drumhr are disgusted by humankind. The clones are tolerated because they are clones and as such considered clean. Some of your ways are being adopted because they will prolong the race. It is all out of need, not desire."

"Okay, but then it won't be equipped to be driven by a human, will it?"

"A mech should be able to pull it quite easily."

"Monster two-oh?" Soon said. "It's a decent upgrade."

"That tractor saved our lives," Donovan said.

"May she rest in peace," Kraeger said, making the sign of the cross toward the remains of the vehicle. "Let's not dally, Major. We've got a war to win."

Kraeger headed off toward the hangar, leaving the others to watch him go.

"He killed Murphy," Donovan said.

"And countless others," Ehri replied.

"He's also a good fighter," Soon said. "I don't know what his background is, but I think he was trained by the military."

"He might have grown up as part of the resistance. That would explain his self-proclaimed soft spot. You're a pretty good fighter yourself, Captain."

"I have a lot to live for," Soon replied.

"We all do," Donovan replied. He stepped over to the remaining rebels. "Good work, all of you. I'm sorry I don't know you very well, but I hope to get the chance to. We're going to be heading to Austin, Texas. There's a resistance base there. Will you be coming?"

"I wouldn't miss it for anything, sir," a woman with short hair and a scar on her cheek said.

"Me neither," one of the others said.

"Let's give them Hell, Major," a third replied.

"Absolutely."

57

THE HUNTER REMAINED OUT OF sight.

Watching.

Waiting.

He had seen the battle. He had followed from the tomb of his brothers, beneath the crashed ship where he continued to observe. The druk'shur had captured their equipment. Their weapons. Their armors. They had done what none of the pur'dahm ever believed possible.

They had challenged the might of the bek'hai, and they had survived.

It was a difficult outcome for him to accept. He knew without question that the bek'hai were the superior race and that the pur'dahm were the most superior of the species. And yet, his two surviving brothers had chosen to chase after the Heil'drek while he had chosen to remain. Was it truly cowardice, as his brother had claimed? Was it caution?

Or was it something else? Something more visceral, more powerful? He was Lex'el dur Rorn'el. A splice from the line of the Domo'dahm himself. He had more reason than most to want to prove his line. More reason than most to want to quell the spreading infection of humankind, to stop the return of their cancerous grip on the planet.

Had he stayed behind because he was afraid, or had he remained because the challenge was not great enough?

He knew the answer for himself, and his brothers had failed to survive to question it. That was just as well. They had always been inferior. Weaker. Slower. Less skilled. None of them could question that. Not when he was the champion of the Cruhr dur bek. Not when he had been undefeated for over two years.

He wasn't *a* Hunter.

He was *the* Hunter, and he had chosen to allow the humans their victory. He knew that it would be short-lived, and when he returned to the Domo'dahm with the Heil'drek's head, and with Ehri dur Tuhrik's head, he would be the one to claim his rightful position in the Domo'dahm's cell.

To the victor went the spoils.

The Hunter remained out of sight as the humans emerged, no longer exposed but within the armored safety of a pair of gur'shah and humorously trailing a ped'ek. He tightened his uneven lips to prevent himself from laughing at the absurdity, and then opened his mouth in surprise as the mechs stopped walking and the people in the ped'ek disembarked, turning to face the facility.

Then the larger human took something in his hand and held it up toward the base. He flicked his finger, and the ground began to shake. Flames and debris spewed from the open areas followed by billowing smoke, and the humans shouted and cheered.

Then they returned to the vehicle and resumed their motion away from the base.

The Hunter shifted his position beneath the ruined transport to watch them, tracking their direction and velocity.

When they had passed, he pulled himself from beneath the wreckage, climbing to his feet and adjusting the feed to his oxygen tanks. He would have to risk breathing the heavier outside air, or he wouldn't have a large enough supply to follow.

He bent down and retrieved his two lek'sai from the dirt, carefully rubbing them clean on the corpse of a nearby human before returning them to their sleeves on his back. His rifle had been damaged in the crash, but that was well and good.

He preferred to get close to his prey.

He looked to the north, where the humans were quickly vanishing over the horizon. He couldn't match their pace on foot, but that too was well and good.

He was the Hunter.

He could be patient.

58

TEA'VA STARED OUT OF THE viewport, his emotions crossing between surprised confusion and impressed respect. The human ship had definitely turned to face the fortress, and now he could see that they had launched their starfighters, the intent of their actions clear.

The Heil'shur and his allies intended to attack. It seemed ridiculous and impossible. What could they be thinking? Gr'el would surely chew them apart.

Tea'va paused to reconsider. Maybe not. Gr'el had been forced to kill a large number of the drumhr on the ship to cement his rise to command. He had also been required to destroy all of the original lor'hai, save for Zoelle and her scientists. While the cloning facility had turned out two replacement batches so far, it was still a number fewer than the ship originally carried.

If the humans had discovered how their technology worked, was it possible they would be able to mount an effective attack? Clearly, they were going to try.

A warning tone began to sound from his terminal as it would at every terminal across the ship, calling all available soldiers to battle. His lips parted in a crooked smile at the sudden turn of events. If the humans managed to cause enough of a diversion, there was a chance he could recover after all.

He kept watching the viewport while the first two squadrons of gi'shah launch away from the ship toward the interlopers. His gaze was intense as the two sides closed the distance between one another. He was sure the Heil'shur was out there. Which one was he?

Three of the ships turned back, giving chase to the gi'shah who were targeting the starship. Two continued forward, dodging the plasma defenses and drawing nearer to the fortress. He saw one of them nearly collide with a gi'shah and then make a smooth flip, let loose a stream of fire, flip and continue again. The Heil'shur! It was him. He was certain of it. Instead of feeling angry, he was nearly gleeful. Let Gr'el deal with that!

He tore himself away from the viewport. It wouldn't serve to linger here. He moved to the door and opened it.

Two soldiers remained outside his quarters. The others had gone running to their battle stations. They turned to face Tea'va, raising their weapons toward him to threaten him back inside.

"You are to be retired," one of them said. "Uphold your honor."

"Honor?" Tea'va said.

He pushed himself forward like a dart, using his hands to slap the soldier's rifles aside. He punched the first in the face, his palm up and out, shoving into the clone's nose. He heard the wet crack of cartilage and the soldier fell to the ground. He spun on his heel, his opposite leg sweeping up, slamming the second soldier's rifle again with enough force that it nearly turned the clone around. He stepped forward, grabbing the soldier's head and twisting until his neck broke.

"That is what I think of Gr'el's honor," he said, bending down to pick up one of the rifles.

He headed across the corridor. The fortress was still fairly quiet, the rush of its personnel already finished. They had gone to their stations to help in the fight and left him alone to move as he wished. Gr'el was a fool to leave him with only two guards. He was being treated like a failed drumhr, not a pur'dahm of the Second Cell. It was insulting, and he was sure his rival intended it to be that way.

It didn't matter now. The humans had given him the distraction he needed to get free. Now that he was out, he could make his way to the bridge, kill Gr'el, and regain control of the Ishur.

He stopped himself a few steps later. What if the humans had figured out how their technology worked? What if they had a plan? What if the infighting between himself and Gr'el had given them the opening they needed to win the battle?

It continued to seem impossible. The firepower of a bek'hai fortress against a ship without any offensive capabilities? How could the humans possibly win against that? Except Gr'el wouldn't be able to field half of the starfighters, or control half of the gun batteries.

Maybe it wasn't completely impossible after all.

He ran along the corridor until he reached another viewport. He looked out in time to see two of the human starfighters rush past, tracking down the side of the ship and out of view. He found the larger starship, taking heavy fire but still vectoring toward them.

The ship had evaded them the first time, sneaking around the fortress to get ahead and begin the chase. He knew Gr'el wouldn't allow that to happen again. The pur'dahm would stand his ground, positioning the fortress so that the human ship would have no choice but to smash right into it.

The ship's commander was smart. He had escaped them twice already. He had to be expecting that this was the case.

Tea'va stared out at the scene, trying to think like the humans. A starship with no weapons and no ability to slip, being chased by an enemy with superior numbers and firepower. A decision to turn around and head directly into the jaws of the gur'uhm. If he assumed that the commander knew he would not be able to circumvent the fortress again, what could he guess that such a commander would do?

A human starfighter rocketed past his viewport again, trailing three gi'shah. The second starfighter was coming up with another gi'shah behind him. They were so close that Tea'va could see the pilots of the human ships. One was old, the other young. They approached one another, the older one shooting at the younger one. Not at. Below. The gi'shah giving chase was hit. So was the older human, his ship vanishing in a small fireball and spitting debris away. The younger pilot followed up the attack by turning his starfighter in an unbelievable maneuver, spraying each of the gi'shah, destroying one and disabling the others.

That one had to be the Heil'shur.

Tea'va ran along the corridor, heading for the nearest transport beam while keeping an eye on the battle. The young human's fighter burst away again, and this time, there were no gi'shah to follow.

Why had he come to engage them so close to the fortress, while the others were staying back to protect the larger ship?

He had a feeling he knew. But could the human starship survive the journey?

He made it to the transport beam, taking it down to one of the decks that adjoined the hangar. Immediately, he could hear the sound of gunfire coming from inside. The Heil'shur was in the fortress, using the fighter's cannons on any of the clones that remained in the hangar.

That was where he decided to go. He turned the corner at the same time a squad of clones did. They stood only a meter apart for a moment, both taken by surprise. Tea'va recovered first, his plasma quickly dispatching the unprepared group of clones. He continued down the corridor, over the top of the hangar and to the control pod that hung above the space. He opened the hatch, shooting the drumhr he caught trying to escape and then descending into the pod. He could see the Heil'shur's fighter clearly now, on the ground and facing away from him.

He looked out past the hangar and into space. He could see the starship from his position. It was beaten and battered. One of the nacelles had already been destroyed. It was coming this way. He was sure of it. The hangar was large enough to house the human ship but just barely. There would be no way to stop the momentum in time, no way to come to a smooth stop. If the ship did enter, it was going to collide. The shielded lek'shah could survive a blow like that. Unless the human ship had a similar shield to absorb some of the force, there was no way that it could.

He glanced down at the Heil'shur's fighter, resting on the floor of the abandoned hangar. He could almost see the top of the pilot's head clearly from his position. He was a human. A regular human. Nothing exceptional. And yet, he was a worthy adversary. A human who had proven he was as skilled as a bek'hai. Most of the pur'dahm believed it impossible; that it wasn't the skill of the Heil'shur, but the failure of those that had faced him. Tea'va had seen him more than any of the others. He knew they were wrong.

The fighter's thrusters fired, and it began to slide along the floor on a small set of skids, headed back to space. Tea'va looked down at the controls. An electromagnetic shield kept the atmosphere out, but the hangar also had lek'shah doors that were normally closed for slipspace travel. He could trigger the command to close the doors. He could seal the Heil'shur in and the human starship out. He could effectively end the resistance for good.

He hesitated, finding the human starship once more. He was caught by surprise when the fortress' main plasma cannon fired, bathing the ship in bright light.

The plasma paused, a sudden impenetrable darkness spreading from the bow. Tea'va watched in amazement, his mouth dropping open as the plasma poured into the darkness and disappeared. Then the light grew too bright to see beyond, the plasma washing over the human ship. Tea'va couldn't breathe. He couldn't move.

The remains of the attack passed over the ship.

It was still coming his way.

It was impossible. Completely impossible. The plasma beam was phase modulated. It would have torn a hole into a fortress if it had struck one. Not only were the humans alive, they weren't even hit.

They hadn't just reverse-engineered the technology. They had improved it.

He put his hand over the terminal, ready to close the hangar doors. It would be so easy to shut them out. To let them slap harmlessly against the outside of the ship. Shields or no shields, they would never get in that way.

Gr'el had turned on him. Zoelle had turned on him. Even the Domo'dahm had turned on him, shunning him for being too human while at the same time asking the bek'hai to accept their evolution and the inclusion of human traits. He owed them nothing. He owed the bek'hai nothing. They had made him into a hybrid freak and then disregarded him for his advancements. They had used him and then cast him aside.

The humans were a different story. If they made it onto the ship, they would need help to control it. They would need help to understand it and to make it function. They would come to depend on him, and that was something that he could use. Not only to get revenge on Gr'el but to strike back at the Domo'dahm and turn the course of his misfortune.

He lifted his hand away, watching as the fighter slid out of the hangar, through the shield and into space. The starship was drawing near, coming right at him, ready to force its way into the fortress. He scrambled from the control room, climbing out and running back toward the transport beam. He needed to get down to the base level. He would have one good opportunity to make this work.

He was halfway there when the impact came. He could sense it before he felt it, the lek'shah phasing as it was struck. Then the shockwave came, powerful enough that the entire fortress groaned in pain, substantial enough that it knocked him off his feet. He stayed on his hands and knees for a moment, waiting to see if the blow was enough to destroy them. When there was no sign of critical failure, when the ship maintained both power and life support, he rose once more and continued his run.

The bek'hai had used him. He would use the humans, first for revenge, and then to regain control.

Then he would end them all for good.

59

THEODORE LOOKED UP. SMOKE WAS filling the bridge, the equipment sparking and shorting, strained beyond its limits at the impact. His chest hurt where the emergency straps had dug into it, reminding him that he had nearly been strained beyond his limit.

Nearly, but not quite.

The ship still had emergency power. He had no idea how. It was some kind of miracle in itself.

"Maggie, you there?" he said, coughing.

"Yes, General," the computer replied, oblivious to their state.

"How's the atmosphere outside?"

"Eighty percent oxygen, fifteen percent nitrogen. Other components include water vapor, argon, helium, and an unidentified gas."

It was breathable, as he suspected. That was good enough. "Patch me in with Colonel Graham."

"Yes, General."

"Colonel," Theodore said. "Status report."

"A little shaken, General," Graham replied. "We're ready to move."

"Do it. Secure the perimeter. We'll meet you outside."

"Maggie, sound the evac." He paused to cough again. "Everybody okay up there?"

A round of affirmatives greeted him.

"We need to get off this thing. Follow along behind me, make sure you grab a gun on the way out. If they're gone before you get there, stay with the people who are armed."

"Yes, sir," the crew replied.

Theodore unstrapped himself, and then transferred into his chair. Colonel Choi appeared beside it.

"Can you get the locks for me, Colonel?" he asked.

She bent down to release the chair from the floor. The rest of the bridge crew was assembling in front of them. He counted heads, happy to see they were all up and about.

"Stay alert. We made it this far, but we haven't won a damn thing yet."

He turned the chair, rolling it from the bridge and out into the corridor. This part of the ship was vacant; the personnel already shuffled to prepare for the incursion. They had managed to survive the crash landing on the alien ship; now they needed to find a way to gain control of it. The Dread used clones for everything, so there had to be a means for a human to pilot it.

And if a human could pilot it, then he damn well could.

The corridors were hazy, and the smell of burning wires and metal was thick in the air. The emergency lighting cast a shadow of light along the haze, which would have made the Magellan eerie if it weren't so familiar. Theodore cursed as they came across the body of one of the crew, who hadn't managed to buckle up in time.

Someone behind him cried out at the sight. Someone else vomited. He couldn't blame them. He tensed his own stomach to keep his emotions in check. This was war. Casualties happened. May God have mercy on their souls.

They kept going, moving at a light run. Theodore had no idea what kind of defenses the Dread were going to have. Unless they had brought the ship full-stop in a hurry, they had a limited amount of time before they could back up into the crease through the dead zone, or move the ship out of it completely. The only shot they had was to hit the enemy while they were still vulnerable.

"General, this is Sergeant Hafizi. Delta Squad is on the ground outside. The area is clear and secure."

His voice was choppy through the damaged comm system.

"This is Graham. Beta squad is out and clear."

"General, this is Alpha Squadron Leader. There's no activity outside the fortress. I don't think they have any other fighters."

Theodore looked over at Choi. "No more pilots, more like," he said. "Something fishy's going on here. I'm not complaining, but I expected this to be a little harder."

"Me, too," Choi replied.

"Maggie, pass a message to Gabriel to bring his squad in. If they had more Bats to send at us, they would have done it already, and we may need the extra hands on the ground."

"Yes, General."

"Send a message to Hafizi, too. Get his team moving into position to cover wherever Beta ain't."

"Yes, General."

They reached the emergency stairwell. Choi, Abdullah, and Locke all helped lift his chair, carrying him down the steps. He hated that they had to do it, but he stayed silent. Now wasn't the time to complain about being independent.

"General, Alpha Squadron is home," Gabriel said through the comm.

"Heh. Home? We'll see about that. Vacation rental, more like."

It took almost five minutes for them to get down the stairwell to the belly of the ship, where the emergency ground access was located. For each second of each minute, Theodore waited to hear from Hafizi that they were taking heavy fire, or from Graham that they were under attack. No such messages came. It was almost as if the Dread were hiding.

Or waiting.

Whichever it was, he didn't like it.

Sergeant Diallo was waiting at the exit with Guy, Sarah, and Reza. She was holding their single Dread weapon.

"General," she said, saluting as he approached.

"Sergeant. That thing still work?"

"Yes, sir," Reza said.

Theodore spun his chair to face them. "I don't have the words to express my gratitude over what you three have accomplished here. I'm proud as heck of each and every one of you, and grateful to have you on my ship. Let's not get too comfy, though; we're not of the swamp just yet."

"Yes, sir," they replied.

"The others are already on the ground, sir," Diallo said.

"No sign of the enemy?"

"Not yet. I think they're afraid of us."

"I think they're working out a nice, proper welcome. And I don't mean good old-fashioned southern hospitality. Maggie, how long until we clear the dead zone?"

"Three minutes, General."

"That's about how long I think we have. Maggie, set yourself to secure standby and power down. Unlock only by command of myself, Colonel Choi, or Major St. Martin."

"Yes, General. It was nice to see you again, General. Farewell."

"Farewell, Maggie."

The emergency lighting dimmed further as the Magellan began to shut down. Theodore stayed behind Diallo as they moved down the ramp to the floor of the Dread fortress. He could see most of the crew assembled beneath them, many of them armed and all of them organized and alert, taking cover behind whatever they could find, their weapons trained on the apparent exits to the hangar.

He saw Gabriel and his dog crouched next to Lieutenant Bale, unarmed but still watching the ingress points. He was alive and unharmed. He could only hope he would stay that way.

"General," Colonel Graham said when he reached the ground. "I've got everyone organized. How do you want to do this?"

"These couillons must have a bridge or a control room or something somewhere in here. We move together, one unit until we find it. We've got one gun that can hurt them, and it needs to go to the best shot." He turned to Sergeant Diallo. "Is that you, Sergeant?"

"Yes, sir," Diallo replied.

"Good woman." Theodore coughed slightly before raising his voice. "All right boys and girls, this is it. I think the fact that we're being ignored in here is a good start. We're still alive, and I plan for us to stay that way. We've got the Dread rifle; now the mission is to find whatever passes for a CIC around here and take control of it. We cut off the head, the rest of the snake will be left flopping around. Any questions?"

Nobody said anything, though they all turned his way, their expressions clearly reflecting the respect they had for him. Even Gabriel. Especially Gabriel. He wanted to go over to his boy, but he wasn't his son right now. He was just another soldier.

"In that case, let's-"

One of the doors to their right slid open, cutting him off. Diallo ducked in front of him, protecting him while raising the Dread rifle to fire back at the incoming soldiers. The rest of his crew reacted in kind, those with weapons training them on the door, the remainder taking cover.

Except there were no incoming soldiers. At first, nothing came through the door. It sat open, the corridor behind it vacant.

Then a single form appeared from the shadows. It was taller and leaner than an average human, with long fingers and small ridges on the sides of its head. It was wearing a skintight suit of some kind and was holding a rifle by the barrel, hands up and out in a submissive posture. It smiled at them as it entered the hangar, a crooked smile that revealed white human teeth.

It scanned the line, starting with Theodore and sweeping across their defensive positions. It stopped when its eyes fell on Gabriel.

"There you are," it said. "The Heil'shur. Much honor and respect to you. My name is Tea'va dur Orin'ek." It bowed low before them. "I am humbly indebted to you for your intercession, and wish to offer myself to you in service."

60

GABRIEL STARED AT THE DREAD standing in front of him along with the rest of the crew. Most of them had never seen the enemy who stole their home world at all. Gabriel had never seen one outside of their impenetrable armor.

Seconds passed in tense silence. The alien, Tea'va, waited motionless for Gabriel to respond to his offer. To respond at all. Gabriel was too stunned to speak. The fact that their opponent looked so human was one shock. That Tea'va had offered to help them was another. This whole mission had felt as if it were being guided by an invisible hand. His mother's, maybe? But this?

This was something else entirely.

He dared a quick glance over to his father, who was already looking back at him. The General nodded shortly, giving him permission to interact.

"Heil'shur?" he said.

"It means honored adversary," Tea'va replied. "We have met before. In the dark above the planet called Earth."

"We've met before? You mean you're a pilot?"

"Yes. You have escaped from me many times. Your skill is unmatched among both our races."

Gabriel wasn't so sure about that. He had seen the damage to his fighter when he climbed out of it. It was luck, not skill.

"Why are you here? Why offer us your help? What are you hoping to achieve?"

"As I said, I wish to offer my services. I am lor'el on this ship. An outcast. Mistreated and dishonored for my appearance. I have done all that they ask, and yet they say I am too human. If I am too human, if I am a failure for that, then I shall become a human." He laughed in a shrill cackle. "Revenge, Heil'shur. That is what I hope to achieve. Revenge against the bek'hai who have stolen your world, and betrayed me."

"And we're just supposed to believe that?" Gabriel asked. He had no idea what the enemy's tactics looked like. Would they send a single combatant in to distract them?

"No. Only a gruk would do so," Tea'va said. "I've brought you something. Two things."

He raised his hands a little higher and then threw his rifle toward Gabriel. Gabriel reached up and caught it, lowering it and checking it. It was active.

"I can take you to more," Tea'va said. "I also have this."

He backed away again, beyond the entrance to the hangar. The movement caused the other members of the crew to tense.

"Easy," Gabriel said to those around him. "Take it easy."

Tea'va dragged something into view. A dead Dread. He held it up to them so they could see he had shot it in the head. Then he dropped it unceremoniously to the floor.

"This one and five others were on their way here, to fortify this position and prepare for the ambush. I destroyed them for you, as a sign of my loyalty if you will have it."

Gabriel looked to his father again. This wasn't his decision to make. It was Theodore's.

His father tapped his wrist. They didn't have a lot of time.

That was all he did. He didn't provide a yes or a no. He was leaving Gabriel to make the decision for them. Trusting his instincts.

They didn't have many options. They had managed to get on board the ship, which was a miracle in itself. But they still didn't know where to go, what kind of opposition they would run into, nothing. What were their chances if they went in blind? Minimal, and they all knew it. They had done it because they were desperate, not because it was ideal. If this Dread, this Tea'va, was leading them into a trap, they were goners, but they would have likely been goners anyway. If he really did intend to help them? They might be able to pull off one of the greatest military victories of all time.

"Very well, Tea'va. I accept your offer. If revenge is what you're after, then there will be plenty of opportunities for you to get it."

The Dread smiled again. Gabriel couldn't help but recoil slightly at the sight of it. It was so close to human, and yet alien enough that his mind couldn't quite accept it.

"They will be coming when the Ishur exits the void," Tea'va said. "When your weapons will be ineffective against them once more. Your tactics and timing were impressive. Was it your idea?"

"My father's," Gabriel said.

"Father?" Tea'va replied. "I have heard of this thing. Bek'hai have no fathers. What you did with your shields, I did not believe it was possible." He made a clicking noise that seemed impressed. "Come. We must reach the armory before Gr'el can adjust to my treachery. He will be reinforcing this position with the few units he has to spare."

Few units to spare? That sounded promising. Gabriel glanced over at Theodore again. The General smiled.

"You heard the Dread," his father said. "Form up and move out. O'Dea, run on over to the other side of Maggie and get Hafizi and Beta in line behind us."

"Yes, sir," Daphne said, rushing away from the scene.

"According to my watch we've got less than a minute," Theodore said.

"Is this your Si'dahm?" Tea'va asked. "Your second in command?"

"No," Gabriel replied. "General St. Martin is the leader of our forces."

Tea'va faced Theodore, sweeping low again, his head down in a submissive pose. "My apologies, Dahm St. Martin."

"Don't worry about it," Theodore said. "Just get us some guns, and you and me will be best friends forever."

"As you command, Dahm St. Martin. This way."

Tea'va moved back across the threshold, out of the hangar. The entire crew of the Magellan hesitated to follow, Gabriel included. It was one thing to verbally accept this apparently traitorous enemy's help. It was another to follow him into the unknown.

"Don't just stand there lallygagging," Theodore said. "We doubled down; now it's time to show our hand." He began rolling forward ahead of them. Sergeant Diallo was caught off guard, but she hurried to catch up.

Gabriel got in motion as well, moving from his cover behind a Dread starfighter. Colonel Graham fell in beside him, along with Bale and Celia.

The Dread stood a dozen meters ahead of them, at the intersection of another corridor. He waited for Theodore and Gabriel to reach him before pointing out the others he had killed, all with a single wound to the head.

Gabriel was as impressed with Tea'va as Tea'va had seemed to be with him. The Dread was not only a pilot, but he was also a crack shot. Gabriel wished he could say the same about his ground combat skills.

"We go that way. We will cross three more corridors to reach the hub. There will be a green light in the center. It is a transport beam. Lower your hands to go down. This one will take you to the lowest deck, where the main armory is located. Pass word to the others in your cell. Once we have taken the weapons, I will lead you to the bridge. Expect strong resistance there."

"How many soldiers does this Gr'el fellow have?" Theodore asked.

"Fortunately for you, not anywhere near as many as he had before. He seized control of this ship from its original commander and destroyed every drumhr and lor'hai whose loyalty was questionable. That is why he is holding back. He won't risk what he has remaining when he can hold out for a better overall position."

"I would do the same thing," Theodore said.

"Gr'el didn't question your loyalty?" Gabriel asked.

"Of course, he did. I was this ship's original commander. He betrayed me with the blessing of the Domo'dahm, our leader, because of my humanity. Your attack allowed me to break free. That is why I owe you a debt of gratitude. Your numbers are nearly equal to his. If we can reach the armory, you will almost be on even-"

Tea'va stopped speaking, darting forward and shoving Gabriel back against the wall. Gabriel felt his stomach clench, waiting for the killing blow. A plasma bolt whizzed past him, right where he had been standing a moment before. Another followed, striking the corner of the intersection as Tea'va released him and urged them back.

Shouts went up from the rear of the rebel forces, followed by opposing bursts of plasma and heavy ions.

The Dread starship was out of the dead zone, and the reinforcements had arrived.

61

"Damn it," Theodore said, throwing his chair back against the wall and turning his head toward the rear of their column. "We need one of those guns back there. Diallo, make it happen."

Sergeant Diallo was crouched beside Theodore, positioned in front of him to take any wayward shots that managed to come near.

"Sir, I should stay with you," she said.

"Are you questioning me during a firefight, Sergeant?" Theodore roared. "I'll court martial you right here."

Diallo headed away at a run, carrying the Dread rifle toward the rear. Gabriel glanced back at her before returning his attention to the incoming forces.

The attack had come from both ends at once, the enemy clones moving in from the intersecting corridors. There was little cover. Nowhere to hide. The area was filled with shouts and cries and screams, with red and blue bolts of energy. The clones weren't wearing armor, but the front line was carrying shields made of the same impenetrable black material and using them to absorb the human counterattack.

Gabriel fired the Dread rifle, impressed by the lack of kick and the ease of use. His bolt struck one of the shields, leaving a score mark in it but not piercing through in one blast. He fired three more times with similar results. A return bolt flashed past him, and one of the crew members cried out a few feet away.

"We're getting chewed apart out here," Theodore said. "We need to retreat and get some cover." He spun on one wheel. "Graham," he bellowed. "Get everybody moving back to the hangar."

"Yes, sir," Graham shouted. The Colonel was pressed against the wall, firing ahead at the clones.

"So much for reaching the armory," Theodore said. "You were too slow getting to us."

Tea'va made a face. Gabriel thought he saw a hint of anger, but it was gone in an instant. "You were too slow in your landing, Dahm St. Martin," the Dread replied calmly. "We must change our tactics if you want your people to live. Send them back. We will go forward."

Gabriel looked back over his shoulder. Diallo was positioned in the intersection, putting down cover fire across the corridor with the Dread rifle and keeping the enemy fire somewhat suppressed. He could see most of the crew retreating, but also dozens of men and women already motionless on the ground. He had known each and every one of them by name. Now they were gone, just like that. He felt a pain in his chest. Where was Miranda? A spike of fear threatened his composure. He couldn't worry about her now.

A squad of soldiers was moving in their direction. Delta.

"Sir," Sergeant Hafizi said, saluting as he reached them. "Diallo sent me to help get you out safe."

"We aren't going out," Theodore replied. "We're going ahead."

"Sir, I don't think-"

"Am I the General here?" Theodore snapped. "Get in line, soldier."

"Yes, sir," Hafizi replied.

Gabriel saw Tea'va smile. The Dread was amused.

"So how do we get out of this?" Gabriel asked.

"Back away down the corridor," Tea'va replied.

"We'll get caught in the center. Boxed in."

"You can trust me and live, or question and die."

"Do it," Theodore said. "Our fate is in God's hands now."

They began backing up, clearing the intersection and avoiding further fire. Gabriel noticed Reza was with them as they did. How did the scientist end up at the front of the line? There was no time to ask him.

"Cover the rear," Tea'va said. He flexed his hands and began moving forward.

"You're going after them unarmed?" Gabriel asked.

"They are lor'hai. I am pur'dahm."

It was the only explanation he gave. Then he rushed forward, leaping across the corridor, hitting the wall with his feet and springing back out of sight. A rush of plasma crossed the hallway, followed by screams.

Gabriel turned to face the second intersection. The enemy was drawing closer, leaving Diallo on the opposite side, trying to keep them at bay. Too many of their crew were on the ground in the middle of it all. He didn't want to look at them, terrified of who he would find in the mix. Miranda? Daphne? Colonel Choi?

He made it to the intersection and began shooting in the opposite direction as the Sergeant. The combined force was enough to temporarily halt the attack, the incoming enemy clones remaining cautious. They could afford to be patient.

"Heil'shur," he heard Tea'va say a few seconds later. He turned to the Dread, who was holding one of the shields in one hand, a plasma rifle in the other. His clothing was burned, but he appeared unharmed.

"Diallo," Theodore said. "Take that thing and get it back to the others. Bar the door to the Magellan with it if you have to."

"Sir?"

"If we can take the ship, we can stop the attack. Ain't that right?"

Tea'va nodded, throwing both the shield and the rifle across the intersection. Diallo scooped up both and began retreating to the hangar. Gabriel could hear more screams from back there, as the Dread forces began closing in around them. He hoped it would be enough to save them.

"This way," Tea'va said, leading them forward again. He ran ahead, his long legs carrying him quickly. He paused at the intersection, checked it, and burst forward again.

Gabriel ran behind the Dread, while the soldiers of Delta Squad kept his father surrounded. Reza stayed close to them, keeping pace.

They crossed the corridors, reaching a longer hallway illuminated by a green beam of light in the center. The transport beam. Tea'va stopped in front of it, waving them past. "The bridge is twenty decks up."

"What about the armory?" Theodore said.

"It will be fortified beyond our capacity to take it. Gr'el reacted more quickly than I estimated. He must have guessed I am helping you."

"Won't the bridge be fortified as well?" Gabriel said.

"Yes. There is another way. One he won't expect. Remember. Raise your hands to go up, try to count the floors. Otherwise, we will be separated."

"Hafizi, here," Gabriel said, handing his rifle to the Sergeant. "Take point."

"Yes, sir," Hafizi replied. He moved toward the transport beam with the squad. They stepped inside, seeming to dematerialize as they did.

"That's some serious voodoo," Theodore said.

"Voodoo?" Tea'va replied.

"I'll explain later." He rolled into the light and vanished.

Gabriel waited for Reza to go through, and then he joined them, stepping into the beam with Tea'va. He looked up, feeling a rush of something for just a second before it all stopped. He stepped forward, coming out into an identical corridor behind Delta Squad and the others. He was nearly hit in the face by an incoming plasma bolt as he did, finding them engaged by another group of clones. The Dread soldiers didn't have a shield to protect them, so they hid around the corners, popping out to attack. Hafizi's team returned fire when they did, keeping them honest. One of Delta's soldiers was down directly in front of Theodore's chair. The unfortunate crewman had likely saved his father's life.

"We must get down this corridor," Tea'va said. "There is a rear access channel to the bridge beyond that point. Even if Gr'el knows about it, which I doubt, it will be difficult to defend in numbers. We can use it to circumvent any defensive positions he has created."

"Maybe we can go another way?" Gabriel said, ducking down as another plasma bolt flew past.

"There is no other way, Heil'shur." The Dread smiled again. It was less alarming now that Gabriel had seen it a few times. "If we die, we die with honor. Yes?"

"Yeah. I guess so."

"You heard him," Theodore said. "We have to push forward and break through the defenses. This ain't no time to be yellow. Let's show these couillons who we are."

"Yes, sir," Hafizi replied. "Delta, we're going in."

The Sergeant took a step forward. A plasma bolt caught him right in the chest, making a sizzling noise as it burned into his flesh. The force of it knocked him to the ground, and he landed dead on his back.

Another soldier was hit a moment later, and he fell with a shout, coming to rest at Gabriel's feet. He heard Tea'va growl beside him, and then the Dread was rushing the enemy position again, pausing momentarily to grab Hafizi's fallen rifle.

"Gabriel," Theodore said. Gabriel looked at his father. He was holding his antique handgun out to him. "I can't roll and shoot at the same time, son. You've already made me prouder than any man has any right to be. Don't be afraid."

He knew what his father was suggesting. He didn't hesitate. There were no other choices left.

He grabbed the pistol, rushing down the hallway behind the Dread warrior.

62

THE VOLUME OF FIRE WAS intense. Plasma bolts streaked past Gabriel, and he did his best to use his skills as a pilot to try to throw the aim of the enemy soldiers, jerking side to side as he ran, following behind Tea'va. He could feel the heat of the energy going past his face, past his arms and legs. One bolt caught the edge of his shoulder, and he clenched his teeth at the burn of it on his arm. He didn't let it slow him. Somehow, some way, he was going to make it through the barrage. They hadn't come this far to lose now.

Tea'va paced ahead of him, moving so much faster than a human. He dropped as he neared the enemy position, sliding forward on his back toward the thick of it. One of the clones rose to track him, and Gabriel aimed and fired, the kick of the gun nearly pulling it from his hand. The shot hit the clone in the arm, the force enough to spin him around. A second clone broke cover and took aim at Gabriel. Gabriel managed to swing the ancient pistol back toward the enemy, pulling the trigger and watching as the clone's entire chest exploded out from the force of the impact.

The rest of the enemy soldiers were down by the time he reached them, with Tea'va standing in the center.

"Much respect, Heil'shur," Tea'va said.

"Much respect," Gabriel replied.

The others caught up to them a moment later. His father, Reza, and the two remaining soldiers, Corporals Kilani and Bush.

"Nice work, Major," Theodore said.

"Thank you, sir," Gabriel replied.

"This way," Tea'va said. "Do not delay."

They resumed their frantic pace through the fortress, passing a number of empty corridors and sealed doors until they reached what looked to Gabriel to be a solid wall. Tea'va waved his hand in front of it, and a previously invisible hatch slid open.

"In here," he said.

Gabriel leaned in. The passage was small and narrow.

Too narrow for his father to follow.

"That isn't going to work," Gabriel said.

Tea'va moved back out into the corridor, his expression confused at first until his eyes landed on Theodore. Again, Gabriel thought he caught a flash of anger from the Dread, but he wasn't sure.

"Come," he said, quickly crossing to a closed door. It slid open ahead of him, revealing a bare room with only a small bed against the wall. "Your Dahm can wait for us here. It will be safe."

"What?" Gabriel said. "I'm not leaving him behind. Forget it. Find another way, Tea'va."

"There is no other way, Heil'shur. There are only five of us, and still many dozens of soldiers blocking our path to the bridge. Gr'el may know this route, but there is a second further down that I am sure he does not. We must take the first to reach the second, and if your Dahm cannot follow, then he must remain."

"No," Gabriel said. "I'm not leaving him."

"Excuse me, Major," Theodore said. "That isn't your call."

"General," Gabriel said.

"I appreciate that you care, Gabe, but I'm an Old Gator, and not suited for this kind of mission. We both know that. You need to leave me here. If Tea'va says it's safe, then it's safe. I need you to go and get me that bridge.

That's an order, Major."

Gabriel gritted his teeth. He didn't like it at all, but orders were orders. "Yes, sir," he said. He held out the antique pistol. "At least take this."

"No. You might need it. Nobody's going to come and check this little cubby hole of a room for a human with no legs. I'll be perfectly fine. Capture the bridge, and then come back and get me, okay?"

Gabriel withdrew the gun. "Okay." More words flowed to the tip of his tongue, and he was tempted to hold them back. He didn't want any regrets. "I love you, Dad."

Theodore smiled. "I love you too, Gabe. Go and make your mother proud."

"Yes, sir."

"Uh, sir," Reza said. "If you don't mind, I think I'd rather stay here with you."

"Go ahead and take a seat, Mr. Mokri," Theodore replied. "Good hunting, Major. Good hunting all of you."

Gabriel backed out of the room. The hatch slid closed in front of him. He turned to Tea'va. "Okay. Let's go."

Tea'va stared at him for a moment. He seemed confused by the exchange, but he didn't say anything. He brought them back to the hatch, waving them in once more. As soon as they were all inside, the hatch closed, bathing them in near complete darkness.

"I can't see anything," Corporal Kalani said.

"Me neither," Gabriel replied. "Tea'va, how are we supposed to do this blind?"

"I can see, Heil'shur. Put your hand along the wall and follow my voice."

Gabriel put his hand out, touching the side of the passage. The material tingled against his fingertips, as though it were holding an electrical charge. Based on what he had learned of the Dread's shields, maybe it was.

"The wall will curve slightly as we move ahead. Then it will continue straight for some distance. Move as quickly as you can."

Gabriel followed Tea'va's voice, letting the Dread guide them through the passage. They reached the end a few minutes later, with no sign of any opposition.

"Curious," Gabriel thought he heard Tea'va say beneath his breath. It didn't seem that he was expecting to make it this far without being attacked.

A new door slid open and light filtered into the space once more. Gabriel squinted his eyes against it, giving them a moment to adjust. Tea'va's form faded into view beyond the bright light.

"We cross here, to there. This route will evacuate a short distance in front of the bridge. You must adjust to the light quickly."

"We'll do the best we can," Gabriel said.

Tea'va opened the second door and once more directed them in. They followed him, using his voice to make their way through the maintenance corridor. Again, they reached their destination without interruption.

"I do not know what waits beyond this door," Tea'va whispered to him. "The bridge will be on your right. I expect Gr'el's defenses to be organized to the left, most likely clones hiding behind lek'shah shields. Or perhaps he has gathered the few drumhr warriors who were loyal to him here. We will only have a few seconds to use the surprise to our advantage, but they will be vulnerable from behind. Do you understand?"

"Yes," Gabriel said. He tightened his grip on his father's gun. "We're ready."

He could hear Tea'va shift ahead of him. A moment later, the door slid open, and the light began filtering in again. Gabriel squinted his eyes to fight through the blinding glare, moving out into the corridor and turning to the left, aiming the pistol, ready to begin shooting whatever was there in the back.

Except there was nothing there. No fortifications. No soldiers. No shields.

He heard Tea'va mutter something foreign behind him, the Dread's tone of voice surprised and confused. He clearly hadn't been expecting this either.

The door behind them slid open. Gabriel turned toward it just in time to see two plasma bolts fire from behind it, one striking Corporal Kalani, the other hitting Corporal Bush. Both soldiers dropped to the floor.

Then a dozen plasma rifles were trained on them, held not by the clone soldiers Gabriel had seen below, but by two other types of clones. Both were female. One was heavyset, with large breasts and hips and a plump face. The other was like the one he had seen on Earth. The spitting image of his mother.

He felt a chill tingle down his spine at the sight of the four identical copies of Juliet St. Martin. They were each wearing long, dark robes, their hair tied back and up. One of them was wearing a shimmering blue pin, and from the way she stood it was clear she was superior to the others.

He was so surprised by them that he didn't notice the Dread standing in the center of them right away. He was a larger, uglier version of Tea'va, his skin lighter, his hair longer, the bony ridges across his head more prominent. he reminded Gabriel of an image Theodore had shown him once of a real alligator.

"Tea'va," the Dread warrior said in thick English. "I would despise you so much more if you weren't so predictable."

63

"GR'EL," TEA'VA SAID. "WHAT HAVE you done?"

"What do you mean?" the Dread asked.

"You know what I mean. The Mothers."

"The Mothers are a tool, Tea'va. Like all tools, it only takes a creative mind to find different uses for them. Do you like what I've done with mine?"

"The Domo'dahm-"

"The Domo'dahm has no dominion out here, Tea'va. You know that."

"He trusted you."

"He didn't trust you. He told me that you would plot against him the moment you were out of Earth's orbit. That you were too human, and that humanity would lead you to resent him and the other pur'dahm for our superiority. He tasked me with removing you quietly, which I have tried to do. Honor and respect for your ability to evade capture, but you are the lowest of the lor'el for running instead of retiring yourself."

"You don't seek to remove me on the wishes of the Domo'dahm. You are plotting to overthrow him yourself, to return with this ship and an army of lor'hai." He thrust his finger out at the Mothers. "Their minds are unfit for the Soldier programming."

"They have taken to it rather well," the Julict clone with the blue pin said.

"Better than I had hoped," Gr'el said. "In any case, none of that is your concern, Tea'va. You are nothing now. You no longer exist to the bek'hai."

"I am the future of our race," Tea'va said.

"No. You are the mistake of an overzealous scientist who took the human genome too far. Rorn'el allowed you to survive because of your potential to reproduce naturally. But you denied the one thing that set you apart, the one thing that might have put you back into his favor, especially after your repeated failures against the Heil'shur." Gr'el looked at Gabriel for the first time. "Honor and respect to a worthy adversary," he said, bowing. "I am Gr'el, Dahm of the Ishur."

Gabriel didn't respond to the greeting. He was trying to put together the pieces of the Dread's conversation, to understand the complete picture of what was really happening on the fortress. He was starting to feel as though for all of their efforts, and for every member of the crew they had lost, their offensive was inconsequential to the infighting that appeared to be going on. Maybe it was. Gr'el had clearly been expecting Tea'va to lead them here. He had been waiting to get the drop on the traitor.

Tea'va was seething next to him, his teeth bared, his pale face darkened. "Mistake?" he hissed. "You owe me Hesh dur bek for words such as those."

"Honor of battle?" Gr'el said. "You have no honor, Tea'va. You surrendered. You agreed to retirement. You didn't even have the courage to go through with it."

"Who are you to speak of honor and courage? You betrayed me. Worse, you sent a Mother to assassinate me instead of trying to do it yourself. A Mother!"

Tea'va took a step forward. The clones raised their weapons, signaling their warning.

"Careful, Tea'va," Gr'el said. "The only reason I haven't killed you already is because I'm enjoying the embarrassment of your defeat. A Mother is all you are worth. I would never dirty my hands with you."

Tea'va's face gnarled in rage, but he stood his ground, drawing a laugh

287

from the other Dread.

"Even now, you care too much for your life to honor it by attacking me." Gr'el looked over at Gabriel again. "You will make an excellent prize. I have no doubt your genetics are of superior quality. Zoelle, this one should be an improvement for the programming, should it not?"

The Juliet clone with the blue pin nodded. "Yes, my Dahm. The Heil'shur is assuredly of impressive genetic stock."

"You would know," Gabriel said. "Or rather the woman whose life was claimed in your making would know."

"What do you mean?" Gr'el asked.

"My name is Gabriel St. Martin," Gabriel said, feeling his hands clenching into fists. His initial fear of the situation was quickly changing to a cold anger. "My mother was Juliet St. Martin. Does that name mean anything to you?"

The Juliet clones all gasped as one. Gr'el seemed surprised as well, his inhuman smile growing even larger at the news. "You are a child of the un'hai? A natural born child? You are a more valuable prize than I could have ever imagined."

"I don't know what you've done to her," Gabriel said, his sudden anger exploding as he spoke. His hand came up, wrapping around the crucifix below his flight suit, clenching it tightly."You and your Domo'dick, or whatever you call him. My mother was kind and gentle, compassionate and intelligent. She wasn't a traitor. She wasn't a killer. She didn't use humankind like a toy to program to her whims, or anyone else's. She wasn't an inconsequential thing, or a tool to be used as a means to your own ends. You've twisted her memory into something foul. You've soiled everything she stood for. You son of a bitch."

He acted without thinking then, springing forward toward the Dread. Unlike Tea'va, he didn't care if that meant dying. The other clone of her he had met, Ehri, was helping the rebellion. She was fighting for humankind the way Juliet St. Martin would have. He didn't know how or why, but she was.

There had been no one to defend his mother's honor before.

There was now.

He got closer to Gr'el than he expected, almost reaching him before one of the Mothers came from the side, slamming him in the head with the butt of her rifle. He tumbled sideways onto the floor, a sharp pain in his jaw.

"Be careful, druk'shur," Gr'el shouted. "You'll damage him."

"My apologies, Dahm Gr'el," the clone replied, lowering her head.

Gabriel pushed himself into a seated position, clenching his teeth as he did. He looked back at Gr'el, and then beyond him to the Juliet clones. He froze when he noticed that Zoelle was staring right at him, a sudden look of concern on her face. It vanished a moment later.

Was he imagining things?

"And what do you intend to do with me?" Tea'va said.

Gr'el glanced over at Tea'va. "Are you still here?" He reached out, grabbing a rifle from one of the clones. "You've ceased being amusing, lor'el."

He pulled the trigger at the same time Gabriel hit his shoulder, sending the plasma bolt wide. Gr'el pivoted with the blow, swinging the weapon back around and slamming it hard into Gabriel's gut. Gabriel doubled over, the air stolen from his chest. He put his hand on the floor to steady himself. He had to get up. To keep fighting. His mother's memory demanded it.

He felt Gr'el's long fingers wrap around his neck. Then he was lifted off the ground, held by the throat and unable to breathe. It didn't matter what he wanted. His strength was vastly inferior to the Dread's.

"How dare you touch me," Gr'el growled, the pressure from his hands increasing. "I had forgotten how willful the un'hai was rumored to be, and what a poor pur'hai she was. It was only the Domo'dahm's weakness that allowed her to become so revered."

He let go. Gabriel fell to the ground again, gasping for air.

Gr'el aimed his rifle again, this time at Gabriel. "Honor and respect to you for your prowess in battle, Heil'shur. Your courage is commendable. I see now that you will be more trouble than you're worth. I would sooner destroy you and your fellow humans than have your lor'hai aboard my ship, or as part of my bek'hai empire."

"My. Name. Is. Gabriel St. Martin," Gabriel gasped, trying to stand again. "Son of Theodore and Juliet St. Martin. Remember that, asshole."

"Very well, Gabriel-"

A small fist came from Gr'el's left, hitting him square across the jaw with enough force to knock him to the ground. Gabriel's eyes darted to his attacker. The Juliet clone he had called Zoelle.

"You wanted your Hesh dur bek, Tea'va," she said. "Now is your chance."

64

"ZOELLE?" GR'EL SAID, HIS WORDS muffled by his broken jaw. "Traitor. Kill her. Kill the Scientists."

The Mothers raised their rifles, turning them toward the Juliets.

Tea'va sprang at Gr'el, kicking him in the face before he could recover and sending him rolling across the floor.

Gabriel pushed aside his shock, forcing himself to his feet.

Zoelle turned on the closest Mother, punching her hard in the stomach, and then in the face, knocking her down.

The plasma followed, Mothers and Scientists shooting at one another at point-blank range. Gabriel didn't know what the difference was between like clones, but Zoelle not only held herself as superior, she clearly was. She danced to the side as a plasma bolt skimmed her robes, twirling and moving forward, grabbing the Mother's arms and lifting them, so the next shot went to the ceiling. She turned again, gathering the Mother's weight and pulling, throwing her over her shoulder while capturing her rifle. The Mother tried to get up, but couldn't before Zoelle shot her.

A second Mother was lining up a shot behind Zoelle. Gabriel stumbled forward, slamming into the clone and falling on top of her. She struggled beneath him while he tried to pin her arms. She pushed back, throwing him aside with a strength he couldn't believe.

It didn't matter. One of the Scientists was over her a moment later, firing down into her chest. She was killed before Gabriel could blink, caught with a plasma blast by a nearby enemy. That Mother went down in a shrill cry, hit by another plasma bolt, this one fired by Zoelle.

Gabriel got back to his feet, finding Gr'el and Tea'va squaring off a few meters away. The two Dread warriors circled one another, their teeth bared like animals, their hands out with fingers curled as if they were claws.

Then Gr'el moved in on Tea'va, his hands a blur as he made a series of quick strikes, slapping and punching at the other Dread. Tea'va moved in time to the attack, shifting his balance and either knocking aside the blows or adjusting to allow them to land harmlessly. He survived the onslaught before countering with a fury of his own, pushing back against Gr'el with a long series of kicks and punches that bore similarity to streams Gabriel had seen of human martial arts. The difference was in the power and quickness of the movements. The Dread were a blur as they attacked and counter-attacked one another in near silence.

And then Tea'va seemed to get the better of Gr'el. He slipped behind his rival, locking a hand around his neck and an arm around his chest. The larger Dread writhed beneath the grip, trying to find purchase on the ground, trying to find leverage to turn the hold.

Tea'va grunted as he bent backward, lifting Gr'el from the ground. Gr'el tried to punch him from behind, landing ineffective blows against his sides. Gr'el also attempted to slam him in the face with the back of his head, but it was just out of reach.

"You are a disgrace to the bek'hai," Gr'el said, his voice growing weak. "There is no honor for you in this killing, Tea'va."

"I need no honor from you," Tea'va replied. "All I need is for you to expire. The true betrayal belongs to you and the Domo'dahm."

Gr'el tried to say something else, but couldn't manage it. He gurgled instead, and then shuddered one last time before falling still.

Tea'va dropped his corpse to the floor.

A silence fell over the ship. The battle between the clones was over as well. None of the Mothers were standing. Two of the Scientists remained, including Zoelle. She was walking toward him from his left. Tea'va was coming toward him from his right.

"Zoelle," Tea'va said.

She raised her hand to Tea'va, ignoring the Dread and locking eyes with Gabriel. "Gabriel St. Martin," she said, a tear running from her eye. "I am Zoelle dur Tuhrik, Dahm of the Ishur."

"You are not Dahm," Tea'va said. "Lor'hai cannot be Dahm."

She continued to ignore him. "My ship is yours, Gabriel. As is my life. It is an honor to meet the son of the un'hai."

She fell to her knees in front of him, bowing her head. The other Juliet clone did the same behind her.

Gabriel opened his mouth, catching himself before he called her mother. "I. I need you to call off the attack on my people," he said, finding it hard to breathe.

Zoelle looked back at the other clone, who headed off toward the bridge. "It will be done."

"You have no authority," Tea'va said.

Gabriel turned on the Dread. "What are your intentions, Tea'va?" he snapped. "You pledged yourself to me to help you get revenge, and now you have it. Will you betray me as he betrayed you? If so, do it now."

Once more, Gabriel thought he saw the hint of anger in the Dread's expression. Once more, it faded in an instant. Tea'va didn't attack him. Instead, he lowered his head.

"My apologies, Gabriel St. Martin."

Gabriel turned back to Zoelle. "Please. Stand up. You saved my life. You saved my crew. You saved my father. You never have to lower your head to me."

Zoelle looked up, her eyes moist. "Did you say your father? He is here?"

"Yes."

"I should very much like to meet him."

65

"IT WAS SIMPLE, REALLY, GENERAL," Reza said. "The Dread modulation follows a predefined pattern loosely based on rudimentary quantum physics and string theory. Once Guy and I broke down the pattern, we were able to work out an equation to describe how to alter it to defeat the modulation. What I'm not clear about is why the Dread use the technology the way they do. It's as if they figured out the most basic principles of phasing, and decided to stop there. Although, I guess it could have something to do with the resources they have available. The use of organic matter has some clear benefits, but it also has some well-defined drawbacks, especially concerning variability. Do you-"

"Mr. Mokri," Theodore said, glancing over at the scientist. "Can you please pipe it for a minute or two? Gabriel is out there, and so are my people. I'm worried sick about all of them, and I'm too damn old and too damn incapacitated to help out. Do you have any idea what that's like?"

Reza stopped talking. "I'm sorry, General. I talk when I get nervous."

"Understood, but that's the fourth time I've had to ask. The next time, I'm not going to be polite."

"Yes, sir."

Theodore looked away, back toward the door. He knew Reza was going to start up again. It was in the boy's blood. In part it was annoying. In part, it was comforting. At least he wasn't here alone.

It had been nearly an hour since Gabriel had left him in the small room. It was a long time. Too long as far as he was concerned. He was afraid his son was dead, his crew lost. He had been tempted to go out there more times than he could count.

Every part of him wanted to be doing something active, something useful. Every part of him knew it would be a mistake.

His value was in his mind, and in his skill at the command of a starship. His days as a foot soldier had been over long before he had destroyed his legs.

And how the hell would Gabriel find him if he left the room, anyway?

He closed his eyes, his lips moving in another prayer that Gabriel would come through that door again, and sometime soon. He was afraid for him, and at the same time, he had that feeling in his gut that he was still out there. Still alive. He held onto it, refusing to let it go. Gabriel was a better man than he had ever been. He was the best of him and Juliet. He would be okay.

Once they took the ship, once Tea'va showed them how to fly it, he would use it to return to Calawan. Alan couldn't ignore him then. He would have no choice but to organize the troops, and to pour every resource into preparing to return home. They would use what Guy and Sarah and Reza had discovered to build better defenses and better weapons. They would return to Earth as the Dread had arrived.

Completely unstoppable.

He smiled at the thought. He had promised her he would go back. That he would find a way to save them.

The smile vanished. Only if Gabriel survived. Only if they managed to win. Had he saved them by flying the Magellan into the Dread fortress or had he sealed their fate?

He wanted a resolution. An answer to the question.

He wanted Gabriel back.

"It's too quiet in here," he said. "What else you got stewing in that brain of yours, Mr. Mokri?"

"You just told me to shut up, sir."

"And now I'm telling you to talk."

"Okay. Well, I was just thinking a little bit more about the organic compounds we found in the Dread rifle. Of course, the composition is nothing we have on Earth, but the thing is that any organic compound will break down over time. Decompose. The compounds in the rifle looked relatively fresh."

"Meaning what?"

"Meaning that wherever they came from, the Dread must have a source somewhere."

"Like a farm?"

Reza laughed. "Yes, sir. In a sense. Although it is more likely that they grow the organic materials from stem cells. That would be more logical, considering the-"

A knock sounded from the other side of the wall. A simple rhythm that Theodore knew instantly. He was already beaming by the time the door slid open and he saw Gabriel standing there, unharmed and smiling along with him.

"Gabriel," Theodore said. He couldn't remember the last time he had been as excited about anything. Probably the day he had met Juliet. "Thank God."

Gabriel entered the room, leaning down and wrapping his arms around him. "We did it, Dad. The ship is ours."

"I'd say I don't believe it, son, but I always had faith in you."

Gabriel stood up. Theodore could tell right away that there was something off about him.

"What is it?" he asked.

"Uh. Dad, I. I'm not sure about this."

"About what?"

Gabriel's face was flushing. "Just try to stay calm, okay?"

"Damn it, boy, what the hell are you talking about? You want me to stay calm, and you're getting me all worked up with your beating around the bayou."

Gabriel stepped aside.

Everything stopped.

Memories flooded Theodore at the sight of her. So many memories. The day they met. Their first kiss. That day on the beach. The first time they made love. Their first house. The cat she had named Bobo because she thought the way he said it was funny, and it stayed funny that darn kit's entire life. It was as though he relived it all in a single breath.

Juliet. He had spent the last fifty years longing to see her alive one more time. Wanting to look at her face, to see into eyes that could see him back. He felt the tears come, sliding down his cheeks as he stared at the woman in front of him. In the back of his mind, he knew she wasn't the real thing. He knew she was a clone. For a moment, it didn't matter.

"Juliet," he whispered.

She came to him, kneeling beside him with tears on her face, and a smile that he would have known anywhere. A smile he had missed more than anything in the universe.

"Theodore," she said, putting soft hands on his. Hands that tingled at the touch. "It's been so long. I thought I would never see you again."

"What?" he heard Gabriel say behind her.

"It's me," she said, her voice as beautiful and soothing as he remembered. "It's your Juliet. I always knew you would keep your promise. I always knew you would come back. I've prepared them for you.

The Domo'dahm has no idea what he has done."

Thank you for reading Weapons of War!
Reviews are appreciated!!!

Don't miss the next book in the series, **Tides of War**, coming soon!

Want to be notified? www.mrforbes.com/notify

More Books By M.R. Forbes:

M.R. Forbes on Amazon

www.amazon.com/author/mrforbes

Starship Eternal (War Eternal, Book One)

http://amzn.to/1xSYZeY

A lost starship...
A dire warning from futures past...
A desperate search for salvation...

Captain Mitchell "Ares" Williams is a Space Marine and the hero of the Battle for Liberty, whose Shot Heard 'Round the Universe saved the planet from a nearly unstoppable war machine. He's handsome, charismatic, and the perfect poster boy to help the military drive enlistment. Pulled from the war and thrown into the spotlight, he's as efficient at charming the media and bedding beautiful celebrities as he was at shooting down enemy starfighters.

After an assassination attempt leaves Mitchell critically wounded, he begins to suffer from strange hallucinations that carry a chilling and oddly familiar warning:

They are coming. Find the Goliath or humankind will be destroyed.

Convinced that the visions are a side-effect of his injuries, he tries to ignore them, only to learn that he may not be as crazy as he thinks. The enemy is real and closer than he imagined, and they'll do whatever it takes to prevent him from rediscovering the centuries lost starship.

Narrowly escaping capture, out of time and out of air, Mitchell lands at the mercy of the Riggers - a ragtag crew of former commandos who patrol the lawless outer reaches of the galaxy. Guided by a captain with a reputation for cold-blooded murder, they're dangerous, immoral, and possibly insane.

They may also be humanity's last hope for survival in a war that has raged beyond eternity.

Join the Mailing List!

"No," you cry. "I will not submit myself to even more inbox spam. I have quite enough garbage coming in from people and places that I care a lot more about than you."

"But," I reply, "if you sign up for my mailing list, you'll know when my next book is out. Don't you want to know when my next book is out?"

"Eh... I'll find it on Amazon."

"True enough, but you see, a mailing list is very valuable to an author, especially a meager self-published soul such as myself. I don't have a marketing team, and I don't have exposure in brick and mortar stores around the world to help improve my readership. All I have is you, my potential fans. How about a bribe?"

"Hmm... Keep talking."

"Picture this... giveaways, a chance at FREE books. There is a 10% chance* you could save at least three dollars per year!"

Silence.

"Where'd you go?" I ask. "Well, I'll just leave this here, in case you change your mind."

http://mrforbes.com/mailinglist

* For illustration only. Not an actual mathematical probability.

M.R. Forbes

Thank You!

It is readers like you, who take a chance on self-published works that is what makes the very existence of such works possible. Thank you so very much for spending your hard-earned money, time, and energy on this work. It is my sincerest hope that you have enjoyed reading!

Independent authors could not continue to thrive without your support. If you have enjoyed this, or any other independently published work, please consider taking a moment to leave a review at the source of your purchase. Reviews have an immense impact on the overall commercial success of a given work, and your voice can help shape the future of the people whose efforts you have enjoyed.

Thank you again!

About the Author

M.R. Forbes is the creator of a growing catalog of speculative fiction titles, including the science-fiction Rebellion and War Eternal novels, the epic fantasy Tears of Blood series, the contemporary fantasy Divine series, and the world of Ghosts & Magic. He lives in the pacific northwest with his family, including a cat who thinks she's a dog, and a dog who thinks she's a cat. He eats too many donuts, and he's always happy to hear from readers.

Mailing List: http://www.mrforbes.com/mailinglist

Website: http://www.mrforbes.com/

Goodreads: http://www.goodreads.com/author/show/6912725.M_R_Forbes

Facebook: http://www.facebook.com/mrforbes.author

Twitter: http://www.twitter.com/mrforbes

Made in the USA
Middletown, DE
17 August 2018